MW01182253

Peace in Paradise

Sara Dotson

Fankaloa Pronunciation Guide

a - ah

e - ay

i - ee

o - oh

u - ooh

ai - sounds like "eye"

ei - ey

oi - oy

au - ow

Other vowel combinations: both vowels pronounced distinctly

' - indicates a sharp break between vowels

Consonants pronounced the same as in English

Examples:

'Ema (sweetheart, dear, honey, etc.) - pronounced EYmah.

Aliakeanu (witch) - pronounced ahLEEakayAHnooh

Aliakeanukea'u (witchcraft) - ahLEEahkeyAHnoohKAYAH ooh

Nama'ea (sanctuary) - pronounced NAHma EYah

Kiliopi (end) - KEEleeOHpee

Pikali (non-Fankaloa) - peeKAHlee

Chapter One: A Guttersnipe Lobster

"Welcome, new students!"

In the five minutes I'd known the headmaster of my new school, I'd decided he was a cheerful man. He had a clipped Leyonish accent, wrinkles and a messy thatch of grey hair that looked in no hurry to recede. The sparkle in his bespectacled blue eyes and how straight he stood made it clear that he was about as energetic as possible for a man of sixty-four - which was a good thing if he was going to be dealing with a hundred nineteen of us for the next year.

I stood in the Garden, hands shoved in my pockets, and half-listened to him explain the rules for the icebreaker game we were going to play. I wasn't the only one not paying rapt attention, either; my wandering eyes met at least a half dozen other pairs before Professor Langley got close to finished.

As I scanned, I noticed a group of girls whispering and giggling to each other, looking at me. They looked away when they realized I saw them, but they did a bad job of hiding a renewed fit of giggles.

I sighed and dug my hands deeper into my pockets.

I had known I would stand out.

I'd had a monster growth spurt over the summer, shooting up from five-two to five-ten in two months flat, and had to wear Dad's old work clothes because Mom was several inches shorter than me. But Dad was six-four and even after trying to shrink the clothes in the dryer, they fit me like a dingy circus tent. I looked like a street urchin, right down to the long ratty hair and sailor's mouth, and in a place like this I stuck out like the sorest thumb ever to have existed.

But at that moment, I wasn't sure I cared. I had wanted to become a Peacekeeper since I attended my first Career Day presentation nine years before; the stories they told sounded like something out of a book, something exciting, something infinitely greater than what even my naive, seven-year-old self could see in the streets of the poor district of Plancint where I lived. I was here now, I had made it out, and no gossipy teenager was going to ruin this for me.

Professor Langley finished outlining the rules and called for order - the second he'd stopped talking, most of the students had started. He took it all in stride and led us out of the Garden to separate us into six teams.

I ended up on the smallest one, the one with

nineteen students instead of twenty. Our captain was a teacher in her early thirties with a sparkle in her blue eyes that made me think of Professor Langley. And no wonder: she introduced herself as Madelie Langley, the headmaster's daughter. She had thick, smooth red curls and her father's straight posture. As the teams started collaborating, she pulled us into as close a huddle as possible.

"All right, troops," she said, "here's how it's going to work. I've a permanent alliance with Oline Malthrin. She's the brown-haired woman over there, the science teacher - captain of blue team. We let them grab the balls they need out of our stash, they let us grab theirs. Don't attack them, at least not until I give the order. Understood?"
A slow, mischievous smile played across her face, and I decided I liked her.

"Yes, ma'am," we said, almost in unison.

"Excellent," Miss Madelie said. "Now, as for the other teams: their red balls first, and then any others you can get away. But don't be stupid. We're short on manpower as it is; we can't afford to mount rescue missions every time somebody goes into enemy territory. Don't take any unnecessary risks. Am I understood?"

This time, our chorus was perfect. "Yes, ma'am!"

"Good,"Miss Madelie said, smiling. "Now, let's get our flags and get into position. I want about eight people to stay in here and defend. You'll have to work out for yourselves who that's going to be, because I'm going to be on offense. Now, red team: move out!"

We joined the other teams hurrying to grab their flags. I snatched mine as quickly as possible and moved away from the jostling crowd, hooking the belt part around my waist. The rest of red team joined me around our base within about half a minute.

"Right," said one of the boys. He had a babyish face, with close-cropped dark hair. "Who's on defense?"

Three people volunteered: a plain girl with flat, shoulder-length brown hair, a skinny boy of about sixteen, and a girl whose short black hair fell in choppy layers.

"We need more than that, guys," said a petite young woman with thick, dark hair that curled wildly around her head and shoulders.

"Would you like to volunteer?"

"Well, no," said the woman. "I was just saying..."

"Cut her a break," I told the boy who had spoken, a lanky guy whose strawberry-blonde hair hung messily around his face. "She's just trying to get us organized. You wanna be back here?" I jerked my thumb at the balls gathered in the circle of orange cones.

"No."

"So don't taunt her." I grinned. "I'll do a midfield job - half offense, half defense. If that's okay, Miss Madelie?"

She nodded. "Sounds like a solid plan. We could use a few more of those, if you think you can get the manpower from volunteers." She smiled. "But you're not getting me!"

"I'll go on defense, if otherwise it'll just be you three," said the baby-faced boy who had spoken first.

We managed to get the rest of a defense through a series of threats and volunteers who were tired of the argument. Finding people to go on offense wasn't hard - we had so many volunteers that Miss Madelie ended up relegating a couple back to midfield with me so we could have a more solid defense. She and the other people on offense seemed raring to go.

When everyone finally finished, Professor Langley blew hard on a whistle. The people on offense - on all the teams - lunged for the borders of their respective wedges, lurking around, searching for an opening so they could grab a ball without getting their flag pulled.

Miss Madelie and Ms. Malthrin made eye contact across purple team's wedge and then sprinted across, trailed by several students on their teams. Several of our people started after the entering blues to grab their flags, but then stopped as they remembered we had an alliance.

I lunged after a yellow who snuck in while the others had been distracted by the blue advance. She jumped back into her own wedge, and I prowled away, glancing back twice to make sure she didn't come back.

A cheer went up as Miss Madelie and the two other offense kids returned with the red ball from blue's stash. They'd all made it through without getting their flags pulled. Across purple's wedge, Ms. Malthrin made her way home with one student. The other had gotten his flag pulled and was languishing in the purple jail.

A familiar-looking brown-haired girl clad in a white dress and leather sandals dashed into our territory. She was a green.

I grabbed at her flag, but she pulled it out of the way and ran on. I lost my balance and very nearly managed to trip over my own feet before resuming the chase.

She was pretty good, I had to admit, as she evaded me and several other reds. She reached the stash and grabbed the green ball - and one of our reds.

"Hey!" I shouted over the multitude of laughing, screeching students. "You can't grab two!"

The girl glanced at me disdainfully and dashed back towards her wedge.

I pursed my lips and lunged after her, stretching my legs as far as they could go. She zigzagged around so much that I almost fell over twice more on our way to green wedge.

I clenched my fists and tried to focus on running without tripping over my own recently gargantuan feet. But having my fists clenched just made me want to punch someone. A very specific someone.

In my distraction, I crossed into green's territory and got my flag pulled. It was only then, as a triumphant green led me off to jail, that I realized why the girl seemed so familiar.

She had been one of the ones laughing at me in the Garden.

After that, getting the girl out became my main goal. While I had been in the green jail, a yellow had come in and tried to grab his team's ball.

The girl in white stepped on it, keeping the yellow from taking it, and had yanked his flag while he'd scrambled to get the ball out from under her foot.

The small curly-haired woman ended up rescuing me. "Thanks," I said when she tagged me. "White Dress over here was really starting to piss me off."

"Good thing I got you out, then," replied the young woman. "You look like the type to do something drastic about someone you don't like." She grinned. "I'm Valie Handrix."

"Lillia Anied," I replied. We shook hands. Then, as we stepped back into red's wedge, I asked, "What exactly makes me look like I'd do something drastic to White Dress?"

***

Purple won the game. I was a little disappointed that it hadn't been us, but at least it hadn't been green. If White Dress had won I would have fought her. And quite possibly killed her.

Valie was nineteen and from Pahn, I discovered, the same province as me, but she came from the port city Arins in the southeast. Her parents ran a small recreational fishing business out of the harbor. She told me that she knew more about fishing than anyone ever should.

I told her that Dad was a construction worker

and Mom had three part-time jobs trying to help with the bills. I did not tell her that up until the minute I'd left, three different gangs had been trying to recruit me, nor did I tell her why.

These were not things you told people you'd just met.

They were not things you told people period.

After the game, the girls and the boys separated to go to their dormitories and unpack. Valie and I stopped by the Garden to grab our things, and then we headed south towards the girls' dorms.

I didn't really want to go inside - it was warm and sunny and not nearly as humid as it usually was in Plancint that time of year - but the inside of the dorm building was just as pleasant. The windows of the common room all sat open, letting in the slight breeze and the sunshine. The common room was airy and bright and had a large video screen that showed our room assignments. My name was the second one down.

Anied, Lillia and Tomsein, Reubyn: room 310.

Valie and I grimaced at each other. "Bad luck," she said. "We're bound to have at least one class together, anyhow."

"Yeah," I said. We walked together partway

up the stairs, but Valie and I separated at the second floor. "See you later."

"'Bye," Valie replied. I continued up the stairs.

Room 310 was at the very end of the hallway - of course I ended up with the longest walk - but it was a nice room; the corner meant it got two windows instead of just one. There were two beds: one across from the door and the other on the far side underneath one of the windows. Each bed had a blue plaid comforter and solid blue sheets. Next to each sat a desk with an old model, keyboard-equipped omnipad. Across from each was a wardrobe.

The windows were wide and open, so the room felt fresh and airy. That was a big change from the apartment in Plancint.

I put my bag on the bed by the window and glanced out. Most of the school grounds aside from the Garden and the boys' dorms were visible from there. I could see the lake, which was nice and clear, most of the school building, the mess hall, and the gym. Paths led into the woods, trails for walking and running. It all looked so open and bright.

Then I heard someone's feet in the doorway, and I turned to see White Dress walking in with all three of her bags.

You've got to be kidding me.

We looked at each other for a second. Then, to break the silence, I said, "Reubyn Tomsein?"

"Roy-been," she said in a nasal voice, correcting my pronunciation. "Lillia Anied?"

I nodded.

She didn't say anything else, which made me happy. Even after three words, her voice grated on my ears.

We turned and busied ourselves at our beds. I yanked out my toiletries, my old green blanket, and two incredibly battered books, rather more roughly than I should have considering that most of it was already beat-up. But my manner changed when I took the last thing out of the bag.

When I'd hugged Mom and Dad goodbye in the lighttrain station, Mom had given me a small package. "Don't open it until you get there," she'd told me. I'd opened it the instant the lighttrain rounded the first corner.

Inside had been a sleek silver rectangle: a Vcomm. It was shiny and clean, newer than anything else I owned. When I'd switched it on, I had found that there was already a contact listed in it: Mom and Dad.

I had almost cried.

Now I let my fingers trace the surface: no

scratches, no dents or dings. This was the nicest thing I owned. I couldn't help wondering how much Mom and Dad had to pay for it.

Gently, I set the Vcomm down on the desk. Then I grabbed my toiletries and headed for the third floor's communal bathroom.

A line of double vanities marched across the back wall of the bathroom, marked according to the rooms that used them. I made a face. *Great.* It looked like I was stuck with Reubyn.

I reprimanded myself immediately. *Dumbass!* I thought. *You're jumping to conclusions. Reubyn's probably just timelagged - Klinds is a long way away, after all. Come to think of it, I'm timelagged. We just got off on the wrong foot.*

But then I heard her giggling with the other girls in the Garden again, saw her disdainful look when I'd caught her breaking the game rules, and I wasn't so sure.

I started unpacking my toiletries, putting my toothbrush in the glass, my toothpaste beside it, and everything else under the sink. Reubyn came in while I was unpacking and started doing the same thing. I left.

Back in the room, I started organizing my things. I put my bag in the floor of my wardrobe, folded my blanket and set it on the middle of the bed, and set my two books on the little shelf above my desk. Then I opened up the wardrobe again and looked inside.

Five green uniform shirts hung from the rack - two collared, two V-neck, and one crew-neck - and some black bottoms sat folded on the shelf: two skirts, a pair of Bermuda shorts, a pair of cargo shorts, and a pair of slacks. There was also, I realized, a pair of black high-tops and an aqua-colored bathing suit. I glanced out the window at the lake. I'd never learned how to swim, but this seemed as good a time as any. Maybe I could ask Valie to teach me.

I grabbed the swimsuit and was leaving just as Reubyn came back in. We whacked shoulders, and glared at each other as we went our separate ways.

I wasn't the first one down at the lake: ten or twelve other students had finished unpacking before me and were now splashing and laughing and swimming. I paused as I splashed into the water. The ripples lapped at my ankles as I looked around to see if Valie was there.

She wasn't.

I bit my lip. Swimming had been a nice

thought in my room, three stories above the water, with the idea of a teacher, but here facing the water without any help, it was a slightly more difficult proposition. The deepest parts of the water easily reached down thirty or forty feet.

"What's the matter?" asked an over-sweet nasal voice from behind me.

I was already scowling when turned to look at Reubyn. She was smiling. "Not scared, are you?"

"Of course not," I snapped, trying not to sound too offended. There was no need for her to know I couldn't swim. I was sure *she* could.

"Good," Reubyn said, and something about her tone made my stomach do an uncomfortable flip. "So what do you say we race?"

Which made my stomach - and all my other internal organs - decide to abandon me altogether.

"R-race?" I said, stammering despite myself.

Reubyn nodded, still smiling. "To the rock out there." She pointed, and I glanced out without thinking. "The rock out there" was about halfway across the lake, in one of the deepest parts. I swallowed.

"Well?" Reubyn asked. "What do you say?"

I stared out at the rock for a moment longer. When the word "yes" slipped out of my mouth, it surprised both of us.

"Okay then," Reubyn said, shaking off her surprise. She moved deeper into the water.

I joined her. What on earth had made me say yes? I couldn't swim. I couldn't even fake it.

"Ready...go!"

Reubyn dove into the water and swam towards the rock with a quick, even stroke. Half on instinct, I flung myself into the lake face-first and tried to follow her.

I spluttered, clawed and kicked my way up to the surface, and tried to force myself through the water. I glanced ahead and tried to copy Reubyn's strokes without inhaling too much of the lake. She was getting farther away from me every second.

I gritted my teeth and tried harder. I would not let her beat me.

And to my surprise, I seemed to pick it up. My strokes fell more evenly, propelling me further through the water each time. I even got brave enough to put my head under. And I was gaining on Reubyn.

She looked at me in shock as I reached her and splashed in her direction. Then she scowled and started going faster.

I realized that she had been going easy on me, counting on my previous inability to swim to take care of humiliating me. We strained towards the rock, first with Reubyn ahead, then me, and then Reubyn again. I was able to see what she was doing much better from beside her. I cupped my hands instead of letting the water run through my fingers and tried to kick more evenly. It seemed to work, and slowly I pulled ahead. I had greater reach, I realized, and my hands and feet were bigger than hers. The advantages of being a lanky mutt instead of a pretty little purebred, I thought, and forced myself not to smile. It would be a shame if I drowned now.

The rock was only a couple dozen yards away now. A tired ache started to spread through my limbs and my chest, but I couldn't stop. Twenty yards - ten - five -

And then my fingers hit rock and I stopped, grabbing onto a crevice to keep from sinking. Reubyn pulled to a stop fifteen yards back, staring at me in shock.

"But I thought - you - what - what?" she spluttered.

I grinned and pushed off the rock, leaving Reubyn there to fume.

That evening, curfew found me sitting on my bed in Dad's T-shirt. I had relegated it to pajama duty, since it was long enough on me to pass for a vaguely modest nightgown. I was looking at my Vcomm, wondering whether or not to call Mom and Dad.

After my race with Reubyn, I had found Valie teaching her roommate, Aniamakolan Mariona, how to swim. Mako of the ridiculous full name was from Naklia, the northernmost of the provinces, where the average summer high was about sixty degrees. But after a few hours with Valie, she swam like a fish.

Once we'd finished swimming, the three of us had put on our uniforms and started exploring some of the trails around the school grounds. We hadn't stopped until the bell rang out for dinner at eighteen hours. Later, Valie had had to give Mako and me some aloe vera lotion, because we'd both burnt ourselves to crisps. Valie, being darker than both of us combined and having worn plenty of sunblock, didn't have to use any.

I stretched carefully, wincing as my burned skin pulled. Then the Vcomm rang. I scrambled to grab it and answer, yelping as I rubbed the sunburn against everything I touched.

But I managed to find the button to pick up the call and was rewarded by seeing Mom's and Dad's faces fill the screen.

"Hi, Mom, hi, Dad," I said, smiling. "I was

just about to call you."

"We caught you at a good time, then," said Dad. "How was your first day?"

"Um, interesting," I replied. Before I could say anything else, Reubyn walked in the open door. She glared at me and slammed open her wardrobe.

Mom and Dad both gave me a look. "And who's your friend?"

"Oh," I said. "That's my, ah...that's my roommate. Her name's Reubyn."

Reubyn stalked back out of the room with a bundle of fabric, slamming the door behind her. I'd really managed to piss her off. I shouldn't have felt as good about that as I did.

I looked back to see Mom and Dad watching me. Dad had raised one eyebrow, a trick which annoyed Mom because only Dad could manage it.

"Okay," I said, "I hate her. And she hates me, too. But I learned how to swim!"

Mom's look told me that my attempt at cheer was thin. "Sweetie, are you sure you're going to be okay there? You two are going to have to live together for the whole year. If you don't get along ..."

"I'll be fine, Mom," I interrupted. "Relax. Sure, we don't get along, but it could be worse. It's not like we'll be stuck together forever, right?

Besides, this is my dream. No pain-in-the-ass roommate is going to mess that up for me."

But I sighed inaudibly.

Dad gave me a sympathetic look. More than Mom, he knew what it was like for me when I got angry. He got the same way. It was his advice that I used to try to control myself.

"Just call us if you have any problems, okay?" he said.

I nodded. "Sure," I said. Then I glanced down at the clock icon in the bottom right-hand corner. "Oh. Crap, I need to get going. We're having a bonfire in the Garden at twenty hours, and it's five til."

"Have fun," Mom said. "Love you, Lil."

"Love you guys. 'Bye."

I hung up and sat on the bed for a moment.

Maybe this hadn't been such a good idea. I had always been a fighter, as little as I liked to admit it, and it scared me. And I was going to have to deal with Reubyn for the next whole year. The things that tried to take control of me when I was angry had only broken through into a fight once before, and I had never let them again. They terrified me. But if Reubyn and I had to live together, there would be a lot of anger, and probably fights, too. I didn't want to think about what might happen.

Then I shoved myself up. There was no point in sitting here all night thinking about what might happen when there was something fun going on. Going to the bonfire would be good. Valie, Mako, and I were going to meet up, and there were supposed to be s'mores. Besides, I loved fires. This would be fun.

I laced on my school-issue black high-tops and left the room, trying not to feel uncomfortable. It felt kind of weird to just be wearing a shirt, even if it was an appropriate length.

Most of the students were already in the Garden, along with the entire faculty. Everyone was in their pajamas. The only light came from the waist-high lamps around the Garden's borders, which left the center pretty dark. It was a clear night, and I could see about a million stars when I looked up.

"Good evening, everyone!" called Professor Langley's voice through the darkness. "Welcome to our Opening Night Bonfire! Are you all ready?"

I cheered with everyone else as I searched through the crowd for Valie and Mako. A dim shape moved as Professor Langley leaned over and struck something. A couple of sparks leapt from his hands to the pile of tinder, and a small blaze started up. I smiled.

Valie, Mako, and I met up and helped some of the other students tend to the fire. I was grateful for the warmth. It was only September first and it had been a warm day, but now that the sun had gone down it was getting a little chilly.

When the fire had been built up enough, the teachers distributed sticks and marshmallows, and we began roasting. The circle around the bonfire was large enough that we didn't have to shove past the other students to get our marshmallows by the fire, but we were still packed in tight.

When I thought my marshmallow was done, I wriggled my way out and headed over to where Miss Madelie and the social studies teacher, Mr. Velsom, guarded the graham crackers and chocolate.

"Ready for the s'more?" asked Miss Madelie. In the flickering light, her vivid red curls almost looked like they were flames, too. I nodded.

"Hold out the marshmallow," said Mr. Velsom. "Careful, it'll be hot."

I moved the marshmallow into place, and Mr. Velsom balanced a piece of chocolate on top of it. Then Miss Madelie moved in and pinned marshmallow and chocolate between two halves of graham cracker.

"Pull the stick back," she said. I did so, and as Miss Madelie pulled on the s'more, it came free. She handed it to me, still smiling. "Enjoy!" she said.

"Thanks," I replied, moving back over to the fire with my s'more. A line had formed by Miss Madelie and Mr. Velsom, leaving me on my own by the fire.

Mako joined me a moment later. The graham cracker part of her s'more was spiderwebbed with cracks, and she had crumbs all down her nightgown. She'd clearly started in on her s'more already.

"Aren't you going to eat yours?" she asked, covering her mouth with one hand to avoid spraying me.

I grinned and said, "I might. But I think you might have made me lose my appetite."

"It's not just me," said Mako in fake offense. As we had all learned at dinner, Mako made a mess when she ate. It wasn't entirely her fault; her family was very traditional Naklian and didn't use forks and knives very often. But mostly, Mako just had a talent for making messes.

I bit into the s'more and found that Mako was right. The graham cracker broke all around the place where I'd bitten. I put a hand underneath the s'more to keep everything from falling out onto the ground.

"It's good," I said, swallowing.

Valie joined us. She was very clean, despite the fact that her s'more was halfway finished and the cracker was broken in about fifty different places. Valie and her roommate were on opposite ends of the mess-making spectrum.

"Hey Makomess, hey Lil," she said. "You like 'em, huh?"

"They're great," said Mako, flushing above her sunburn at the new nickname. "How did you not get any of that on you?"

"Talent," Valie replied, taking on a superior air and a Leyonish accent. Mako and I both laughed, and Valie broke down and joined in. "Seriously, though," she said through the giggles, "I don't know why you think it's so hard to keep from making a mess."

"I don't know why you think it's so easy," I shot back, chomping down on my s'more as messily as I could. Crumbs showered down onto my shirt and stuck around my mouth as I chewed slowly, making as much of a mess as possible. Valie and Mako both laughed.

"Okay, well, don't waste it," Valie said as I moved to take another bite.

I nodded my agreement through a slightly less messy mouthful.

Whatever might have been said next was interrupted as Ms. Imok, the language teacher, called for everyone to join in as we sang some campfire songs. I rolled my eyes. This was bound to be silly.

Which it was, but it was also really fun. As we headed back to our dorms at twenty-one hours, I decided that it had probably been the best evening of my life. I was chilly away from the fire, but it was a beautiful night; I could see the stardust spattered in an arm across the sky, one of the other arms of the Milky Way. I'd never seen the stars so clearly before.

Valie and Mako left for the second floor, and I headed up alone to the third-floor bathroom. I brushed and flossed quickly, sighing as I looked at my lobster-red skin. Tomorrow, I thought, I would have to find some sunscreen that I could use. I was sure I would end up outdoors again; the school grounds were great. I headed back to my dorm room in high spirits.

A moment or two later, as I was figuring out how to start up the omnipad on the desk, Reubyn came in and my spirits sank down to the first floor. We exchanged glares and looked away from each other.

I found the right button and brought up the main screen of the omnipad. The first icon I clicked was the one for the Interweb. I'd never really gotten to go on it before.

When I hit the icon, a search screen popped up. I grinned. This was kind of fun.

My returning good mood was punctured as Reubyn's voice piped up from the other desk. "Heeey!" she said.

I glared over to see her leaning back in her chair, talking at a purple Vcomm.

"Hey, Reubyn," came a woman's voice. It had the Klinds accent, too. I wondered who it was, and then decided I didn't care. I went back to the omnipad and the Interweb, trying to ignore my roommate's conversation.

When she hung up, Reubyn was silent for a moment. Then she said, "You should have worn sunblock."

It took me a second to realize she was talking to me. I turned away from the omnipad slowly, looking at her for a long moment. She smirked. I raised my eyebrows.

Reubyn snorted. "I'm just saying," she said.

"You look like a guttersnipe lobster."

I scowled. "Well, apparently lobsters are faster than manatees."

Reubyn's chair scraped against the floor as she stood up. "Faster than what, exactly?"

Oops. I had managed to instigate something. But since it was already happening, I saw no reason to derail the insult train.

"Manatees," I replied, looking back at the screen. Reubyn was far from fat, but I had needed something, and that had come without any effort.

I could see her reflected in my screen, looking like she wanted to strangle me, but then she got control of herself and said, "I think manatees are cute. Besides, I'd rather be one of those than a stickbug."

"Thought I was a lobster. You're going to have to control that short-term memory loss when you talk to people, dear." If there was a time to derail, it was now, before Reubyn got irritated past the point of no return. I couldn't fight.

That was what my brain said, anyway, but I felt my blood rising. Surely it couldn't hurt just to punch her once. Just once. Right in the middle of her smug, delicate little face...

In the end, Reubyn made the decision for me. She tackled me from across the room, tipping me out of my chair and onto my bed. I writhed and kicked her off, and we sprang up onto our knees on the bed. We glared at each other.

Stop! screamed the rational part of my brain, like a mini-Lillia rattling the bars in a mental cage. She seemed cold and tiny compared to the heat filling my veins and quickening my pulse. My instincts.

They awoke nearly every day, sometimes two or three times if I was particularly unlucky. If I grew angry or frightened, if I was backed into a corner or pushed into a fight, they woke up and pulsed through my body, filling me up with an energy and a will that terrified me on a deeper level than anything else. I knew without having to think about it that if I let them have free reign, I could kill. Would kill.

Almost had killed.

I moved slower than I could have, but I needed to control myself more than I needed to be lightning-fast. I still managed to match every one of Reubyn's blows with one of my own. It was closer to a no-rules wrestling match than a fistfight - fingernails and elbows and knees and teeth got involved just as often as kicks and punches, and one or the other of us were usually on our backs or our knees instead of our feet. My skin stung from scratches and sunburn.

Then I heard a ping, and a voice came on over the intercom. "It's twenty-two hours thirty," it said. "Lights out, please!"

Reubyn pushed off to her own side of the room without hesitation. I was pleased to see that she had to limp over there - the result of a kick I'd landed on her thigh. We glared at each other until she flipped the switch and the lights went out.

Then I lay there in bed, unwilling to curl up. I hurt all over.

Well, the Academy was great. I'd made some friends. And at the end of the year, I would achieve my dream and become a Peacekeeper.

If Reubyn and I didn't kill each other first.

Chapter Two: Mass Destruction

Over the next two months, life at the Academy fell into a steady rhythm. Every morning, I woke up at six hours sharp. Four days a week, I went on a run; two days I spent some time on one of the bike machines at the gym; on Sundays I just took a walk.

Every few days, I worked out after the cardio. All of this was a routine I'd been doing for about a year, but it was only after reaching the Academy that I could actually use a gym on a regular basis.

Once I finished all of that, I showered and get ready for the day. Breakfast was served in the mess hall from seven hours to eight hours thirty, and I usually started eating around eight hours. Usually Valie or Mako or one of my other friends was in there, so I didn't have to sit there and stare at my food like a loner.

The school day itself started at nine hours. I loved it. Even though it covered a lot of the same subjects, it was much better than the school I'd attended in Plancint. There was the schedule, for starters. Mine went like this:

900 - 940
Language
(Nessa Imok)

945 - 1025

Health

(Mart Ibsroo)

1025 - 1055

Break

1055 - 1135

Mathematics

(Antrea Mag)

1140 - 1220

Science

(Oline Malthrin)

1220 - 1300

Lunch

1305 - 1344

Law and Justice

(Madelie Langley)

1350 - 1430

Social Studies

(Torp Velsom)

Then there were the classes themselves. They fascinated me. All the teachers were great, and I loved how small the classes were. There were only about eighteen or twenty students in each.

Altogether, one hundred nineteen students called the Academy home that year: sixty girls and young women, and fifty-nine boys and young men. By the end of the second week, I could recognize everyone, and name most of them. I liked how small it was.

Of course, that meant that Reubyn and I had plenty of chances to clash.

We tended to avoid each other as much as possible to keep it at a minimum. I woke up before she did in the mornings, so my only trouble was trying not to pull pranks on her while she slept. I couldn't count the number of times my hand itched for a marker or a bowl of warm water.

I tamped down the itch, though. Keeping the peace was essential - not just for people once I graduated, but in my dorm, too. If I rocked the boat too much, things would get worse.

On Sundays and after classes ended every other day, we did a variety of things. Sometimes we had workshops - survival skills or basic things like sewing or cooking. Sometimes we-d be brought together to play some sport or other. Then sometimes, we had mock-up missions.

These were different every time. For one we would be in a group with three other students; another we would work solo. Unfortunately,

Reubyn and I ended up together a lot. We usually managed to agree on a course of action, but when we didn't the whole mission went down the toilet. Both of us were stubborn, and it was only fueled by our deep lack of love for one another. Even when we cooperated, we traded jibes and insults back and forth the whole time. Keeping myself under control proved to be much more difficult than I'd hoped.

But I was coping. Valie, Mako, and I were growing closer, and I had made a few other friends as well. We explored the grounds and sat in the Garden or the common room and talked or helped out or started random projects, like the production of "Romeo and Juliet" we tried to put together in October, which straggled through broken props and ripped costumes to a couple terrific death scenes and appreciative applause from the audience at all the humor we'd caused them trying to get the show together.

But once the fun ended, it would be time for a mock-up mission or some activity where Reubyn and I had to interact. Monday through Friday, we were together for three periods a day.

And one day, all that togetherness finally got to us.

It was mid-November, and we were in the middle of

the Chemistry unit in science class. Reubyn and I had partnered up, though not intentionally. Ms. Malthrin had put everyone's names into a hat and drawn out two at a time to work together. It was just bad luck that Reubyn and I had ended up working with each other. Again.

I had a headache, and I hadn't slept well the night before. Sometimes, especially if I was angry or irritated when I fell asleep, I had strange dreams. They all featured the same place: a cold, dark, twisted otherworld full of people with instincts like mine who didn't hold them back. Strange monsters populated the world along with the people, and always I spent the dream feeling that something icy and powerful watched over everything - watched over me, cold, evaluating, grasping.

But the frightening part wasn't the monsters or the instinct-driven men. The most frightening part was the pull I felt towards it all - towards letting my instincts flow like theirs, towards the cold, malevolent force that watched. Even now in the bright light of the science room, the feeling made me shiver.

So dealing with Reubyn was not high on my list of priorities.

Ms. Malthrin spent about ten minutes detailing what we were supposed to do for the lab, accompanying the explanation with drawings on the board. The chemical we were using wasn't too dangerous, she told us, but we needed to be careful anyway. "After all, anything can go wrong in a science lab."

Which wasn't the most encouraging thing, but I shrugged it off. Ms. Malthrin had a way of making everything sound about twenty times worse than it really was, and we had all learned by now that she didn't really expect the worst to happen. She just wanted to prepare us in case it did.

I retrieved the materials we'd be mixing from the front table, while Reubyn grabbed everything else.

"What's the first step again?" I asked, putting on my goggles. Faraway things looked kind of mushy to me, and I didn't want to take any chances mixing chemicals. God, I needed glasses.

Reubyn rolled her eyes. "Why don't you look yourself?"

"Sure friggin thing," I said. "Just don't blame me if I misread a word and blow us all up."

"Forget it," muttered Reubyn, and looked up at the board. "Cup of sugar."

We started mixing the ingredients: one cup of sugar, one and a half cups of potassium nitrate. I turned on the Bunsen burner and set the skillet over it so our mixture could heat.

"You set it to the right heat, right?" asked Reubyn.

"Of course," I replied. "Even without glasses I can see that much."

Reubyn took the spoon and started to stir the mixture - way too quickly, it seemed to me.

"You look like you're trying to whisk eggs or something. Slow down or it's not gonna work right."

"Shut up, would you?" asked Reubyn, looking up from the skillet to glare at me. "For someone who can't read the board, you're awfully sure of what I'm supposed to be doing."

"For someone who can, you're messing it up an awful lot," I retorted. "Give me the spoon so you don't screw it up."

"I've got it," Reubyn said, twitching the spoon away from me. "The only reason I'd screw this up is if you don't shut up and let me do it!"

My mouth tightened, and I reached across the table. "Just give me the spoon," I snapped.

"Stop -" said Reubyn.

I felt my arm hit something hot, and I yelped. My heart jumped into my throat as I heard a clatter. The skillet had fallen to the floor, spilling the hot, half-liquefied mixture.

"Shit," I hissed. My first thought was to run

cold water over my burn, but Reubyn grabbed my good arm. "Help me clean this up!"

"How?" I asked.

Ms. Malthrin strode over to us, clearly angry. Every student in class stared at us. Valie sat over in the corner with Ril, one of our other friends, and I could see the sympathy in both of their faces.

"What do you think you're doing?" asked Ms. Malthrin, almost yelling. "Every time, you two! Every time! You need to learn to work together or else this -" she pointed at the mess spreading across the floor - "is going to look like a Sunday picnic!"

She picked up the pan with a potholder she had apparently brought with her. "Lillia, go rinse that burn," she told me.

I stalked over to the sink.

The water soothed the pain, but not the worry that had started gnawing at me. Reubyn and I had clashed too many times in Ms. Malthrin's class. Last time, she had told us that if it ever happened again we would get detention.

Ms. Malthrin pulled us away from the rest of the class as they continued the lab.

"Listen to me, both of you," she said. Her voice was quiet, but I could hear the suppressed anger underneath her easy drawl. "Y'all need to learn how to put up with each other without causing mass destruction."

"We've done pretty well so far," I said, unable to help it. "We've been rooming together two and a half months and this is the worst that's happened."

"That's not the point," said Ms. Malthrin. "I want both of you in here by fourteen hours forty for detention."

Both of us started protesting, but at the look in Ms. Malthrin's eyes, we subsided. I crossed my arms, welcoming the pain as my burn rubbed up against my shirt. It distracted me from wanting to rip something to shreds.

I realized several seconds too late that Ms. Malthrin said something else.

"Huh?"

Ms. Malthrin gave me a look. "I said go to the nurse," she said. "You need to get that burn taken care of. Reubyn, I want you to go with her."

"You what?"

Another look from Ms. Malthrin, and Reubyn and I both shut up.

"Go, now. Come straight back when Mrs. Opni finishes patching y'all up."

With that, she turned away and left.

Reubyn and I left the classroom.

"This is your fault," I told her when the door

closed behind us.

She turned to stare at me. "How?" she asked. "You're the one who tried to snatch the spoon! If you hadn't done that, none of this would have happened."

"I wouldn't have tried to snatch the spoon if you hadn't been so stubborn about the project," I snapped. "If you'd have let me do it the right way, we'd be letting that stupid smoke bomb cool in the fridge right now."

"You know what, let's just not talk," said Reubyn.

Sounds good to me.

We walked down the hall in silence, resentment simmering in the air between us.

Mrs. Opni fixed my arm up quickly, and after she applied a burn cream and wrapped it up, she sent us on our way. I didn't really want to go back to class, but Ms. Malthrin had told us to. Besides, class was better than ten minutes with nothing to do but talk to Reubyn.

Ms. Malthrin didn't let Reubyn or me do anything else for the rest of the period. We sat at our lab table and stared around the room while everyone else finished putting the smoke bombs together and put them in the back to cool. We were supposed to light them off the next day. Reubyn and I, of course, wouldn't be doing any such thing.

It was a relief when the bell released us for lunch. I joined Valie and Ril as we headed to the mess hall.

"I'm so sorry, Lil," said Valie as we walked.

I shrugged. "It's not like it was your fault," I said. "I just can't believe I've got detention. And with Reubyn, no less. Half an hour of just sitting there with her. I can't even do homework." I shoved my hands into my pockets. It was chilly.

We joined Mako and two of our other friends - Jannei and Zula - at our table once we got our food. Valie and Ril filled the other three in about science class as we dug in.

"That sucks, Lil," said Jannei when the story was done. "Man, you and Reubyn are like cats and dogs, huh?"

"Yeah," I said, sighing. "Could be worse, though. I mean, it's only for a year, right? It's not like we'll have to room together forever."

Eurgh. What a thought.

When the bell rang for the end of lunch, the six of us left the mess hall. Mako and I turned left as soon as we entered the building and went to Miss Madelie's room for Law and Justice.

I dreaded the end of sixth period.

The detention was every bit as bad as I had expected. Ms. Malthrin had Reubyn and me sit at our lab table silently for half an hour. We couldn't do anything - not homework, not read, nothing. And since Ms. Malthrin was in the room, we couldn't so much as kick under the table like three-year-olds. I didn't breathe properly again until Ms. Malthrin told us that the half-hour was up and we could go.

That was the worst half-hour I've ever spent, I thought.

Reubyn and I went opposite directions as soon as we left the classroom. And as I headed down the hall back to the girls' dorms, I decided I wouldn't mind if we went opposite directions for the rest of our lives.

Chapter Three: Safe-ish

PING!

"Five minutes to mock-up mission assignment! All students to the Garden for assignment, please!"

I shut off the water and groped for my towel. I'd just finished up in the gym, so even though I knew we had a mock-up mission soon, I'd taken a brief shower. I figured everyone I ended up working with would appreciate it.

A gust of cold wind sliced through me as I stepped out of the gym. It was December 23rd, and the coldest day I'd seen at the Academy so far. I pulled my jacket out of my gym bag and put it on, shivering. It took a few moments to warm up the lining.

I reached the Garden with about half a minute to spare. Aside from a few stragglers - others who had been at the gym or eating breakfast - we were all there.

Once all the stragglers arrived, Professor Langley called us to attention. "All right, everyone," he said. "Who's ready for a mock-up mission?"

A cheer cut through the icy air. I enjoyed the mock-ups, even if I did get stuck with Reubyn more than I liked.

"All right, settle down, settle down," called Professor Langley, chuckling behind the exquisite white mustache he'd grown the month before. "Now, today will be your first mock-up in truly wintery weather. It's going to make things different."

He went on to talk about the importance of keeping warm as we worked, moving quickly but not sloppily, and a bunch of other things that started to mush together in my ears. We'd been over all of it several times in different workshops.

When Professor Langley said my name, my head snapped up.

"Miss Anied, you'll be with Miss Tomsein..."

Son of a bitch.

Ever since our spat in science class, the teachers had put us together for every assignment. I suspected Ms. Malthrin. She had been serious about us learning to get along.

Miss Madelie was waiting in the Law and Justice room, where Reubyn and I were supposed to meet. Reubyn entered only a moment after me.

"Good, you're here," Miss Madelie said. When we had a mock-up, the teachers went into Leader mode. It usually seemed silly, but according to the teachers it made things more realistic. "Here's the situation, you two..."

She turned away from us and tapped the video screen with her finger, and it came to life. A hi-def image of the lake, which had been frozen over for about a month, filled the whole thing. Translucent temperature and heart rate gauges lined the right edge of the screen.

"We've got a person injured and trapped out on the ice," Miss Madelie said. "Here." She tapped an area about three-quarters of the way across the lake from the school to zoom in on the image. I could see the dummy serving as our trapped person lying spread-eagle on the ice. It had on a thick down jacket, long pants, and boots. One of its legs was bent at the wrong angle, like it was badly broken.

"Your mission is to rescue this person before his condition gets too much worse," Miss Madelie said. "But be careful. It's cold out there. The two of you are going to have to work together every step of this mission."

Of course we were.

"Go get ready," Miss Madelie said. "And then get going. We haven't got much time."

I kitted myself out in long pants, a pair of warm

black boots, a long-sleeved green shirt, and a thick purple vest. Reubyn had on a skirt, which I thought was impractical, but she had on thick white leggings, boots, and a vest of her own. Her vest and boots were a very bright shade of fuchsia.

"At least if we get stuck," I said, "they'll be able to see us to get us out."

"Shut up," said Reubyn. "I understand that you have the emotional capacity and fashion sense of a toddler, but there's no need to flaunt it."

I muttered an insult in her direction and left the room, trying to be sweeping and grand about it, but the toe of my boot   snagged on the threshold and I found myself sprawled on the floor, palms burning, nose feeling decidedly squashed.

Reubyn laughed. I pushed myself up and headed out the door, trying to pretend nothing had happened.

"Aren't you forgetting something?"

I turned. Reubyn had two satchels: one hanging over her shoulder, and one dangling from her hand. My cheeks went warm, and I knew my face was going vivid red. How had I forgotten my satchel?

Each student had one, though the teachers usually kept them in storage until mock-ups. They held basic supplies we'd need for each one, like first-aid kits.

I grabbed the one Reubyn held out to me, slung it over my shoulders, and went on pretending nothing had happened.

As we headed down to the lake, I checked my omnipad for details. The main screen showed a live video feed of the part of the lake where our dummy lay sprawled, with boxes along the side showing heart rate, internal body temperature, ice thickness, and external temperature. The first two numbers were simulations, but the last were real enough. It was negative fifteen degrees Celsius, and the ice under the dummy lay half a meter thick.

Because of the cold, our satchels had been equipped with earmuffs, several baggies of mixed nuts each, and thermal blankets. Everything had been tested and retested to make sure the conditions would be as safe as possible, but nobody wanted to take chances.

I put the omnipad away, put the earmuffs on, and shoved my hands in my vest pockets. I would much rather have been rescuing a summer hiker caught in a precarious position or someone caught in a rip current than wandering out onto the ice like this. It would have been dangerous, sure, but at least it wouldn't have been cold.

When we reached the edge of the ice, Reubyn

and I both hesitated. I saw her hand go to her necklace, something I had unwillingly noticed her doing during difficult tests and once or twice in the middle of the night when I woke up from a dark dream and happened to roll over so I was facing her. The pendant was a round blue stone carved with symbols, hung on a leather thong. I'd never seen her without it.

"What are you looking at?" she asked, noticing my gaze.

"Nothing," I said. "Shouldn't we get out there?"

Reubyn glanced out over the frozen lake, expression inscrutable. "Of course." She looked at me, and I was almost glad to see the familiar disdain in her expression. "What, scared?"

No, I thought. *...But I think you are.*

Reubyn didn't wait for my answer. She put her foot on the ice and tentatively increased the pressure.

Nothing happened.

She lifted her other foot off the ground and set it down on the ice, too.

Still nothing.

We started moving across the ice slowly, carefully. Every time I heard the slightest groan, I froze. My heart jumped into my throat and stayed there. I didn't care that the ice had been checked and re-checked before our mock-up; I didn't want to be out on it. It freaked me out.

Nervous as I was, though, Reubyn seemed to be even worse. She looked calm enough if I just glanced at her, but longer scrutiny when she wasn't looking revealed something oddly fragile in her expression. I'd never seen her like this. Usually - around me, at least - she looked annoyed or hostile. Honestly, I thought I preferred that. I was used to that. This freaked me out even worse than the ice.

I looked up to see clouds scuttling in from the edges of the dome of sky around the Academy. As they settled in over the sun, I shivered. It felt like the temperature had just gone down another five degrees.

"I think we're going to be in for some serious snow soon," I said, glancing at Reubyn. "We'd better hurry."

She grunted her agreement and began to move faster. I hurried to keep up with her while trying to squash my own fear. We were about a half a kilometer away from shore, over one of the deepest parts of the lake. But the dummy was only a few meters further. I figured on maybe ten more minutes before we made it back to shore, dummy and all.

We reached the dummy and knelt down next to it. I checked the internal body temperature and heart rate monitors as Reubyn pulled out supplies. The temperature gauge was dropping, but the heart rate was rising. Hypothermia. But I needed to take care of the leg before I could do anything else.

"I need a bandage or something," I said. "The leg's broken."

"I'll get it," Reubyn said. "Take care of the blankets."

She grabbed a stick and a roll of bandages and moved to splint the dummy's broken leg. I pulled the blankets over top of it, which was the most I could do while Reubyn patched it up. Once she finished the splint, we gently rolled the dummy up in the blankets to keep it as warm as we could.

The wind worked its way up to a screech, and the temperature still felt like it was dropping. The snow started to fall in big, thick flakes.

"Let's get back quick," I said. "The weather's turning nasty."

"No, really," murmured Reubyn, but she didn□t argue. We shoved our supplies back into our satchels and prepared to pick up the dummy.

"Urgh!" I grunted. The thing weighed at least a hundred fifty pounds. Reubyn and I were both pretty strong for a sixteen-year-old and a recent seventeen-year-old, but given the conditions, lifting the dummy was tough. It was deadweight. There was no way it could help us with the load.

It was slow going back towards shore as the conditions worsened. The wind keened faster than ever, flinging the huge snowflakes into our faces.

Soon I lost sight of shore. The snow blowing around us grew heavier, and it felt like we were blown back a pace every time one of us picked up a foot.

"We have to stop!" I yelled over the wind.

"We can't!" replied Reubyn. "How are we supposed to get back otherwise? We have to keep going."

"If we do, we'll get lost!" I said. "Can you see land? Because I sure as hell can't! For all I know we're walking in circles." *Oh, God, don't let us die out here.*

"We can't stop," Reubyn insisted. I heard a note of panic in her voice. "Who knows how long this'll last? We could be stranded out here for days!"

As we argued, something shifted beneath my feet. Reubyn and I both shut up, freezing to the spot.

"That's not good," whispered Reubyn.

The next time, a cracking sound accompanied the shift. My heart stopped for a second, then started up again at double speed. "Oh, no," I breathed. I flashed through what I knew about staying on top of thin ice.

"Lie down," I told Reubyn. "Use your hands and your legs to move."

We did just that. I couldn't feel any cracks with the snow piled fifteen centimetres deep on top of the ice, but I knew they were there. I could still feel the ice shifting every so often.

"Careful," Reubyn said.

We began to shimmy through the snow, dragging the dummy behind us. It had the blankets wrapped around it, after all. We were going to want those when - I tried not to think if - we got off the ice.

The ice cracked again, louder now. The world had turned into a blinding white wall around us. All I could see was Reubyn to my left and maybe a meter of ice and blowing snow on either side of me.

Next time the ice cracked, Reubyn shrieked and I heard a splash.

"Reubyn!" I shouted.

Most of her body dangled beneath the ice, in the freezing-cold water. She clung to the ice for dear life, but I could see how thin it had gotten. We must have turned and headed towards the lake center in the whiteout.

I let go of the dummy and shimmied over to

my roommate, preparing to hoist her out of the water somehow. But the ice gave out beneath me, and I fell into the water myself.

The breath huffed out of my lungs. The water soaked through my clothes in an instant, even the boots and vest. It burned like fire and stabbed like thousands of needles all at once. It took three long seconds before I could make myself breathe and move again.

Every time I tried to grab onto the ice around me, it cracked. The ice was much thinner here, too thin even to hold a hundred nineteen pounds of lanky teenage girl.

Finally, I found a spot that supported me and looked around for Reubyn. I made out the vivid fuchsia of her vest across the hole from me. "Help!" she screamed. "Somebody help!" She sounded hysterical.

Bracing myself, I pushed off the ice and swam over to her. The hole in the ice had grown; I had to struggle across almost ten feet of icy water before I reached the other side. Below the surface, I saw the dummy. It must have fallen through. But I didn't have a second to waste on the now-useless blankets. I grabbed Reubyn's shoulder.

"Help!" she screamed again, and I realized she was sobbing. "Somebody help, they're drowning!"

They? Reubyn must have been hysterical. I put an arm under her shoulders and tried to pull away from the thin platform of ice. I felt a slight current beneath us, which meant we were above the spring that fed the lake. It was on the opposite side of where we had started, but at least I knew where we were now. The shore was only about two hundred meters away.

"Reubyn, paddle!" I shouted. "Help me out here!"

But she seemed determined to do exactly the opposite. She strained against me, trying to go back. "They're drowning!" she half-screamed, half-sobbed. "We have to help them! Josoh! *Dad!*"

I didn't waste brainpower trying to make sense of what she said. Reubyn continued sobbing as I dragged us towards the shoreline. The snow and wind were still getting stronger. If we didn't get out of here soon, we'd both be in serious trouble.

I made out the faint shapes of people on the shore. They seemed to be shouting, but I couldn't hear them over the wind. The ice was getting thicker, harder to push through, but it was still too thin to walk on and besides, I wasn't strong enough to pull us both out of the water. I had to keep swimming.

"Lillia!" came a faint yell. "Come on, Lil!"

"We're coming after you!"

They were. Not Valie and Mako, the two who had yelled - a couple people held them on shore so they didn't run out and break through the ice themselves - but some of the teachers ventured towards us. I decided my current position was solid enough and stopped pushing forwards. I treaded water instead, struggling to keep both myself and the now-still Reubyn afloat.

Then a pair of arms wrapped around me. Someone grunted maybe twenty centimeters from my ear, and I felt myself being dragged out of the water. I let my eyes drift shut, but I wrenched them open again when I felt Reubyn slipping from my grip.

"No! Reubyn!" I shouted, grabbing for my roommate's limp body.

"Calm down, Lillia!" ordered a woman - Miss Madelie. "I can't pull both of you up. Mr. Velsom's got hold of Reubyn."

I subsided. Miss Madelie put an arm around me as I got free of the icy water. "Try to help me," she said as we moved back towards shore. I did try, but I didn't think I did much good. In the instant after I left the danger, exhaustion I hadn't realized I felt had all caught up to me. It was like someone had attached lead weights to my feet.

When we reached shore, people swarmed us. Someone put a warm blanket over my shoulders.

"Let's get them to the nurse," said one of the students. And then Ms. Mag: "Come on, hurry!"

I let my eyes close again as we walked. When we entered the warmth - the main building, I assumed - I sighed in relief. As we walked down the hall, the brightness turned the backs of my eyelids orange. Finally, in the infirmary, I was able to sit, sinking down onto one of the beds.

"Everybody clear out," said Mrs. Opni. "Give us some privacy so I can get them into something dry."

The people who had come in with us filed back out, and Mrs. Opni handed me a towel and a set of flannel pajamas. She handed the same things to Reubyn. "Change," she ordered. "Tell me when you're done - I've got hot chocolate waiting."

She left the room. Reubyn and I undressed and dried off, too cold and wet to care about modesty. When I had on the pajamas - which were wonderfully warm, like they'd just come out of the dryer - I sat back down on the bed.

"Lillia?" came Reubyn's voice from behind me. I stiffened in surprise. Aside from our first day, I didn't think I had ever heard her said my name.

And certainly not in the tone she used then - soft and hesitant, almost like she was talking to a friend.

I turned to look at her. "Yeah?"

Her hand was back on her necklace. She looked down at the floor. "You saved my life," she said. "I... Thank you."

I didn't know what to say. Two hours ago the only reason she'd have said a word to me would have been to make a snide remark. How were you supposed to respond in this kind of situation?

"What else could I do?"

Reubyn smiled and looked up at me. "Still, thank you," she said. "I'll tell Mrs. Opni we're done."

I stared at her as she crossed the room to Mrs. Opni's office. A moment later, she returned carrying a steaming mug. Mrs. Opni was putting a blanket over her shoulders. The nurse had another blanket, too, and another mug.

"Here," she said, handing it to me and putting the other blanket around me. "Try to stay awake for a little while, please. I'm going to set up the space heater."

She bustled around for a moment or two, putting on the space heater right by Reubyn and me, making sure we were drinking the hot chocolate, advising us to try to do a few aerobic exercises to warm up a bit more. Then she left. I looked at

Reubyn.

"What happened out there?" I asked, quietly so Mrs. Opni couldn't hear us. "After the ice cracked, I mean. You said something about somebody drowning. Somebody named Josoh...and your dad."

Reubyn looked down at her hot chocolate and rubbed at her necklace. For a long moment, I thought she wasn't going to answer.

"My dad was a Peacekeeper," she said eventually. Her voice was still as quiet as it had been earlier. "He was my idol. I wanted to be just like him when I got older.

"But he died, almost three years ago," she continued. "Just after Christmas. The twenty-eighth of December. We'd all gone out to the pond near our house - Mom, Dad, Josoh and me, I mean. Josoh had gotten new ice skates for Christmas. He wanted to be a hockey player." She smiled. "He was a forward. Brilliant at it. So we went out to the pond so he could break in the skates."

Reubyn had looked up from her mug. Now she looked off towards the window, like she could see the scene just outside.

"I was awful at ice skating - still am, actually - so Mom and I stayed near the edges of the pond while Dad and Josoh skated out closer to the middle. I remember I felt so jealous. Dad and Josoh were so good at things like that. I wished I could be, too. I wished I could skate well enough that I could go out there and join them. But I guess it was a good thing I couldn't, in the end.

"Josoh was close to the middle - too close. There was this awful crack, and suddenly he was under the water. I tried to skate out after him, but Mom grabbed my arm and stopped me. You can't go out there, she told me. You'll get hurt.

"She didn't tell Dad that, though. He skated over to the hole in the ice and jumped into the water after my brother. Josoh was sixteen, strong and a great swimmer, but with the skates and all the cold-weather clothes on, he just couldn't make it up to the surface. I guess he drifted to the side or something. The hole was really small."

Her eyes glimmered in the fluorescent hospital wing lighting. She looked back down, and I would have sworn I saw a tear fall into her hot chocolate.

"Everything would have gone all right," she said, "if Dad had had his stuff. But he'd left it all on the shore so he wouldn't have to tote it around. He didn't have his Aquabreath. I guess between trying to find Josoh and then trying to get back up again, he ran out of oxygen. The next time Mom and I saw them was when a few more Peacekeepers showed up and went after them with Aquabreaths. It didn't take very long, but it was already too late. Dad and Josoh were both dead."

I didn't know what to do with that.

Finally, feeling more than a little awkward, I slid an arm out from under my blanket and laid a hand on top of hers. "I'm sorry," I murmured. "I - I shouldn't have asked. It was a stupid-ass question -"

Reubyn shook her head. "No. I'm kind of glad you asked." She looked at me, and even though there were still tears in her eyes, she smiled. "Which is weird, considering that an hour ago I hated your guts."

I smiled, too. "Crazy, right?"

An hour before, I'd hated Reubyn. And now I felt like we'd been best friends our whole lives. Was that what a life-and-death experience did to you?

"My dad gave this to me that Christmas," Reubyn said, showing me her pendant. "I've seen you looking at it a few times. That's why I wear it. I didn't really like it much when I got it, but now it means the world to me."

That explained a lot. Like why she never seemed to take it off. Even swimming or at the gym she had it on. And when I got up in the mornings, I always saw the leather strap hanging out of her fist.

"The symbols," I said, looking at it. "They're Oisian, aren't they?"

Reubyn nodded. "This one means peace," she said, touching it. "And this one means beloved. Dad wasn't Oisian, but he thought the characters looked nice. Mom said that he spent weeks working on it."

For a moment, we sat there silently, thinking and drinking our hot chocolate. Finally, I said, "Thank you. For telling me."

"Thanks for listening," Reubyn replied. "I don't think I've ever told anyone that story except for the grief therapist." She smiled wryly. "Guess I'm still more messed up than I thought."

I couldn't help giggling. Neither could Reubyn. Then everything sort of caught up to me, and I found myself doubled over on my lap, laughing my ass off and holding my mug of hot chocolate up over my head so it didn't spill. It took almost ten minutes before the two of us could do anything else.

Then we dragged two of the hospital beds close together on either side of the space heater and sat talking as we nursed the cooling remains of our hot chocolate. Mrs. Opni came in once or twice to check on us or bring soup, but otherwise she left us alone. The two of us sat there for most of the rest of the day, exchanging stories, daydreams, likes and dislikes. I told her about Mom and Dad, the Career Day presentation that had made me want to join the Peacekeepers, about fights on the streets and friends of mine who'd gone down in them - all the things you didn't tell people. Reubyn had already told me her deep dark secret, so she told me that her mom was an image consultant and did hair and makeup styling. She said that she knew the business as well as her mom did.

"I could give you a makeover," she offered, grinning.

I laughed. "Maybe some other time," I said. "After Mrs. Opni sets us free."

We both laughed at that. Mrs. Opni could be a little overbearing about her patients.

"She can't keep us too long," Reubyn said. "Once she makes sure we didn't catch pneumonia or anything, she has to let us go."

I glanced over at the window and saw, to my surprise, that it was dark out. "Wow," I said. "How long has it been since we went out this morning?"

Reubyn looked at her watch. "I don't know," she said. "My watch must've stopped in the water." She showed me the face. Sure enough, it was stuck on eight hours fifty, thirty-nine seconds.

The clock above the infirmary read eighteen hours forty-five. "Ages," I said. "More than ten hours."

"Wow," murmured Reubyn. "What a day."

I nodded in agreement. "What a day."

***

"I changed my mind. I really don't want to do this."

Reubyn slumped her shoulders in an exaggerated sigh. "Come on, Lillia," she said. "You already agreed to this. Besides, you trusted me to do everything else. Why not?"

"Because this involves me getting a needle stuck through me," I replied. "Three times. Hair grows back, dye washes out, and I can take off makeup - and I'm going to, I don't like having this shit on my face - but what am I supposed to do if I don't like having pierced ears?"

"Take out the earrings," Reubyn replied. She turned off the water and looked at me, newly sterile needle raised. "The holes close up if you do that. Trust me, okay?"

I squeezed my eyes shut for a long moment, then sighed. "All right," I said. "Just do it quick, before I lose my nerve again."

Reubyn moved quickly. I felt a chill as the ice pressed against the back of my earlobe, and I gritted my teeth. *It'll be all over soon,* I told myself. *Don't think about it, don't think about it...*

"Yeeow!" I yelled.

Reubyn had poked the needle through my ear. I felt a couple little tugs as she slid the needle out and put a stud into place, but mostly all I felt was a sharp, throbbing pain. My eyes teared up.

"Can't lose your nerve now," Reubyn said, starting on the other ear. Again, I yelped. On the positive side, the first ear was starting to throb less.

"Ready for the cartilage?" asked Reubyn.

"No."

"Don't be chicken. It'll only be a second. Then you can look at it and decided whether you want to keep them or not."

As she said this, she held the ice behind the top of my left ear. I gritted my teeth.

The needle didn't hurt as much as I expected. Reubyn ignored my flinch and slid the stud in just as deftly as she had the other two.

My breathing and heart rate started to slow, and I stood up. There was a full-length mirror by the bathroom door. Even though I'd seen the makeover Reubyn had given me - minus the earrings - before, I really wanted to see it again.

And when I looked in the mirror, I saw the girl Reubyn had made me into. My dyed auburn hair was side-parted, cut into a bob at my jawline with side-swept bangs.

She'd helped me with makeup, too - in other

words, she'd put it on my face while I held still and tried not to wince or move the wrong way. I had on brown eyeliner and mascara, greenish-brown eyeshadow, and tinted lip moisturizer. She'd also managed to get her hands on some foundation that matched my skin tone. It looked good, but I hated how it felt. That shit was coming off ASAP.

I could see all of this perfectly clearly, courtesy of my new square, black-framed glasses. Mrs. Opni had gotten my prescription after an eye exam she'd administered while Reubyn and I had been in the infirmary. I hadn't realized until I put them on that paradise was not angel choruses and pearly gates - it was vision that didn't blur everything in my path.

"I hope you like the colors," Reubyn said, interrupting my thoughts. "It'll be about six weeks before the lobes heal, and three months or so before the cartilage does. I've got stuff to keep the piercings clean while they're healing."

I looked away from my reflection. "Thanks, Reubyn," I said, smiling. "As much as I hate to admit it, I kind of enjoyed most of that. And it looks really good."

Reubyn smiled. "Thanks. I enjoyed it, too."

I laughed. "I know you did," I said. "You're a control freak, you know that?"

"Yes I am," Reubyn replied. "I'm just glad you aren't. What do you say we do the real dye tomorrow? The permanent stuff, I mean."

I glanced back at my reflection in the mirror. I had to admit, I loved how I looked.

Slowly, I nodded. "Yeah. We can do the real dye."

Chapter Four: Five More Minutes

The sun shone brightly over Reubyn, Valie, Mako, a few of our friends, and I as we sat on the rock in the lake. What little conversation sprang up among us was quiet and short-lived. None of us knew if we were ever going to see each other again.

Today was September first, one year since entering the Academy, and that meant graduation. Soon it would be time for all of us to leave.

Professor Langley would give us our duty station assignments as we graduated, but I couldn't help wishing we could know beforehand. If I was going to have to leave my friends, I would have liked to have more time to say goodbye and know I was saying it. As it was, we had to sit here on the rock and imagine that we might all be going our separate ways.

I sighed and looked up at the sky. It was almost noon. "We probably ought to get going," I said.

The others murmured their agreement, and we slid off the rock and into the cool, clear water of the lake.

The swim and walk back to the dorms was almost completely silent. I could feel the melancholy in the air. We all could. No one wanted to leave.

We split off one or two at a time, heading for our rooms, until Reubyn and I were alone on the slow walk to room 310.

"I guess this is really it," Reubyn said. We paused outside our door. Reubyn looked out the window at the empty grounds.

"Yeah," I agreed. "Listen, Reubyn..."

She turned her attention from the window to me. "Mm?"

I fiddled with the doorknob, looking for the words.

"I just want you to know," I said finally, "that even if we don't ever see each other again...you're my best friend. I never imagined that I would have a friend like you." I cracked a weak smile. "And I definitely never imagined that if I did, it would be you."

Reubyn smiled. "I know what you mean," she said. "You're my best friend, too. I'm gonna miss you if we don't get stationed together."

"Maybe we'll get lucky," I said. "They spent half the year trying to get us to work together; maybe now that we do they'll put us in the same place."

"That would be nice," Reubyn said. She glanced out the window again, graceful shoulders sagging under what looked like the weight of the entire school's sadness.

"Come on. We'd better finish packing."

Ping.

"All students report to the Garden for graduation, please. All students report to the Garden!"

Despite myself, I felt excitement rise up.

I picked up my bag and looked around at the room one last time. Then I joined Reubyn, and we left together, closing the door behind us.

By the time we left the building, we had been enveloped by the stream of girls headed for the Garden. On the other side of the path, I saw the boys coming from their dorms. I waved to a couple whom I knew.

The students crowded into the Garden, leaving our bags by the entrance. It was easier that way; besides, nobody wanted to be carrying a bag for graduation.

I wiped my palms off on my shorts and shoved my hands in my pockets. Nobody needed to know that they were trembling. Maybe even I'd forget about it in a minute or two.

"Welcome, soon-to-be-graduates!" called Professor Langley. The low level of chatter dampened down to nothing. "We're sad to see you go, but I'm pleased to know that each and every one of you has passed this year of schooling and chosen Peacekeeping as your official duty! With you all protecting the Confederacy, I'm sure we'll all feel a little safer in our beds."

"Yeah, because a hundred nineteen teens and twenty-somethings are going to keep the whole Confederacy safe," whispered Reubyn. Everyone within earshot giggled.

Then Professor Langley went off on some spiel about how the burden of the safety and peace of the Confederacy was now to be shared by us, and starting on the next stage of our lives, and something about friends and family that I mostly missed because I got bored and started whispering to Reubyn and the others halfway through.

Professor Langley brought our attention back to the ceremony and called Rhian Klaoskah, the valedictorian, up to the front. We were starting.

Rhian looked more than a little nervous about having to talk in front of so many people. She opened her mouth, closed it, cleared her throat, opened her mouth again, and stood there for several long, silent seconds before she managed to speak.

"Well, I guess first and foremost I should say congratulations to everyone," she said. "We survived!"

A collective snicker ran through the crowd

"Um, well," Rhian continued, "just remember, I suppose, that even though we're done here, it's not an ending. This is really the start of our lives, right?"

It took everyone a few seconds to realize that she wanted an answer, and the following murmur of assent sounded halfhearted. Rhian shifted and started talking again.

"If there's one thing I learned over my year here," she said, "it's that the most essential part of Peacekeeping is keeping peace inside yourself. I'm sure all of us have had that day when we were nervous or angry, and everything we tried to do went straight to hell..."

Reubyn and I both chuckled quietly. "You got that right," I murmured.

"Anyway, well, I guess what I really mean to say is, always keep the peace first and foremost inside yourself. It's only when you've taken care of that that you can effectively keep the peace everywhere else. Um...Professor Langley?"

Rhian stepped back as Professor Langley addressed us again.

"There's little left for me to say," he said. "Let's begin!"

He gestured, and Mr. Ibsroo stepped forward. He held a stack of papers - our diplomas.

"Penze Adronis!"

Penze was the strawberry-haired boy who had been on my team on the first day of school. In January, he'd cut his messy mop of hair, and the ensuring crew cut almost blended into his complexion. He stepped out of the throng and moved up. Mr. Ibsroo handed Professor Langley the top diploma, and Professor Langley gave it to Penze.

"Peacekeeper Adronis," Professor Langley said, "you have been stationed as a Province Keeper in Klinds." The two of them shook hands, and then Penze started making his way down the line of faculty and staff.

I was third to be called, right after Nit Akli, a pretty, dark-haired girl who was stationed in Mandis, the capital of Leyon. Professor Langley handed me my diploma and said, "Peacekeeper Anied, you have been stationed as a Province Keeper in Fankon."

Fankon!

As I moved down the line of teachers, shaking hands, I ran through what I knew about the province. It was a remote group of six small, semitropical islands to the southeast of Pahn. It had been formed by a volcanic hotspot, but only one island still had an active volcano. Actually, that was all that island was. I made a mental note to avoid it. What had it been called - Kali-something? I couldn't remember. All the islands had names made up primarily of vowels. Kalinuea, that was it. What a mouthful!

I watched the rest of the ceremony from the growing group of new Peacekeepers. Jannei, Mako, Valie, and Zula came to join me one by one.

None of them had been stationed in Fankon. Jannei had ended up in Plancint, along with several other students. I could understand why; Plancint needed a lot of Peacekeeping.

Valie had been stationed in Ranoe, a major city in the province of Carloan. Mako was going to be a Province Keeper in her native province of Naklia. Zula had been stationed in Cialo, the capital of Oisi.

Finally, after too many other T's, Professor Langley called Reubyn to the front. My stomach knotted itself up even more than it had when Professor Langley had called Valie, Jannei, Mako, and Zula.

"Peacekeeper Tomsein," Professor Langley said, "you have been stationed as a Province Keeper in Fankon."

I stared. *No way...*

But as Reubyn started moving down the line of teachers, seeming just as stunned as me, I felt my shock slowly giving way to excitement. In the time it took Reubyn to reach us, I recovered enough from the surprise to shriek a little with her and exchange excited hugs.

"I can't believe it!" Reubyn said. "I would have thought they'd put us on opposite sides of the Confederacy after how we started off."

"Me too," I said. "But I'm not complaining. Reubyn, this is great!"

We kept our little party quiet until Professor Langley had given everyone their diplomas. Then he turned to the group of new Peacekeepers.

"Congratulations!" he cried in unison with all the teachers and staff.

A loud cheer came up from our throats and went on solidly for over a minute. Reubyn and I grabbed onto each other's hands and half-danced, half-jumped around in a circle. Mako screamed, "I'm going home! I'm going home!" Valie hugged everyone in sight. A couple meters away, a big group of kids had broken out into a loud, off-key rendition of an old military victory song.

When we finally started to quiet, Professor Langley waved for our attention.

"Now then, before you disperse," he said, "the Peacekeeping Ministry has paid for your lighttrain tickets. But if you miss your scheduled departure, the cost will be on you! Departure times are posted on the video screens in your old common rooms.

"And now I suppose there's only one thing left for me to say. Go well, new Peacekeepers!"

This time, the cheering lasted much longer.

Reubyn and I had to leave right away to catch the lighttrain to Arins. The ride was an hour and a half long, and I spent a lot of it watching the scenery flash by at enormous speed. Lighttrains moved incredibly fast on the reduced friction tracks, almost seven hundred kliks per hour.

We got off the train at Harn Station.

"Now down to the harbor, right?" I asked. The next step for us was a little trading vessel across the Prentic Ocean. Not many boats went out to Fankon this time of year.

Reubyn nodded, consulting the map of Arins posted on the wall to our right. She put a finger on the lighttrain station, and then traced a line to the harbor. "It's not far," she said. "Right when we exit, and then follow the road until we reach the ocean."

"Sounds simple enough," I said. "Let's see if we can screw it up, shall we?"

Both of us cracked a grin as we set off.

Gulls circled over the street, calling to each other and dive-bombing garbage dumpsters. It was a warm, sunny day, and the streets were thronged with people: tourists and locals and musicians strumming guitars or singing or playing drums or violins for spare change, interspersed with the kind of people I recognized from years in the bad part of town. At one point, I saw a young man in a Peacekeeper uniform and gave a small salute. He smiled and saluted back.

Reubyn and I stopped under the arch marking the entrance to the harbor and looked at each other. "What was the name of the boat again?" Reubyn asked.

"Um..." I said. "Oh, no."

This was not good. There were at least a dozen boats in the harbor; any of them could have been the one we were supposed to take to Fankon.

Then I heard a voice calling, "Peacekeepers! Over here!"

Reubyn and I both turned to see a man with thick black hair waving to us, smiling. We hurried over to him.

"Tomsein and Anied, right?" asked the man. "I'm Harndel Rishar. I'll be taking you two out to Fankon."

"Thanks for calling us over," said Reubyn. I could hear the relief in her tone. "We weren't sure where to go."

"No problem," replied Harndel. "Climb aboard. I'm all ready to set sail."

During the next few days, I made some discoveries.

One: I loved being at sea. The wind in my face, the fresh, salty air, the endless blue waves; all of it seemed like heaven to me. From the start, I felt perfectly fine on the boat - unlike Reubyn, who had a half a day of seasickness before she grew accustomed to the motion of the boat through the waves.

Two: until Reubyn and I had been stationed there, there had been only one Peacekeeper in Fankon.

I had known it was a peaceful province, but that seemed insane. Usually, the minimum for any province was three Province Keepers. Most had more. But I supposed that most of the force had been used for areas that really needed more Peacekeepers. Now that the crime rates were finally going down again, the Confederacy could afford to bring Fankon up to standard.

Three: Harndel was a merchant. He had been on his way to Fankon to trade and pick up taxes.

He had been given Reubyn's and mine Peacekeeper equipment - green shirts with the emblem of the Peacekeepers, a brown Greek cross inside a white circle; plain satchels; goggles, and an Aquabreath and omnipad each. Reubyn and I had both fixed some of our shirts so that they were a little more in touch with our own preferences. I liked that the uniform rules were lax enough for that.

All in all, the first two days on the boat were heaven to me. As I lay in one of the hammocks we'd strung across the deck, listening to the motor as Reubyn took her shift driving, I looked up at the stars and smiled. This was great.

***

A loud rumble and a sudden downpour of cold water woke me up in the middle of the night. I spluttered and sat up too quickly. The hammock swayed wildly from side to side and dumped me off onto the damp deck.
"Ow!"

I wasn't entirely sure I'd woken up at first; I'd been having another one of my dark dreams, and the storm left the boat so dark that I couldn't tell much difference.

"Lillia?" came Reubyn's voice, confirming that I was awake. "Come on and help me wake

Harndel!"

We'd learned that the merchant was a heavy sleeper. It looked like even the rising storm hadn't managed to rouse him.

As we readied ourselves beside the hammock, a flash of lightning revealed that the waves were enormous - which I'd already inferred from the wild rocking of the boat. Before I could count to two, thunder crashed again.

"One -" I yelled over the noise of the storm, "two - three!"

Reubyn and I yanked the hammock up to our side, sending Harndel tumbling onto the deck. We'd discovered that this was one of the only ways to wake him up.

"What's going on?" he asked groggily.

Another flash of lightning and a roll of thunder answered for us. Immediately Harndel was on his feet.

"Get below deck," he ordered. Reubyn and I wasted no time arguing.

If anything, it was worse in the hold than up on deck. The wind and rain couldn't cut into us down here, but Reubyn looked distinctly sick, and even I felt a little nauseous. Every time lightning struck, the sea outside the portholes lit up an angry, foamy white. And now the storm was close enough that every bolt of lightning matched exactly with a shattering boom of thunder.

I grabbed an empty bucket from beside a large box of merchandise and brought it over to the small clear space where Reubyn hunkered down. She looked really, really ill, and I wanted to be prepared.

"Thanks," Reubyn said.

"When did this start?" I asked, gesturing up towards the storm.

Reubyn swallowed. "Only a minute or so before you woke up," she said. "It came out of nowhere. I mean, it started clouding over about eleven, but the rain and everything started up at full strength all at once. I was just about to wake Harndel up for his shift when - oh!"

Another combined roll of thunder and lightning strike crashed, the ship gave a particularly violent lurch, and Reubyn lost the battle with her stomach. I managed to shove the bucket in front of her just before she threw up. Loudly.

Eurgh, I thought, reaching over to get Reubyn's hair out of the way. She gave one more heave, wiped her mouth, and said, "Sorry." It came out weakly.

"It's okay," I said. "You have an excuse."

"Don't remind me."

My own nausea had been exacerbated by Reubyn's episode, but I swallowed it down. This was nasty enough already.

We sat there for a long while listening to the storm. Occasionally, Reubyn had to lean back over the bucket and empty her stomach again. Even though we were both tired - Reubyn had taken a three-hour shift driving the boat and I had been woken up in the middle of the night - neither of us could sleep. I usually liked storms, but this one seemed a little too strong to be normal. Of course, the fact that we were out on the ocean probably didn't help.

I checked the time about a thousand times during the storm but the minutes only struggled past - it felt like nearly ten would go by, but I'd check the time and it had only been one. Two if I was lucky. But the storm finally quieted at about three hours.

Harndel came down then to check on us. He wrinkled his nose at the scent - I'd ended up adding to the bucket after all - but didn't say anything about it.

"We're good," he said. "The storm's passed. How are you two feeling?"

I still felt a little queasy, and Reubyn looked ready to barf again, but we both shrugged it off.

"Well enough," Reubyn said. "Nothing a nap in the sea air won't fix."

"I'll take my shift," I offered. "It's about that time anyway."

The three of us headed out of the hold and back onto the decks. I sighed with relief. Away from the smell of the vomit, my stomach felt much better. Reubyn and Harndel headed for their hammocks, and I headed up to the wheel to take us through the last few hours of the night.

As the sun began peek up off to the east, I caught a glimpse of a low dome of land rising on the horizon ahead of us. "There it is," I whispered. "Fankon."

I glanced at the clock to the right of the wheel. It was five hours fifty-seven, three minutes before the end of my shift. The only clouds left in the sky were tatters of white like cotton caught in a fence, and they skulked around the edges of the sky behind us. It looked like we would be in for some real island weather when we arrived.

Since we were on a straight course for the nearest island, I let the wheel rest and checked my omnipad, which was plugged in charging next to the wheel. According to the map, we were about thirty miles offshore.

Three minutes later, I heard someone moving

around on deck. It was Harndel. He had strange sleeping patterns, I thought; he woke up instantly at six hours every morning, but otherwise you had to all but shove him off a cliff to get him to wake up.

"There it is," he said, joining me by the wheel. "We should be there within half an hour. I'll take the wheel now, if you like. Go and wake up Peacekeeper Tomsein. She's out like a light over there."

How? I wondered. The hammocks had to have been soaked once the storm finally subsided. They were probably still wet.

I shook Reubyn, who grunted and rolled over. I rolled my eyes and shook her harder.

"Five more minutes."

I narrowed my eyes and decided to do the same thing Reubyn and I had done to Harndel the night before. Reubyn hit the deck and snapped awake.

"What was that for?" she spluttered.

"You weren't waking up," I said, grinning. I enjoyed that more than I should have. "Come on. It's only half an hour until we get to Fankon. You can see it on the horizon."

I offered Reubyn my hand and she yanked me down onto the deck next to her. "Let's go see it, then," she said, standing up and muffling a laugh.

We headed up to the bow of the ship to watch Fankon grow on the horizon.

Here we go.

I made out several people waiting on the dock as we drew closer. One of them was a man with red hair, wearing a green shirt and black shorts. That must have been the other Peacekeeper, Vrenchard Alindes. There was a woman with him, with thick dark hair and light brown skin, and a smaller girl who looked a lot like the woman. They waved at us.

Harndel waved back. "That would be Peacekeeper Alindes," he said. "And it looks like he brought his wife and daughter, too." He stopped talking long enough to maneuver the boat into place at the dock. Vrenchard and the woman and girl - his wife and daughter - moved to the side of the dock.

"How are the seas running, Rishar?" asked Vrenchard, tossing Harndel a rope. I liked his voice. It was warm and slow and deep, like a bass drum.

"Well, up til this morning," Harndel replied. "We had an awful storm. I've never seen the likes of it before."

"We had one early this morning, too. Maybe Maunei is agitated," said Vrenchard's wife, and chuckled.

"Or fighting with Kaiko," interjected their grinning daughter. "About time one of them started it! Maybe it won't be so tense now."

"If they were fighting, it was one helluva spat," said Harndel. He rolled his eyes at Reubyn and me in a good-natured sort of way, like someone poking gentle fun at a friend's quirks. Reubyn and I exchanged glances. "Anyway, I've brought more than just goods today."

"Ah!" said Vrenchard. He looked at Reubyn and me and smiled. "You must be the new Peacekeepers. It's been a while since I've seen any others in person."

He extended a hand and helped us off the boat. "It's nice to meet you, sir," I said. "I'm Lillia Anied."

"I'm Reubyn Tomsein," Reubyn said. "And you must be Vrenchard Alindes, since you're the only other Peacekeeper here."

Vrenchard nodded. "It's good to meet you," he said.

His wife and daughter moved forward. "I'm Manialua," said the woman. "Vrenchard's wife and resident island archaeologist. And this is our daughter Nikiani."

We shook hands all around. Then Vrenchard turned to Harndel. "Thanks for bringing them," he said. "We rounded up the export goods; they're waiting in the storehouse on the other side of town. Want me to go get them?"

"Actually, would you mind helping me unload first?" asked Harndel. He had finished tying the boat to the dock.

"Of course," Vrenchard said. He clambered aboard.

"Vrenchard, I've got to get home," Manialua said. "I left Aiene in charge of the house; if I don't get back soon, he'll be so deep in the books that he wouldn't realize if Pegu himself came and set the place on fire."

"You left who doing what and who's the arsonist?" whispered Reubyn. I tried to keep a straight face.

Nikiani looked over at us and grinned. "I wouldn't be so flippant about Pegu if I were you," she said. "We might have to leave you on Kalinuea for him!"

"You're going to have to explain who these people are," I replied. "Otherwise that's just a jumble of vowels to us. No threat at all."

Nikiani rolled her eyes. "I'll get Mom to explain it. Dad, can I help?"

"Uh-oh," muttered Vrenchard. "Niki, I think it would be better if you went back to the house with

Mom and the new Peacekeepers. They need to get acquainted with the islands, not stand here on the docks."

"Fine," Nikiani said. "Bye, Dad, bye, Mr. Rishar!"

She waved for Reubyn and me to follow her, and she took off after her mother. Reubyn and I followed behind.

"So who's Aiene?" I asked, catching up to them. "Your brother?"

"No, he's Mom's apprentice," Nikiani answered before Manialua could say anything. "An amateur archaeologist. He isn't Fankaloa, but he's really into the history of this place."

I probably shouldn't ask questions, I decided. *They just make more.* Such as, what was Fankaloa?

Manialua read the confusion in my face. "Let's get back to the house," she said, smiling. "I can explain things a lot better there. Niki, no!"

Nikiani had stopped and closed her eyes like she was thinking about something. Her eyes snapped open when her mother spoke. "Aw, come on, Mom," she said. "We'd get back so much faster -"

"No," said Manialua. "Give Lillia and Reubyn some time before you introduce everything about these islands to them."

Reubyn and I exchanged glances again as we resumed our journey towards Vrenchard's house. It seemed there was a lot to learn about these islands. I couldn't help feeling that it wasn't going to be anything like I'd ever heard.

The Alindes' house was a small, one-story affair with some sort of loft in the top. It had a ton of windows, all of which sat open to catch the breeze that seemed to blow everywhere on this island. Instead of a door in the front doorway, there was a bamboo curtain painted with the symbol of the Peacekeepers. The property sat a little inland of Lanekea, the town where we'd landed. A forest of tall, branchy trees grew off to the west, and a domelike mountain loomed in the southeast.

Manialua and Nikiani led us into the house. The inside was open and bright, and seemed more spacious than it had looked from outside. The first area we encountered was a clean, neat kitchen. Dried herbs and vegetables hung from the ceiling, so the whole place smelled like a garden. A little ways off, separated by the kitchen counter, was a simple living area made up of a low table, cushions, and a few shelves of games and music. Another doorway covered by a bamboo curtain - this one painted with hibiscuses like the one behind Nikiani's right ear - led out the back. In the back right corner was a sturdy-looking, wooden spiral staircase that led up to the loft.

"I think you two will be staying here," Manialua said. "We don't have a Peacekeeper Base, since for the past nineteen years Vrenchard's been the only one here. Nikiani Akeanialua Alindes, get your feet off that table!"

Looking sheepish, Nikiani took her feet off the table and crossed her legs on her cushion.

Manialua bent down and took off her sandals, sliding them into an empty spot in the shoe rack beside the door. "It's a tradition in the islands to not wear shoes inside," she told Reubyn and me. We hurried to unlace our sneakers and put them in empty places on the rack. As I put my shoes on the rack, I noted that none of the shoes looked like they could be Nikiani's.

When I asked about it, Manialua smiled. "We don't wear our shoes in the house," she said, "but Niki has been boycotting them entirely since birth. And then she goes and puts her island-covered feet on the table where we all eat." She gave Nikiani a motherly glare. Nikiani grinned back.

"I'm gonna get Aiene," she said, hopping up. "I think he'll want to meet the new Peacekeepers."

She headed up the stairs. As she disappeared into the loft, her long skirt flapped up so that I could see her ankles. She wore anklets that looked like they were made out of leaves - very island-y. I wondered about that for a moment. But then Nikiani came back down, trailed by someone who distracted me.

He was tall, especially compared to the tiny Nikiani. Longish black hair fell into his almond-shaped dark eyes and made shaggy curtains around an angular face with high cheekbones and a strong jawline. He had on a tight red T-shirt with cut-off sleeves, which accentuated the sleek muscles beneath his tanned skin.

My cheeks went warm. *Hot damn...*

"Hey, Manialua," said the boy. "Nikiani said the new Peacekeepers were - oh! Sorry," he said, looking at Reubyn and me. He smiled. "I'm acting like you aren't even here. It's good to meet you."

When he smiled, his warm eyes almost crinkled shut and I got a glimpse of a mouthful of clean, straight teeth. I automatically smiled in return and held out my hand. When he took it, I almost swooned. His palm was calloused and comfortably cool.

"I'm Aiene Kimatsuro," he said, distracting me slightly from the fact that he was holding onto my hand. He was holding my hand. Holy crap.

"Lillia Anied," I responded. My brain was detached enough from my mouth that the words were probably only coming out of habit.

Aiene moved on to shake hands with Reubyn, and I curled up my right hand.

Oh, boy, I thought.

This could get interesting.

Chapter Five: Fishing Pole

"So, asked Mom, "how's the island life treating you?"

I was sitting on the roof of Vrenchard's house, one bare foot dangling over the edge. It had been three days since we'd reached Fankon - or Fankaloa, as Manialua told us it was called in the native language. Personally, I preferred Fankaloa. It fit the islands better than the Confederate name.

"It's great," I said. "The weather's amazing, the islands are beautiful, and all the people are really friendly."

Reubyn and I had learned all of that firsthand on the trip round the islands Vrenchard had taken us on the day we arrived. Manialua had talked about the history of the islands, and Nikiani had been a major icebreaker, because she knew everybody just as well as her parents did - if not better, in some cases. I noticed a couple dozen people with the same sort of leaf anklets that Nikiani had, none of whom wore shoes. They were especially friendly towards her.

Aiene had come along on the trips, but I'd kept my distance as much as possible. I worried that if I tried to talk too much in front of him, it would come out garbled and nonsensical. I didn't feel like coming across as a silly teenager with a crush, even if that was what I was.

"You know there's only one Peacekeeper here aside from Reubyn and me?" I asked, pulling my mind away from Aiene. "We're staying at his house with his family, since there isn't a base here."

Mom raised her eyebrows. "Only one other Peacekeeper?" she asked. "Wow. You three must really have your hands full over there."

"Not really." I shrugged. "It's really peaceful. I mean, Vrenchard told us that even when it was just him, there wasn't much trouble keeping everything together. Fankon's just got a much more peaceful mindset than the rest of the Confederacy."

As Mom absorbed that, I looked out to the trees of Kamo Nakae, the island's main forest, which was about half a mile away. Birds called from within the trees. I could smell all the different flowers that grew in the shade and hear the sound of rushing water. Even on the largest island, it was rare to be out of earshot of the sea or one of the small rivers that ran down from the islands' extinct volcanoes.

"I'm glad to hear you like it over there," Mom said finally. "It sounds wonderful."

"It is," I said. "I love it. I mean, Plancint is great, but the islands...there's something about them that I fell in love with as soon we landed. You can walk around barefoot much all the time, which you know I like."

Mom and I both laughed. I had been all but allergic to shoes for most of my life. Unfortunately, Plancint - especially where we lived - wasn't really the kind of place where you could run around barefoot. To step outside without shoes was to risk stepping on broken glass or a blade or something else that nobody wanted sticking out of their foot.

"Dad's working, I guess," I said then. "Is the new project going well?"

"So far it's great," Mom said. The firm Dad worked for had been hired to build the new financial tower in downtown Plancint, the biggest project he'd ever done. "He's been put in charge of one of the work teams."

"Cool," I said. "How far along is it?"

"Not very," Mom said. "The designs are all put together, but they're only just starting on the build. Right now I think they're laying the foundation."

"Lillia!" interrupted Nikiani's voice from below me. I glanced down to see her hanging out the doorway, looking up at me.

"What's up?" I asked.

"Mom said to come get you," Nikiani said.

"She's gonna take us all down to the sanctuary on the south shore."

I glanced back at Mom's image on the Vcomm screen. "Sorry," I said. "I'll call you later, okay?"

"Tell me all about the sanctuary," Mom said. She smiled. "I'll try to get your dad here so you can talk to him, too. Love you, Lil."

I smiled. "Love you too, Mom."

I hit the End Call button and turned off the Vcomm. Then I stashed it in my satchel and slid down onto the ground. Nikiani moved to steady me.

"What kind of sanctuary is it?" I asked.

We headed into the house as Nikiani said, "It's Kaiko's *nama'ea*."

Which sounded like gibberish to me.

Manialua, Vrenchard, Reubyn, and Aiene waited in the kitchen. When Manialua saw the confusion on my face, she smiled. "I'll explain everything when we get there," she told me. "There's a side to these islands that you and Reubyn haven't seen yet, and it's a big part of our culture. It'll be best to learn about it as soon as possible."

"Are we all ready?" asked Vrenchard.

Five heads bobbed.

As we headed out the door, I grabbed a pair of flip-flops - or slippahs, as the islanders called them. *Just in case.* My feet didn't have tough soles like Nikiani's yet.

I put them in my satchel as we rounded the house and headed southwest across the island. Aiene fell into step beside Manialua at the head of our little group. I ended up behind him, between Reubyn and Nikiani.

Manialua led us towards the sound of the river that flowed west from Makanea Pua'e, the volcano that had formed the island and now stood in a wide, low dome on my left. On the western edge of the old caldera was the Transmission Tower, which gave off the wireless signals that let Reubyn, Vrenchard and me send out reports to the Peacekeeper headquarters and also let me connect to Mom over my Vcomm. Dark specks wheeled in the air around it - uamaki, a breed of hawk that only lived in Fankaloa.

Our walk to the sanctuary was only three kilometers, so it didn't take long. I stayed close to Reubyn for most of the journey, but she didn't say much. She had been quiet ever since we arrived.

The nama'ea sat on the edge of a cliff that overlooked the ocean. To the west, about twelve klicks away, I could see Amikea, one of the other islands. But the sanctuary was what held my attention.

The place was in amazing condition. It consisted of a stone dais with a slim pillar at each corner, and in the center, an exquisite statue of a young woman whose loose dress billowed out to become waves beneath her waist. The whole thing - statue, dais, and pillars - was done in some sort of bluish stone. I couldn't help wondering where it had come from. The islands were too small for any sort of quarry, and I couldn't imagine that this was a new build. Despite its excellent condition, the structure was weathered, and clearly old.

'This is the *nama'ea*," said Manialua. "Kaiko's sanctuary."

The waves crashed against the base of the cliffs, eighty meters below. No other sound disturbed the silence except Manialua's voice.

"Kaiko is the Spirit of Water. She is the embodiment of the sea and the rivers and the rains, and she provides us with much of what we need to survive. She is our way of reaching the other islands where our people reside. From her, we learn calm and fury. We respect her, as we do all things, for despite her calmness and kindness she can be among the angriest of the Elementals when she is aroused. This is where we come to honor her."

When Manialua's voice subsided, none of us spoke for a moment. Then I asked, "So Kaiko is...like a deity?"

"No," said Vrenchard. "Neither Kaiko nor the other Elementals have ever been considered deities. Like Manialua said, she's the embodiment of water."

I traded glances with Reubyn.

Then a new voice spoke up. "I think I can explain if you're having trouble."

We all looked over to see a boy - he was probably twelve or thirteen, around Nikiani's age - walking over to join us. He had messy blonde hair that looked like it hadn't been cut in a while, dark green eyes, and tanned skin. He had on shorts and wore a blanket like a cape, but he didn't have a shirt. Over his shoulder he held a simple fishing pole.

"Nico!" said Nikiani. "What are you doing here?"

"I felt you coming," Nico said. He joined our small group by the *nama'ea*, bowed in greeting to each of us, and then looked towards Reubyn and me. I say towards because he didn't look either of us directly in the eye; his gaze rested squarely between us, and he made no effort to look anywhere else. I wondered briefly why, but then he started talking and I pushed the thought aside.

"Kaiko, Iemalu, Maunei, and Pegu are embodiments of the four traditional elements," he said, "meaning water, earth, air, and fire. They aren't deities. They're more like werewolves or vampires, supernatural creatures who have a great deal of power but aren't all-powerful in the manner of gods, except that they're essentially good and basically immortal. And to forestall your question, they aren't legends. They're as real as you and me. Does that clarify things?"

"Yeah." He seemed confident about their realness, but I wasn't convinced, and I could tell Reubyn wasn't either. There was no need to tell him or the others, though. Manialua let me sleep in her house; the least I could do was respect her culture.

"Glad it helped," Nico said. He dipped his head without smiling. He was a strange boy, I decided. I'd never met a kid who acted like him. "Nikiani, could I talk with you for a minute?"

"Sure," Nikiani said. "Ignore us, guys, just go on with the island stuff." She flashed a grin, and then headed off along the cliff with Nico.

Once they were out of earshot of the others, Nikiani stopped and turned to Nico. "Okay," she said. "What is it?"

Nico didn't look her in the eye, but that didn't surprise her. He never looked anyone in the eye.

He had a peculiar ability. He could see about people - their past, their likes and dislikes, hopes and dreams, who they were, and sometimes even who they were going to be. It was something that he said he hated. When he saw people he got too close for his liking. He understood too much. And, he said, it was a violation of privacy.

"Something's happening," he said in Fankaloa. Everyone resorted to the native language to discuss island matters. "You can feel it, can't you?"

Nikiani hesitated, biting her lip. "Yeah," she said, replying in the same language. "I can. But I don't know what it is - it's too weak for me to sense completely. All I can tell is that it's not good. And it's getting stronger."

She shivered. The rising sense of unease carried with it a sort of chill. It wasn't a physical one; this chill made her spirit feel cold. She had a bad feeling about it all.

"Can any of the others sense it yet?" asked Nico.

Nikiani shook her head. "But they will soon. Whatever it is, it's getting stronger, and with that it'll be easier to sense. Right now all I can feel is a little prickle. I've got a feeling that when it's stronger it's going to make me feel a lot worse. You can sense it too, then?"

"I don't have to look darkness in the eye to

tell what it wants," Nico said, shaking his head. "And I can't reign in my abilities entirely. I can feel the dark coming."

Nikiani grimaced. "You're encouraging," she said, trying to sound dry. It didn't come out that way. Of course, the shiver that went through her then didn't help.

"I'm sorry," Nico said. He pulled his blanket off his shoulders and held it out. "If it'll help," he said, "you can use this."

With effort, Nikiani shook her head. "It won't," she said. "But I appreciate the offer. How're you holding up?"

"Well enough," Nico said shortly. He pulled the blanket around his shoulders like he was suddenly cold. "There are plenty of fish and the land's doing well. As of yet, the darkness is too weak to affect the natural world."

"Just the supernatural and freaky," Nikiani said, trying to joke.

It worked, a little bit. The corners of Nico's mouth twitched in a partial smile. He changed the subject then: "What do you think of the new Peacekeepers?"

Nikiani sensed an edge beneath his casual tone. She looked at him suspiciously but said, "They seem all right. They're nice, at least, and they seem to love the islands. I don't know how they'll handle trouble, but it's not like they'll have to deal with much here. Why?"

Nico looked over towards the *nama'ea*, where Nikiani's parents, Aiene, and the two new Peacekeepers still stood. Then, without looking back to Nikiani, he said, "It's not an accident that they're here now, when the darkness is rising."

Nikiani bit her lip and looked over at the *nama'ea*, too. "Are you sure?" she asked. "I mean, Dad was the only Peacekeeper in this entire province. And the others are peaceful enough now that the Confederacy could spare a couple for us out here. It might just be a coincidence."

"It's not, Nikiani," Nico said. He rolled his eyes. "You're aliakeanu - you of all people should know that nothing is a coincidence, especially here. They're here for a reason. We all are. And I've got a feeling that the reason is closely twined with the darkness. Too close for my liking."

Nikiani shivered again. "The next meeting at Aliakeanu Kea is tomorrow night," she said. "Do you think I ought to bring it up?"

"I don't think so," Nico replied. "Not unless one of the others says something. If darkness is coming, everyone's going to need all the peace they can get before it arrives."

"Ugh," Nikiani said.

Nico nodded.

"I guess there's nothing we can do for now, then," Nikiani said with a sigh. "We'll just have to keep watch and pray that nothing bad comes of this."

"I'll keep my eyes open," Nico said. His mouth twisted ever so slightly. "Who knows, this ability could come in handy for once."

Nikiani looked at him sympathetically. "Nico," she said, laying a hand on his shoulder, "I'm sorry. If I could help, I would."

"Please don't touch me," Nico said in a voice much huskier than his usual early adolescent timbre. He looked away. "I don't need anybody else's emotions right now. You'd better get back to the *nama'ea*," he said, shifting tone abruptly. "They're waiting on you to leave."

For a second, Nikiani stood there, hand pulled back. Nico didn't notice her gaze. He stared out over the ocean, arms folded under the blanket, fishing pole leaning up against him. Then Nikiani whispered, "I'm sorry," and turned away.

She did her best to bring her usual cheer back to her face.

Her family and friends were waiting for her.

***

An hour after our return from Kaiko's *nama'ea*, I found myself back on the roof of Vrenchard's house, playing a game of chess against the CPU on my omnipad.

It wasn't going so well.

My eyes flickered around the board, and I decided to move my knight to D3. Then I groaned as I realized my mistake. The black bishop darted in from the side and took my knight. *Crap. There goes the other one.*

I plopped the omnipad down on my lap and lay back on the roof, sighing. It had been months since I'd played chess, and much as I enjoyed it, I wasn't much good. Even against Dad, I'd never won; what chance did I have against a computer?

I grunted and sat back up, deciding that I wasn't going to let a computer outsmart me, although looking over the board, I really wasn't sure what I could do. Most of my good pieces were gone. My queen had been taken a long time ago on a reckless mission to take out the black king. Both of my knights, one of my rooks, and most of my pawns were gone, too. I still had both my bishops.

As I pondered, I heard a voice from half beside me and half behind me. "Try moving that rook here," it said.

I jumped, feeling my cheeks go hot, and

twisted to see Aiene looking over my shoulder at the screen.

"You scared me!" I said.

Aiene smiled. "Sorry," he said. "I saw you earlier, and from your reactions it looked like you could use a little help."

"You play?" I asked.

He nodded. "My dad and I played all the time before I came here," he told me. "And I play against one or the other Alindeses every so often. Nikiani kicks my ass."

I couldn't help snorting. "And you're going to offer me help?" I asked. "If you can't beat a twelve-year-old, I can't help thinking that you're not going to be much good against a computer."

"She's ridiculously good," Aiene said. "Vrenchard told me she started beating him at the age of five." He tapped my rook, and the possible paths it could take lit up. I glanced over the options, trying to pay attention to where the black pieces were this time. The spot he'd shown me earlier seemed safe enough. I tapped it, and the rook slid across the screen.

"Thanks," I said.

Aiene smiled. "No problem. You're not doing so well, are you?"

"Well, I haven't played in a while," I said.

"But I've never been too good at chess. I enjoy it, but I'm awful at it."

"Yeah," Aiene said. "No offense."

I laughed. "None taken, trust me. I know my strengths, and this isn't one of 'em." I turned and lay face-down on the roof, laying the omnipad down. "You want to help out?"

"Sure," replied Aiene. He lay down next to me, and I moved the omnipad so that we could both tap the screen without having to reach across each other.

After a few moments of looking over the board, Aiene sighed. "I don't think anyone's going to be able to pull you out of this hole," he told me. "Computers are too tricky to play a friendly game of chess with. There's a set hidden away in the loft somewhere; you want to play me?"

"Sure," I said, closing the chess app. I switched off my omnipad and climbed back into the house behind Aiene.

We spent nearly ten minutes searching for the chessboard in the chaos that made up the library part of the loft. Books seemed to have multiplied across every available surface, mixed in with piles of notes in two sets of handwriting - a neat, even cursive and an almost illegible scrawl. I could guess which ones were Aiene's.

"Yeah," he said, running a hand through his hair. "Usually my writing's neater, but when I take notes on something I go too quickly. Manialua makes me copy them out neater once we get back to the house."

I laughed. "You're better about it than I am," I said. "I apparently can't be bothered to slow down ever. I had to translate for my friends at school."

We finally found the board underneath a pile of notes on Pegu and Fankaloa's volcanoes. It was a little magnetic set, like the kind you'd take with you to travel. I picked it up and we headed downstairs.

"Hey, look who's finally getting along!" said Manialua. "It's about time, you two."

Aiene and I looked at each other. I smiled sheepishly. I'd been too shy around Aiene to really be friendly towards him over the past few days.

I sat down on one of the low cushions and opened up the board, spilling little black and white magnet-bottomed pieces all over the table. Aiene and I scrambled to recover them before they could spill onto the floor and roll away.

As I reached for one of the last pieces, a black pawn, my hand touched Aiene's, who was reaching for it at the same time. My heart skipped a beat. Aiene and I both snatched our hands back. I felt my face go hot, and I stammered, "Sorry."

"It's all right," Aiene said, grabbing the piece and putting it into place on the board.

I heard Vrenchard chuckle loudly from behind me. He sat down a couple cushions away. "Don't mind me," he said, "I just want to watch the game." He met Manialua's eyes. I decided to ignore the snicker they shared.

Aiene and I set up, after deciding that I would play white, since I was the worse player. Then I looked over the board, thinking.

I hated the first part of a game. I had not yet figured out a way to start off that wasn't moving pieces at random, and I had no way of knowing whether or not my early moves would come back and haunt me. Usually, the beginning was where I made a mistake - without even realizing I'd done it at the time.

As we played, Manialua, Reubyn, and Nikiani drifted over to watch, too. Nikiani offered to play winner, but Aiene and I turned her down. I hadn't forgotten what he'd said about her being ridiculously good at chess.

As it turned out, so was Aiene. Within ten minutes he had me beat almost as badly as the computer, and finally, after a spectacular chase involving my king, Aiene's white-space bishop, several pawns, and a rook, I lost.

"Ohh!" I groaned, grinning. "You're too good!"

Aiene gave a mocking bow, grinning impishly. I couldn't help laughing.

"All right, good game," Aiene said. "You're not that bad, either - I've just had the misfortune to practice against this little brat." He crooked his thumb at Nikiani, who stuck her tongue out at him. Everyone laughed this time.

As everyone in the room turned Nikiani down for a game, to great teasing and laughter, I smiled. Already, after only three days with these people, I felt a real sense of family with them.

My eyes met Aiene's across the table, and I started to blush. Well, I felt a sense of family with most of them. And I had a feeling that whatever I felt with Aiene was going to turn into something great.

I stood at the top of a tall mountain, looking down. Beneath me, the islands of Fankaloa spread out like a huge map. The colors of the islands shone more vivid than usual, like it had rained recently.

The beauty took my breath away. Nothing could match this.

As I stood, drinking in the view, something stirred at the edge of my sight. I turned to look, expecting to see a bird fluttering out of the bushes. But there was nothing there.

Disturbed, I looked back down at the islands. But I couldn't enjoy the beauty like I had before. Now I noticed that there was something off about the view. It seemed to be concealing something.

I shivered, a sense of unease rising inside of me. Whatever the peace hid felt like it was getting stronger. Then I noticed the first ripple.

It started across the sea, so I didn't know at first if I'd really seen it or if it had just been a wave. But then it repeated. As it passed, I saw a thick darkness beneath. The sea returned to normal again, but I couldn't shake the feeling of wrongness that the darkness gave me. As another ripple came, I thought I heard a shriek, faint and distant.

Then the ripples spread to the land. Another shriek joined the first. This one was louder, closer. The ground beneath me shivered from the sound.

A third shriek began. This one was deeper, like it came from a guy, but he couldn't have been very old - no more than eighteen. With that shriek, a ripple went through the air around me.

The fourth shriek belonged to a man, too, a grown one. His shriek began when ripples began to spread through the volcano-mountains.

As the voices grew louder and more pained, I

clapped my hands over my ears and squeezed my eyes shut. But I couldn't block them out. They echoed inside my head with even more force than in my ears.

"Stop!" I shouted, falling onto my knees. "Stop hurting them! Stop it!"

But the shrieks didn't stop, and I knew the ripples didn't either. I could feel them around me, strengthening. A horrible, soul-chilling cold spread through me, replacing the warmth of the tropical sun. The ripples pained me now, too. They stretched at my skin, ripping it apart and forcing it back together, again and again and again. My shrieks joined the others echoing across the islands. I curled into a ball, trying to hide from the pain.

Other screams joined mine. They grew in number, until I realized that they belonged to everyone in Fankaloa. Aiene's was among them, and Reubyn's and Vrenchard's and Manialua's and Nikiani's.

No! I thought. Don't... Not them! Don't hurt them! Leave the others alone!

But the darkness and the ripples didn't heed my pleas.

"NO!" I shouted. "NOOOO!"

I sat bolt upright, breathing heavily. My heart raced, and it felt like someone had stuck pins into my skin. Around me, the room was dark, but it wasn't the cold darkness of my dream. It was warm and gentle.

The others were asleep. I heard them breathing. Nikiani snored once, very softly. Reubyn murmured something unintelligible to herself and shifted in her sheets. I couldn't see them through the thin bamboo screens that made up the walls of our rooms at night, but they were all there. Sleeping peacefully, not shrieking in pain. It had only been a dream.

But even though I lay there for hours on my futon, I couldn't fall asleep again.

I was glad that the next day was Sunday. After my nightmare, I hadn't been able to fall back asleep, and I was exhausted - running and working out would not have been an option. I was restless, but that didn't change the fact that all I really wanted to do was go to sleep. I probably would have, if those horrible ripples would have just stopped flooding my mind every time I closed my eyes.

I forced myself to get up at sunrise for a short walk - which helped to wake me up, a little - and then I showered, trying to use the time to figure out the nightmare. I stopped dead in the middle of washing my face when the thought hit me to try looking in Manialua's library. She had tons of books on Fankaloa and the spiritual history of the islands - maybe one of them would be able to explain what I'd seen.

I finished and toweled off hurriedly, leaving my hair almost dripping, and then I headed upstairs, taking the steps two at a time.

None of the others were awake yet, so I made an effort to be quiet as I put away my futon and finally got to the books. I let my fingers trace over the spines, wondering where to start.

"I wouldn't read that one if I were you," came

Aiene's voice from behind me.

I jumped nearly out of my skin. "Why do you always do that?" I hissed. My heart hammered in my throat.

Aiene grinned. "Sorry," he said, but he didn't sound it.

To change the subject, I asked, "So why shouldn't I read this one?" I pulled it off the shelf.

"This," Aiene said, taking the book. He opened it to reveal that it was written in Fankaloa. "I know you haven't started yet on the written form."

Nikiani had started teaching Fankaloa to Reubyn and me the day after we'd arrived, but Aiene was right: even with a teacher like Niki, we weren't advanced enough yet to read much.

"So picky," I said. "What would you suggest then, O archaeological genius?"

"Depends," Aiene said, grinning at his new title and replacing the book I'd taken out. "What are you trying to read about?"

"Um," I said. How to explain this without sounding morbid or crazy? "Spiritual entities, like Kaiko and the other Elementals. And any others that might be hanging around. Like ones that might not be as...good as the Elementals?"

An odd expression crossed his face, but it vanished just as quickly as it had come. He shook his head. "Sorry." Then he cleared his throat and said, "I'm sure there's something in here about that. It's going to be hard to narrow it down, though; unless you want something more specific, you could be reading for days."

"Not that that would bother me," I said, thinking. "Um...well, I had this dream about something dark sending ripples through the islands, and it's kind of freaking me out. Are there any dark entities in Fankaloa lore?"

Aiene's face grew serious. "One," he said, "but...no, that's impossible on so many levels. Let's look around. What happened in the dream?"

I opened my mouth to explain just as Reubyn pulled back her bamboo screen, yawning widely. "Hi," she said through the yawn. "What's up, you two?"

"Lillia was just about to tell me about a dream she had," Aiene said.

"Um, yeah," I said.

"Cool," Reubyn said. She grinned at me when Aiene wasn't looking, and I slashed a finger across my throat. If he saw that -

"Well," I said, pushing that particular worry off my mind, "it was pretty freaky. And it felt incredibly real for a dream. I remember everything."

Reubyn joined us by the bookcase, looking

interested. I cleared my throat, and then launched into the story.

When I finished, Aiene looked worried. "That doesn't sound good," he said. "I think you're right to be concerned about it."

"So you don't think it's just a random nightmare?" I'd been afraid that was how they would brush it off. It hadn't been an ordinary dream, even by my dark-world-nightmare standards, I knew that. This was something else entirely.

Aiene shook his head. "Nothing's ever a coincidence," he said. "And especially not in a place like Fankaloa. The physical and spirit worlds are too closely intertwined here to dismiss anything as chance."

Reubyn and I exchanged glances. She seemed to be taking me seriously, too, which relieved me. I had been worried that everyone would think I was crazy for   worrying over a nightmare.

"Honestly," she said, "I'm kind of glad you had that dream. I've been feeling strange since we got here, sort of...cold. Not physically, more...inside, like my soul or something, like the way you described it a minute ago. It's been getting worse, bit by bit. And I kept thinking I was just going crazy." She laughed nervously. "Not so nuts after all, I guess."

Aiene looked at us, his brows drawing together in concern. "Let's grab some books," he said. "I remember something about a dark entity in Fankaloa history, but I...I don't know. I can't remember exactly." He frowned. "I'm not sure I want to remember."

We started browsing through the books, looking for anything to do with the spirits. There was a lot to choose from.

"It's lucky there're three of us," Reubyn said. "You know what they say, many hands make light work."

I nodded in agreement, and then glanced down at the sizeable pile of books I'd already collected. "Although I'm not sure how light it'll really be."

Aiene snorted. "It could be worse," he said. "We've at least got a good idea of what we're looking for. Can you imagine trying to sift through every single one of these books? That would be awful."

"Yeah," I agreed.

By the time the others woke up, Aiene, Reubyn, and I had about two dozen books off the shelves. Manialua laughed at the sight of us sitting at the table with all the   books spread around us.

"You're going to drown in that," she said.

"Don't say I didn't warn you. Do any of you want pancakes?"

"Yes, please," the three of us chorused.

Manialua smiled and caught up to Vrenchard as he started down the stairs. "'*Ema*," she sighed, "I think we're going to empty the stores."

Vrenchard laughed. "You three had better come down if you want 'em hot off the griddle," he said. "And Aiene and Reubyn, you two might want to get ready. Church starts at nine hours."

As they headed down, I looked at Aiene. "Church?"

"Yeah," Aiene replied. "It's over on the west shore, on the other side of Kamo Nakae. Do you two go?"

I shrugged. Reubyn said, "Yeah." Then she stood, rolling her neck. "I'll be down soon," she said. "Make sure Nikiani doesn't eat all the pancakes."

"No promises," I said, laughing. Nikiani had a big appetite for a twelve-year-old girl, and it was pretty risky to leave food within her reach if you had any plans to eat it yourself. More than likely it would end up in Nikiani instead.

"Are you going?" Aiene asked.

I wrinkled my nose. "Normally I don't," I said. "I'm not a big fan of organized religion." I shrugged. "I might go today, though. It'd be nice to think for a little while that maybe somebody up there knows what he's doing."

We marked our places and then headed off to get ready. I might not have usually thought much of religion, but I would readily admit that it did one thing well: reassurance. And after that dream, I needed all the reassurance I could get.

An older Fankaloa man named Mamo Kaniu led the service, which was simple, outdoors, and almost entirely in Fankaloa. I could follow along a little - Nikiani had an overenthusiastic but effective teaching style - but I decided that I caught at most half of the words. But it sounded beautiful. I loved the way the island language flowed.

Afterwards, we had fellowship. I didn't know what I expected, but everyone was quite friendly. It seemed odd to me - I was used to Plancint, where people hardly even looked at you unless they knew you well - and it threw me off for a while.

In spite of that, I couldn't help feeling cheerful when the people and weather were so nice. Conversations flew across heads and all around the patch of beach we'd claimed for fellowship. I found myself laughing and smiling like I'd known these people all my life.

All the same, my concern stayed an

undercurrent to my thoughts. Just when I'd be completely distracted, laughing at a joke or in conversation with someone, some little thing would pop up and my worry would return. Usually it was harmless - a cooler gust of wind in the breeze, a little bit of pain when I stepped on a pebble. Harmless or no, my heart hammered up to twice its normal speed and I felt myself go white as a sheet every time. Half the beach probably thought I had some sort of nervous condition.

About a half-hour into fellowship, a young woman with leaf anklets and bare feet pulled Nikiani aside and talked to her for a moment, very quietly. It was mostly that that caught my attention, because no one else on the beach made any effort to be quiet at all.

"I don't think we're the only ones worried right now," murmured Reubyn.

I looked at her. "Huh?"

"They're freaking out," Reubyn said. "Let's find Aiene; I'd rather have three heads than two for figuring this out."

We managed to snag Aiene at the tail end of his conversation with 'Ela Kaminu, a man who owned a taro farm on the northeastern shore of Niu'u. "What's up, guys?" he asked as 'Ela walked off.

Quickly, Reubyn explained. "I overheard Nikiani and Damao talking about something. All I heard was the end, but they're both really worried about it. I could feel it from halfway across the beach. I don't think we're the only ones who've noticed something weird going on. And there's some sort of meeting tonight. They were speaking Fankaloa, so I couldn't catch everything, but it sounds like it's a pretty regular thing." Her brows drew together. "I've got a bad feeling about this."

Aiene ran a hand through his hair and looked off over the ocean. "Okay," he said. "We need to figure out what that meeting is. It can't be anything bad - I'd know if it was, you can't hide anything living in close quarters like we do - but we might be able to figure out something about whatever's going on around here. Did either of them say where it was?"

Reubyn shook her head. "They mentioned a *kea*, whatever that is -"

"A grove," Aiene said.

"- but that could be anywhere."

"Okay," I said. "So we just follow Nikiani when she leaves tonight." I shrugged. "Until then, I say we go back to the house and read some more. Maybe we'll find out something before tonight."

"Good idea," Reubyn said. She bit her lip and

looked away. For half a second I thought I saw a tear in the corner of her eye, and then it disappeared. It must have been a trick of the light.

Still, a chill ran up my spine. My hand curled into a fist.

"We've got to find out what's going on," I said. "There's no way I'm letting anything bad happen here."

Even though we spent most of the rest of the day combing through books, none of us found anything useful. It was like the darkness had been wiped out of history. I suggested once that maybe it hadn't been there before, but Aiene shook his head at that.

"It's come before," he said. "I know it. Whatever it was, it's as old as the Elementals, maybe even older. It's definitely not new."

I decided to take his word for it, but as the hours dragged on, I couldn't help but wonder.

None of us brought up the idea of asking Manialua. We had a tacit agreement not to drag anyone else into this unless it became somehow necessary. I wasn't even sure why I'd told Aiene and Reubyn about it; I couldn't make anyone else worry about it, too.

By the time it got dark, all three of us were

tired of reading. The glasses I'd gotten at the Academy did nothing to keep me from getting a headache after hours of staring at books, straining to find some new information in the sea of text. It was a relief when Manialua called up that dinner was ready.

We kept quiet during the meal, despite concerned looks and a couple questions about what we had been doing, sitting up in the loft reading all day. I just shrugged and turned my attention to my pizza. Manialua had mixed jalapeño and onion in under the sauce, which I thought was amazing. It made it spicy.

After dinner, I climbed out onto the roof to watch the stars come out.

It was a full moon that night. The island looked like another world in the light, one made of onyx and silver, caught in dreamless midnight sleep. An owl hooted once, far off. Nothing else moved except the stars, popping silently into the air as the last of the light gave way to onyx in the west.

I'd been sitting up there a few minutes when I heard a voice say, "Hey."

I twisted around to see Aiene standing on the roof by the window we used to get outside. "Oh," I said. "Hi, Aiene."

He joined me on the slope. "How's it going?"

he asked.

"Oh, great," I said. "Just a little worried about this nightmare I had about the world being invaded by darkness and pain and stuff. But, you know, it's all good."

Aiene laughed. "Okay, stupid question," he said. "Are you ready for tonight? You don't have to come if you're too tired. I know you were up early this morning."

I shook my head. "I've got to go," I said, then grinned. "Besides, someone needs to make sure neither you nor Reubyn screws up."

"I resent that remark," came Reubyn's voice from the window.

Aiene and I both laughed. "Hey, Reubyn," I said, turning. "You want to join the party?"

"Not if you're gonna insult me, I don't," she replied, but came down to join us anyway. "So what are we going to do about following Nikiani? Just wing it and hope for the best?"

I shrugged. "I figured we'd stay awake until she leaves, and then sneak out behind her. It's a full moon tonight, so it shouldn't be too hard to keep on her trail unless she ducks into a shadow or something. I mean, it's not like she'll be covering her tracks, right?"

"Not unless she's doing something wrong,"

Aiene said. "And like I said earlier, I don't think she would. Vrenchard and Manialua might even know what the meeting is."

Like we would ask them. If they didn't know about the meeting, I didn't want to tip them off; and if they did, they'd get suspicious about why we wanted to know.

I felt a yawn rising in my throat, and didn't manage to fight it back. Reubyn looked at me sympathetically. "If you want," she said, "we'll wake you up when it's time to go. Or Aiene and I can go on our own."

"Tempting," I said, "but no. We need to trail Nikiani as closely as possible if we're going to be able to find the grove, and even the minute or two it takes to wake me up could make us lose her trail. I'll be fine."

I ran a hand through my hair and leaned back against the shingles. I was tired, but I wasn't going to admit it. Besides, what I'd said was true. We couldn't afford to lose any time if we were going to find the meeting. I pushed my tiredness to the back of my mind and looked up at the stars.

They were clear as they'd never been in Plancint. Even at the Academy, there had been enough light from the buildings and the lights along the path to keep the star count lower. Here, the only lights were indoors, and they shone just bright enough to see by without eye strain. The resulting sky spread out almost more silver than black.

"Hey," hissed Aiene then, looking down over the edge of the roof. I sat up and followed his gaze. A small figure slipped out of the door and started east.

"Nikiani," I breathed. "Come on." I slid to the edge of the roof and lowered myself down. Fortunately, I was at one of the relatively few windowless portions of the walls, so neither Manialua nor Vrenchard would see me sliding off. Aiene and Reubyn followed, and we stole off into the night after Nikiani.

None of us had thought it would be hard to follow her, but it was even easier than we expected. She made no effort to hide what she was doing, and she never once glanced back. The only thing that made it even slightly difficult was the fact that she walked quickly.

As we went on, a couple more people started heading the same direction. I recognized Damao's thick, spiky pixie, which despite being as dark as Nikiani or Manialua's hair still shone silver in the moonlight; several dozen yards ahead, I saw Nico's blanket and realized he was going, too.

"What is this thing?" I murmured. Reubyn

shrugged.

"But did you notice," she whispered back, "that everyone who's going - except for Nico - has on those leaf anklets?"

She was right.

"Nikiani, Damao, and Nico are all worried about something," Reubyn murmured. "The other two aren't. I don't know if they can't sense what's going on or what."

Aiene and I both looked at her. "How do you know that?" Aiene asked.

Reubyn bit her lip and looked at the ground. "I don't know."

"Well, whatever you're doing, keep it up," I said. "It might -"

That was when my stomach lurched like someone had just jumped out and scared me - and I knew who. "Nikiani!" I hissed, whirling around. "Don't you dare!"

The other two stopped, startled, and Nikiani came out from the shadow of a tree, looking sheepish and surprised. "How did you know I was back there?" she asked.

"You were about to jump out and scare us!" I said. "I thought you were worried about something. What happened to that, huh?"

That pulled her up short. "You knew that,

too?"

"Reubyn did," I replied. "So I guess for you, worried equates to jumping out from bushes and scaring us to death?"

She looked from me to Reubyn and back again without answering my question. Then she strode forward, grabbed Aiene and me by the wrists, and commanded Reubyn to follow. The three of us exchanged helpless, confused looks as Nikiani dragged us along behind her to the head of the group heading towards the *kea*.

The grove sat at the foot of Makanea Pua'e. By the moonlight, I could see a group of several dozen people milling around inside like they were waiting for something.

Nikiani led our group to join them. We had gotten a couple questioning looks from Damao, Imana'a, and Kemau when Nikiani had returned with us in tow, though none of them asked any questions and Nico didn't seem surprised at all. The people in the grove glanced over when we entered, and most of them perked up a little. "Nikiani!" called one, and then in Fankaloa: "Finally! You get a little busy at home?"

"Just picking up some stragglers," Nikiani replied. "Let me get the meeting started and I'll explain everything." She let go of mine and Aiene's wrists. "Just stay back and listen," she told the three of us.

"What -" Aiene started to ask, but Nikiani hurried off, leaving us standing there with our mouths open to ask a billion different questions.

The small crowd in the grove started to quiet down as Nikiani bounded through towards a rock at the northern end. She climbed on top, apparently not at all hindered by her usual ankle-length skirt. Her voice carried impressively as she called, *"O'a Ae Came'a onohani!"* That basically translated to God be with you, a formal greeting in Fankaloa that she had taught us the day before; and she kept speaking the same flowing, vowel-heavy language through her speech.

"It's great to see everyone...only I'm afraid that it's not all good news tonight. There have been keiturai around the islands recently, and I'm not the only one who's noticed it. Damao and Nico -" she gestured at the two of them - "have sensed it too, and I thought it was only fair to tell all of you." She took a deep breath, and said, "Something dark is coming."

The breath came out of my lungs in a huff. *Shit...*

"I don't know how many of you have sensed it

too, but you're going to soon. This wasn't something I wanted to bring up until it became *luna'i* necessary, but it looks like that's what it's become. Whatever's rising is bad, and everyone with the slightest trace of *aliakeanukea'u* in their veins is going to know it soon. Nico has noticed it, and he's not even an *aliakeanu*. And we've got a return of the *lao.*"

This time, she gestured at Reubyn, Aiene, and me. The islanders in the grove turned to look at us. I froze. Nikiani said something else, but I didn't quite catch it.

"*Aliakeanu!*" Aiene whispered. "Witches..."

I looked at him, then at Nikiani, and then at all the people starting at us. All the people who were barefoot, and wearing leaf anklets, who had been so friendly towards Nikiani.

Holy shit.

I had been right before. This had gotten interesting.

Chapter Seven: SPF Fifty

"So you're telling me," I said, "that you're a witch?"

Nikiani nodded. "Only we use the Fankaloa word, *aliakeanu*. It's a cultural thing; and also, witch tends to carry the idea of black magic and evil. That's something no one wants hanging around them, right?"

Her nervous laugh made it clear that she'd intended it as a joke, but the three of us were all a little too shaken up to appreciate it. Nikiani sighed and leaned against a tree.

"Listen," she said, "it's not something dark like it's considered in legends from the rest of the Confederacy. *Aliakeanu* powers are natural, an inborn ability to use your energy to affect the world around you. And since we can affect the world, we have to be able to sense it, too. It's kind of like *emelao*, present-sense."

"Yeah, and that's another thing," Aiene said. "What do you mean about the *lao*? I've read most of the books in your mom's library, but I've never seen anything about them."

Nikiani shrugged. "*Lao* have always been rare, even before the time of the Confederacy," she said. "And as far as I know, there hasn't even been one in the past three hundred years or so. I doubt you'd find more than two or three references to them altogether in all the books written about Fankaloa."

"...Okay," I said. "So what are they?"

A lot, apparently. According to Nikiani, they were people born with the ability to sense different times - *demakao*, Nikiani called them, realms of time. They were usually Fankaloa - though Nikiani admitted that during the times when *lao* had been less rare, Fankaloa had had hardly any contact with the outside world. The birth of a *lao* was supposedly a hallmark of coming trouble, because *lao* had their abilities so that they could fend off whatever trouble was on its way.

And apparently, a *lao* was always one person with all three senses - past, present, and future.

"Or that's what the legends say," Nikiani concluded. "Apparently that's not always the case. I mean, if you sensed the future -" she gestured at me - "and you sensed the present -" she gestured at Reubyn - "then there are obviously exceptions."

"There were," Aiene said. We all looked at him, surprised. "It only happened once, and it was a long time ago, but they were split among three people." Then his skin went dark and he shrunk in on himself. It was kind of cute.

Nikiani beamed. "And there's your *ealao,*" she said, leaning back against her tree. "Past-sense.

It figures you'd be the one with it, Aiene, considering you're an archaeologist and everything."

Aiene shook his head. "No, I...I knew that," he said. "I read it somewhere, I think."

"And have never read anything else about lao that you remember?" asked Nikiani. "Not likely. Don't make excuses."

She seemed completely unfazed by this, but she was the only one. I couldn't convince my brain to wrap itself around the idea, and from the looks on their faces, neither could either of the others. Finally, Reubyn said, "I'm sorry, Nikiani, but I don't think we can be really. Maybe you and all these people here are witches, maybe Nico has some weird eye-contact-activated ability, maybe these *lao* existed once, but none of us are even Fankaloa. I don't think we're what you think we are."

"Oh, really?" Nikiani asked. Even in the relative darkness under the trees, I saw the glint in her eye as she leaned forwards. "Maybe you're right. But before you close your mind to the idea, just listen to me for a moment. You can't tell me that you've never felt a sense of empathy so strong you could actually feel what was going on inside the person. That you've never known something about someone without them telling you. Think about it, Reubyn. Just for a moment."

Reubyn stopped. Slowly, one hand moved to her mouth.

"Dad," she whispered. "And Josoh."

I stiffened. *That's why...*

I slipped an arm around her shoulders, hoping it would comfort her. She blinked at me gratefully, and I saw a tear drip out of the corner of her eye.

"And Lillia," Nikiani said, turning to me. "How else do you explain how you knew I was back there earlier? No one could have known until I jumped out and scared you, unless of course Reubyn had noticed that my presence had moved from in front to behind and sensed what I was about to do. And she couldn't have, because I cloaked my presence so that no one would realize I was being dorky enough to pull a stupid prank like that. But since I intended to throw off the cloak when I jumped out, you were able to sense that uncloaked version of me in the future, and you knew what was coming."

I blinked. "Um, okay." It did sort of make sense. Plus, there was proof Nikiani didn't know about: my dream.

"Aiene," Nikiani said. "First, the most obvious proof: you've been Mom's apprentice for a year and a half and haven't caved under the sheer volume of knowledge you've had to learn. That alone says that you and the past have something! And your little spark of knowing just a moment ago, about the *lao kama*, the three lao. You've always been good at history, haven't you?"

"I, uh," Aiene said, "well...yeah. But so are lots of people."

"Did you ever once study for a history test?"

"No."

"Did you ever get less than a perfect grade?"

He opened his mouth, paused, and then shut it again. "I...no."

Nikiani's beam was back. "And there you have it!" she said. "You're *lao kama*, there's no denying it!"

We couldn't argue with her. Everything had rung true, with all of us. But I still had a little trouble wrapping my mind around the idea of having some sort of future-sensing abilities. It brought up all sorts of paradoxes that I'd always enjoyed thinking about but gave me a bit of a headache if I did too much.

I shook my head in an attempt to divert my thoughts. I could ponder out paradoxes some other time. Right now...

"The darkness you mentioned to the aliakeanu earlier," I said, fixing Nikiani with a steady look. "What is it?"

She shifted uncomfortably against the tree. "I'm not really sure," she hedged. "At first it was only Nico and me sensing it, and even then it was really weak. But it kept getting stronger. Damao started sensing it a couple days ago, and even tonight I heard a couple people mention that something felt off. I had to make it public. But I don't know what it is exactly."

"It's getting stronger, all right," I agreed, thinking of the ripples in my dream. "Are there any dark entities in Fankaloa's past, something that might not like the light that's here now?"

A sudden image flashed through my head of a mock-up Mission when we'd questioned witnesses. It was the stupidest analogy ever, but it worked.

"Um..." Nikiani said. She chewed on her tongue for a moment, and her tiny eyebrows knotted up in the middle. "Let's...Let's just go home. It's too late for me to think about this rationally." She shook her head hard. Then she sat up, looking at us suspiciously. "You knew about the darkness before I mentioned it, didn't you?"

I nodded, and proceeded to explain my dream. When I finished, Nikiani rubbed her neck, looking worried.

"I knew it was getting bad," she said, "but I didn't know to what extent it'd go. That's not good.

The ones you heard screaming first must have been the Elementals." Her eyebrows drew together in concern. "I hate to think of what could hurt them like that."

She stood, brushing dirt and leaves off the rear of her skirt.

"Home?" asked Reubyn. The rest of us rose, too.

"Home," Nikiani agreed. "We need to sleep, and then we need to tell Mom and Dad about this. Dad's a Peacekeeper, after all, and this is going to be a major breach of peace. And Mom's our best bet of figuring out what this darkness is. Come on, guys; I know a quick way back. I only took the long way around because the others were walking with me."

She held out her hands. "Two of you grab on," she said, "and whoever doesn't hold my hand hold one of the others'."

Reubyn and I were closest, so we each took one of her hands. My face went a little warm when Aiene took my hand, and my pulse sped up, but I made myself ignore it.

Nikiani closed her eyes.

The hairs on the back of my neck started to rise. I had sort of come to terms with the idea that the skinny little girl was an *aliakeanu*, but knowing it and seeing it in action were two very different things. I could feel a strange, thrumming energy gathering around us, and I couldn't even imagine what Reubyn felt with her *emelao* thing.

"*Ai iki hai'o!*" Nikiani cried - let us go.

Half a second passed in utter silence, and then the world imploded. The grove vanished into a swirling vortex of color. A rush of confused sounds battered at my eardrums, so wild I wanted to cover my ears and scream to block it all out. We hurtled through it all, dragged along behind Nikiani so fast I thought my arms would come out of their sockets, and picked up speed until I knew that my grip on Nikiani's hand had to fail -

And we slammed into the solid ground hard enough to make my legs buckle beneath me. Everything seemed quiet and colorless compared to the vortex. It took me a moment to adjust.

Then I stood up and looked around. We stood in the clearing in front of Manialua's and Vrenchard's house. I whistled softly. The idea of having enough energy to transport four people through space as quickly as Nikiani had - it was amazing. But I pulled my mind back on track before I started myself thinking about all the mechanics involved in what Nikiani had just done. Right now I needed to sleep.

The lights were on downstairs. I felt a little trepidation about going inside after having disappeared, but Nikiani didn't seem to have any problem with it. She looked decidedly more tired than she had moments before in the grove, but she strode on through the bamboo curtain in the doorway with her chin up and the usual bounce in her walk. Aiene, Reubyn, and I exchanged glances and followed her in.

Manialua sat at the table, head bent over a thick book from her library. She looked up when we entered.

"Hi," she said. She didn't seem at all surprised to see the four of us traipsing in her door at twenty-two hours thirty.

"Hi, Mom," Nikiani said.

"How was the meeting?"

"Um, interesting," Nikiani said. "I'll tell you about it tomorrow, okay? I jetted us home, and I'm pretty tired."

"All right," Manialua said. "Be quiet when you go up there; your dad's sleeping."

We nodded and headed upstairs. The screens were already set up, and Nikiani headed straight into her little section. I heard her collapse onto her futon.

"Night, guys," Reubyn said.

I was too tired to even bother changing into pajamas. About five seconds after I fell onto my futon, I passed out.

I woke up late the next morning. The house was unusually quiet; I was a little creeped out until I went downstairs and found a note on the table written in Manialua's neat script.

Lillia:

I'm sorry we couldn't tell you we were leaving, but we know you had a late night last night and none of us wanted to wake you. Vrenchard and Reubyn are out on patrol, I'm visiting Pegu's nama'ea on Kalinuea, Nikiani left to talk to Nico, and Aiene is running, I think; he got up before the rest of us and his sneakers are gone. There are bagels, peanut butter, fruit, and a number of other foods in the kitchen if you get hungry. I'll be gone until evening, but unless there's trouble Reubyn and Vrenchard should be back not long after noon. I don't know about any of the others.

I hope you have a good day!

Manialua

I raided the kitchen and grabbed an apple, which I crunched down while I got ready to go out for a run. As I headed out the door, I glanced down to see that Aiene's sneakers were indeed missing. It was weird to see; he wore shoes only a little more often than Nikiani. Even when we had gone to Kaiko's *nama'ea* and the *kea* - Aliakeanu Kea, Nikiani had called it, Witch Grove - he'd been barefoot.

I stretched briefly, and then headed west to start my run.

By the time I had got back, finished my exercises, and showered and dried off, I heard someone moving around in the kitchen. I dressed, combed my hair, and brushed my teeth, then headed out to make my actual breakfast. My stomach growled.

There were actually three people in the kitchen: Aiene, Nikiani, and Nico. When my feet hit the stairs, thumping as I hurried down, all three of them looked over.

"Hey, Lil," Nikiani said. "Glad to see you're alive!"

"Please," I said, joining them by the kitchen counter. "I've already been on a run, worked out, and put myself together. What have you done?"

"Not quite as much," admitted Nikiani. "You hungry?"

My stomach answered for me, and all four of us smiled. "Omelets, you think?" asked Aiene, heading for the fridge. "We've got ham and mushrooms in here."

"I'll help," I said, getting a couple pans out from under the oven. "Four?"

Nikiani and Nico nodded and moved to help us. "We've been filling Nico in on what's happened recently," Nikiani said as she whisked eggs and cheese together in a bowl. "The emakalao dream. And I've been picking his brain about what the darkness could be."

"Wasted time," Nico said. "I don't know any more about what it might be than any of the rest of you. What did you say we had - mushrooms and ham?" he asked, turning to almost look at Aiene.

Aiene nodded. "What does everyone want?"

"Mushrooms."

"Ham."

"Both," Nikiani said. "I'm hungry."

"You're always hungry," I said.

"Hey," she said, "it takes a lot of energy to do what I do."

"What, eat everything in the house?"

"Okay," Nico interrupted. "I need to ask you something, Lillia."

"Mm?"

"You haven't had any more dreams, have you?" he asked. "Last night, I mean. Or any sudden forebodings, anything to indicate what might be going on here?"

I thought for a moment, but then I shook my head. "Not as far as I can tell," I said. "Or at least not anything clear. The only forebodings I've had were the dream and when I realized Nikiani was going to jump out at us last night. Why do you think that is, by the way?" I asked, looking at Nikiani. She looked up from pouring the eggs into their respective pans.

"Why do I suppose what is?" she asked. "That I jumped out at you?"

I shook my head. Then my eyes widened. "Nikiani, pull the bowl up!"

"Wha -?" Nikiani said, but that was all she got out before I launched across the kitchen and yanked the bowl out of her hands, pulling it upright before the eggs could overflow the pan.

"That's what," I said, handing the bowl back. "The pan was about to overflow."

Nikiani glanced back to see that I was right. "Geez," she said. "Thanks. That would have been a huge mess."

I felt everyone's eyes on me and went pink. "Anyway," I said, "no, I wasn't asking about that. I was wondering if you had any idea about why the powers never showed up before. With Reubyn and Aiene, you pointed out evidence, but I don't remember any manifestations of *emakalao* ever happening to me before that dream."

Nikiani turned back to the pans, this time keeping her eyes on them as she spoke. "The future's a tricky thing; in the legends I've heard, it was always the hardest power to pin down. And you lived in Plancint before, right?"

I nodded. "Yeah."

"Well, that's about as far as you can get from any sort of connection to the earth. And *lao* powers need a connection to their source for them to manifest, just like *aliakeanukea'u* or any other *iemalu uema* - that's earth ability to you."

I took the ham and the mushrooms off the cutting board where Aiene had set them and started putting them on the omelets. Then I retreated to the other side of the kitchen. Nikiani had the spatula, and she seemed intent upon wielding it against the omelets. It was safer on the other side. Aiene and Nico joined me over there.

"I guess you were pretty tired, huh?" asked

Aiene. "How early did that dream wake you up yesterday?"

I wrinkled my nose. "I think it may have actually been very late the day before yesterday. I couldn't figure out what time it was until things started getting light. And then of course, I didn't get to bed until twenty-two hours thirty." I chuckled. "I guess it's no wonder I didn't dream last night."

"Good grief," Nico said. He wasn't looking at either of us, not even in his indirect way. He was watching Nikiani wage war against the omelets. I saw a crease between his brows, like he was thinking about something serious. For what felt like a long time, the house was silent except for the noises outside and the sound of the omelets cooking.

Then Nico sighed. "I don't like to think of what's going on here."

"None of us do," Nikiani said without breaking her concentration. I couldn't see what there was to focus on, really - she was making omelets, for the islands' sakes, not some complex dinner for twelve - but she seemed pretty into it. I guessed she wanted to distract herself. "Somebody get some fruit out, would you? These are going to be done pretty soon. And we need plates, too - and if you want anything to drink, you'd better get it."

The kitchen turned into a flurry of activity as

I pulled out the plates, Aiene got a veritable orchard of fruit out of the fridge, and Nico got out some glasses. Nikiani turned off the burners and flipped the omelets onto the plates. When we finally figured out whose omelet was whose, we grabbed our breakfasts, piled on the variety of fruit Aiene had retrieved and moved to the table to eat.

As we ate, I suggested that we take some time to try combing Manialua's library again for references to the darkness. "After all," I said, "she won't be back until tonight, and I think it'll be better to explain about the *lao* powers when everyone's here so we don't have to do it twice. Vrenchard probably won't know anything that can help anyway."

Before I even finished, Nikiani started shaking her head. "Nu-uh. None of us are going to sit around searching through old books all day; you two and Reubyn did that enough yesterday. Dwelling on this won't make it any better. If anything, it'll only make it worse. No," she said, shaking her head again. "Reubyn's having an island day, trust me - she's not going to find much trouble out there on patrol. We're going to have one, too." She grinned. "And I know just where to go!"

We finished breakfast and, under the direction of

Nikiani, put on bathing suits and sunblock. Mine was a special kind Mom had sent me when she'd found out where I would be stationed: SPF 100, which I would have thought was overkill if I didn't have my skin. I'd learned during my summer at the Academy that I burned like a dry leaf thrown into a bonfire. Even with the 100, I'd still have to reapply it after an hour of sunshine or else risk becoming lobster-ized.

I put on Dad's old T-shirt - the one I used as a nightshirt - as a cover-up, put the sunblock back in my satchel, and grabbed my glasses case and put it in with the sunblock.

When I joined the others by the door, Nikiani nodded at my satchel, eyebrows raised. "SPF 100?" she asked. "Don't you think that's a little much?"

In answer, I got out my omnipad and pulled up the photos. "Look at this," I said, clicking on one from August. Reubyn had taken it, ambushing me with my omnipad when I came back into the dorm after washing off the lake water. It wasn't flattering - not only was most of my skin only a few shades less red than my hair, but my eyes were wide from surprise and my mouth was half-open. Plus I hadn't combed my hair, so it stuck out in every direction except the one in which it was supposed to go. I had no idea why I hadn't deleted the picture the instant

I'd gotten the omnipad back.

"Um, wow," Aiene said. He looked at me, eyes sparkling with humor. "How lobster can you get?"

I snatched the omnipad back and turned it off. "I was just trying to make a point," I said, tucking it back into my satchel. "That was with SPF fifty covering every inch of me that wasn't covered with swimsuit, and I was only out for an hour and a half. So no, it's not too much - not even a little." Then I grinned. "'Course, I make it worse on myself - I always feel like such a party pooper when I insist on getting out of the water every hour to put sunblock back on."

"I'll remind you," Aiene offered. "That crap hurts. It's not going to happen on my watch."

Nico half-smiled. "Punny," he said. He didn't have on a swimsuit, just his usual raggedy brown shorts. His fishing pole rested against the doorframe, on the outside of the house, with the blanket draped over it.

We headed out. Nikiani led us west, along the same path we'd taken to get to church the day before. "The ocean there is perfect for swimming," she told us. "As long as there's not a big group using it, it's fair game."

So for the next few hours, the four of us did

our best to put all of our worries out of our minds.

Reubyn and Vrenchard did indeed finish patrol early, just as Manialua had predicted. We found them at the house when we got back at half-past noon. Reubyn sat at the table, eating some sort of fruit salad with chicken and navigating her omnipad. Vrenchard was making his own lunch in the kitchen.

"Hi, Dad," Nikiani said. "How'd the patrol go?"

"As usual," Vrenchard said. "I hope you had a good time at the beach."

"The best," Aiene said. "What all have we got to work with for lunch?"

I had almost died when we reached the beach and Aiene had taken his shirt off. By now I'd gotten used to it (or at least I didn't start to hyperventilate every time I looked at him), but shirtless Aiene definitely topped my list of "Most Distracting Things Ever." I hadn't realized I had such a list until today.

Vrenchard waved us into the kitchen, taking his own lunch out to the table. I started perusing the cabinets. I was really hungry, but nothing sounded good. After a moment, I sighed and started making a salad. It would at least tide me over until I decided what I actually wanted for lunch.

When I'd filled a bowl, I joined the others at the table. Reubyn had finished her lunch and was now typing away on the omnipad. "My report," she said when I asked about it. "It's not like there'll be much in it, but you know. We have to do it anyway; might as well get it out of the way."

"No escape," Vrenchard said, shaking his head. "Nineteen years of Peacekeeping in these islands and I still can't get off without making a report on my patrols. And then there're the monthly reports."

Reubyn and I groaned in unison. We'd had to learn how to make the monthly reports during a special unit in Language class, and as I'd expressed it so elegantly one day under my breath but not quite quietly enough for Ms. Mag to miss, they sucked ass. Normal post-patrol reports weren't so bad - all you had to do was tell what you'd done or seen, if anything. But the monthly reports had to be properly formatted and written in the government shorthand-jargon that our class had decided had been created for the express purpose of frustration and confusion. You had to report everything of Peacekeeping interest that had happened in the past month, from locals' requests for help to huge, earth-shattering events. Thankfully the next due date was

September tenth, by which point Reubyn and I would only have been in Fankaloa for about a week, so we were excused.

"Let's not talk about that," Aiene said, "those things stress me out and I don't even have to write one. Anything interesting happen on patrol, Reubyn?"

"Well," Reubyn said, "I rescued Ika Ame'ei's cat from up a tree. And I have the scars to prove it," she added, laying her forearms out on the table. A network of thin red scratches webbed across them, courtesy of cat claws.

"Ouch," I said. "What did you do to piss it off like that?"

"I have no idea," Reubyn said. "I swear the thing was screaming at me. It was insane." She tapped a few more keys, hit Send, and took her bowl into the kitchen to wash it out.

"Mom's not going to be back until dinner, right?" asked Nikiani, looking to Vrenchard.

"I don't think so," Vrenchard said. "You know how she gets. I think she's trying to get in touch with Pegu; all the spirits have been a bit restive lately. Remember the storm the night before Reubyn and Lillia arrived?"

Vividly.

"And Kalinuea has been going crazy lately,"

Vrenchard continued. "I've never seen such a high-volume eruption."

Nikiani's face drew. "I hope Mom'll be okay up there."

"Manialua's a smart woman," Nico said. "She knows better than to mess with nature. She'll be fine."

Just as the sun set over Kamo Nakae, Manialua returned. She looked okay - no lava burns or anything - but she seemed tired. I sort of felt for her. After lunch, Nikiani had declared that she would continue Reubyn's and my Fankaloa lessons, and even though Aiene and Vrenchard had been there to curb her enthusiasm, my whole brain hurt from trying to deal with her full-force teaching style.

"Hey, Mom," Nikiani said. She had taken charge of making dinner, so she was in the kitchen, simultaneously baking garlic bread, making meatballs in a pot of sauce, and boiling a pot of noodles. "How'd it go?"

Manialua shrugged tiredly. "All right," she replied. "I managed to make contact with Pegu, but he seemed distracted. He didn't materialize fully. Do I smell garlic?"

"Yup," Nikiani said. "I think dinner should be pretty much ready. Would you guys get out plates and stuff?"

We did just that, and then queued up by the stove as Nikiani started the food line. I had my fork hallway to the noodles before I realized they were green. I stopped.

"Um, Niki," I said, looking over at her, "you know these noodles are green, right?"

Nikiani nodded, smiling. "They're spinach noodles," she said. "Mom makes them all the time, and with sauce and meatballs they taste just fine. Plus I didn't feel like making any veggies, so this was my solution to Mom's vegetables-every-dinner rule."

I shrugged and hooked a pile of the weird green fettuccini onto my plate. Then I doused it with sauce and meatballs and took a piece of garlic bread. I balanced the plate and my glass of milk, and took it back to the table.

Aiene joined me. "Do we tell them now?" he asked quietly.

"No time like the present," I replied. Just then, Reubyn joined us, and I informed her of the plan. She nodded. She didn't seem surprised.

When the others reached the table, we dug in. Nico looked towards me, eyebrows raised, and I nodded. Then I looked at Manialua.

"Um," I said, my usual brilliant starter.

"Listen, Manialua, we wanted to ask you something."

She raised an eyebrow at the word "we," but only said, "All right."

I had no idea how to phrase the question, so I looked to Aiene for help. "We were wondering," he said, "if there are legends anywhere about the islands having dark spirits. I know plenty about the Elementals, but I think there was a dark one too, and I can't remember much about it. We were...we were curious."

My hero.

This time, Manialua exchanged a questioning glance with Vrenchard. Then she replied, "I've told you about one. I'm a bit surprised you don't remember; you usually have a good head for this sort of thing. It was Harimako."

Something about the way she said the name made the short hairs on the back of my neck stand up. On my right, Aiene stiffened; a couple places down from me, Nikiani had somehow managed to go white as a sheet. Nico froze, and Reubyn inhaled a sharp, frightened gasp. Even Manialua and Vrenchard shivered.

"Why were you wondering?"

And now it was my turn to speak again. "Well," I said, "the other night, I had this dream..."

I proceeded to explain again about my emakalao dream. Then Nico picked up with the darkness and chill that he and the others had sensed rising, and finally Nikiani told Manialua and Vrenchard about mine, Reubyn's, and Aiene's *lao* powers. With every word, the fear on their faces deepened.

When we finally finished, the house fell silent for several long moments. Reubyn's pasta-filled fork sat still halfway to her mouth. I imagined it would have looked to someone watching as if we'd all frozen.

Finally Vrenchard, adjusting his wire-rimmed glasses, said, "That...wow. Just...ugh." He shook his head.

"It's a lot to take in," Manialua said, looking at Vrenchard sympathetically. "Even for me, and I was raised on this. Are you absolutely sure?" She looked around at the five of us almost imploringly.

"One hundred fifty percent positive," Nikiani said. She reached out and took her mom"s hand. "It's impossible, right? Please tell me it's impossible."

Manialua ran her free hand through her thick, wavy hair. "Give me a minute," she said. "Vrench, come with me."

Vrenchard followed Manialua upstairs. The

five of us left at the table looked at each other.

"Maybe we shouldn't have told them," Nikiani said, brows knitting together in worry.

Aiene shook his head. "They're strong people, your parents," he said. "And they deserve to know. What worries me is the name she said. Harimako."

Again, the name gave me a bad feeling. "What is...Harimako?" I asked, shivering as the name passed my lips. "The name gives me chills."

Manialua emerged from the loft before Aiene could formulate an answer. She held a very old-looking book in her arms. Vrenchard came down behind her. The worry had grown into the dominant emotion on their faces. They sat down at the table, and Manialua pushed her plate out of the way for the book.

I could see the confusion on both Nikiani's and Aiene's faces. "Where'd that come from?" Aiene asked. "I've never seen it in the library."

Manialua shook her head. "I don't exactly leave this thing lying around," she said. She opened it carefully, like something might jump out of the pages. "This is one of the oldest books of Fankaloa lore there is. And it's the only one that goes into detail about Harimako."

She scanned through the book, flipping pages. As she stopped on one, a sudden icy chill flooded through me and I gasped at the feeling, like a cold hand squeezing my heart.

Someone touched my arm, but I couldn't tell who. The room had all of a sudden gone pale and transparent, and something much more vibrant overlaid it.

I saw a dark palace in a dark landscape, patrolled by inhuman guards. I was moving towards it with Aiene, Nikiani, and Nico, and I knew we were on a mission. I didn't know where we were exactly, but it seemed unsettlingly familiar.

"This way," I hissed. "There's got to be a way in."

We moved around the palace, somehow escaping the notice of the monstrous guards. Then I heard Nikiani's voice. "Lillia," she said quietly, "what if we don't find her?"

I straightened my shoulders. "We will," I said. "I don't need a vision to tell me that. We're going to find her." My jaw set. "And then I've got a promise to keep."

I felt a surge of energy as I glared up at the palace. "Come on," I said. "Follow me."

I led us across the darkly familiar landscape to the palace. When we reached the wall underneath a carving, I ran my hand along the stone, searching. Then my fingers caught on a round bump, and I grinned. "Excellent," I said. "Got it."

I pushed on the bump. It yielded, sinking into the face of the rock. Lines spiderwebbed outwards until they reached the edge of a rectangle. The cracked rock within the rectangle flashed white, then vanished, revealing a passageway even blacker than the rock.

"Nice!" said Aiene quietly.

Nikiani murmured a word in Fankaloa, lighting the stone set into her staff. We stepped through the doorway, into the palace.

At that moment, Nikiani's staff went out.

"Ohhh," I moaned, seeing the small spark vanish. I slumped forwards and felt my face land in something strangely squishy.

"Lillia!" came Aiene's voice, and along with that the feeling of someone shaking me. "Lillia, wake up!"

I raised my head and opened my eyes to find that I was still sitting at the table and that the thing I'd fallen into was my spaghetti. I made a face and tried to wipe off the sauce. Then, realizing that everyone was staring at me, I went red.

"I'm sorry," I said. "I don't know what came over me - it just...happened..."

"You had a vision, didn't you?" asked Nico.

I just nodded, a little too freaked out to trust

my voice. Now that I had woken up, I knew the setting of the vision, and that was almost the worst part, because it was the dark world from my nightmares.

I had to force myself not to shudder.

Manialua gave me a concerned look, and then bent her head to the page. As she looked for her place, Aiene leaned over and whispered, "Lillia, are you all right?"

I shrugged, looking down at my plate of face-splattered spaghetti. "I don't know right now. I'll know better in a little while, I think."

Aiene touched my arm, and instead of making me flush bright red like it normally would, it reassured me a bit. As Manialua started reading, Aiene slid his hand down to rest on top of mine.

It soon became evident that Harimako was bad news. Very bad.

According to the book, he was the oldest of the islands' spirits, and by far the most malevolent. Millennia ago, long before the old continents, almost back to the first great Ice Age, Harimako reigned over the islands. To say the least, it hadn't been a good time. Famines, storms, volcanic eruptions, tsunamis, epidemics, creatures of the dark, and pretty much every other awful thing you could imagine had tormented the islands and the islanders. Harimako held the people back from every innovation that could have helped them, like advanced weapons or irrigation or dams.

Then, according to the legend, Ae Came'a (the Fankaloa deity, whose name literally meant "the father" and who had, over the centuries, blended in with the islanders' witchcraft and the religion the first missionaries brought to the islands to create a very interesting version of Christianity) intervened. He sent the Elementals, the embodiments of the four main elements that had been forced to trouble the islands, to fight against Harimako. For a time, the Elementals had kept in disguise, slowly accumulating Fankaloa to help fight. Among the ones recruited was the first recorded *lao*, Simai.

Finally, the Elementals led the islanders into battle against Harimako's army of dark creatures. It was a long, hard battle, described by the book in considerable detail; but finally the spirits of the islanders won through. Only no one got the chance to celebrate, because then Harimako himself left his dark palace to fight.

At first glance, the islanders, the *aliakeanu*, and even the Elementals had thought he was an innocent, maybe someone who had been captured by Harimako. He appeared as a tall, slender, handsome young man with fair skin, blue eyes, and jet-black, shoulder-length hair. But Simai, whose lao powers allowed her to see past his façade, had raised her weapon and charged.

That was when Harimako had shed his disguise and appeared as he really was, and according to the book his true form had been enough to terrify even the Elementals. He still had the shape of the tall, slender young man with jet-black hair, but everything else had changed. I grasped Aiene's hand under the table to steady myself as Manialua read the description.

"'His skin, already as light as the plumeria flower, whitened yet more until it was the color of a sun-bleached bone, and what the people had taken to be burns resolved themselves into black stripes like those of the great eastern cat. The rags in which he had been dressed as part of his disguise formed themselves into a red warrior's robe, stained black with blood. A sword was tucked into his belt, without sheath so as to reveal the layers of blood from centuries of killing, which had dried on the blade. The whites of his eyes turned red, as though his blood vessels had burst; and iris and pupil merged into a black pit in the center. Darkness ran down in a line from his eyes, black tears of evil. When he opened his mouth, lips tinged a bloody red against the whiteness of his skin, it was revealed that his teeth came to points, and the hearts of all who looked upon him grew still with fear.'"

Manialua continued reading, and even though I hardly heard her, I registered what she said, and none of it made me feel better. Though his army was gone, Harimako was still a force to be reckoned with, and he cut down a huge number of the islanders. Even in the end, they weren't able to destroy him, just weaken him enough that the aliakeanu could work a binding spell on him.

"And ever since then, he's been bound," Manialua said, looking up from the book. "Or at least, that's what we thought. But from what you've said, it sounds to me like the old binding is starting to fail."

"It shouldn't have," Nikiani said. "Every *aliakeanu* in the islands worked that spell. Some of them used so much energy that they lost their powers. That's why I thought...that's why I hoped I was wrong when I thought it might be him."

Her voice was quiet when she said that, and after she spoke the room fell into utter silence.

I looked down at my spaghetti unenthusiastically. For some unimaginable reason, I'd lost my appetite.

If it had taken all that to defeat Harimako before, what chance did we have now? The book had gone into detail about the size of the island army that had gone to fight Harimako: five thousand, half of whom had been *aliakeanu*, plus the four Elementals. There were only about sixty *aliakeanu* now, not the twenty-five hundred of the first battle. And even though there were more islanders now than there had been then, it wasn't by much, and lots were children. Even though everyone on the islands knew the legends were real, we would still be lucky to get maybe five hundred people to fight against Harimako. The book had said the size of Harimako's army had been about double the size of the islanders'. Even if its numbers were lower - which would make sense, since it had been decimated by the first army - it would still be a force to be reckoned with. And once we defeated the army, there was still Harimako...

"What are we going to do?"

It took me a moment to realize it was Reubyn who'd spoken. I'd never heard her so quiet in the year I'd known her.

It was our fault she seemed so bad, I realized: Reubyn didn't just have to feel her own fear, but all of ours as well. I wished then that we weren't across the table from one another; from over here, I couldn't try to comfort her by taking her hand. But I wasn't sure it would help. What if physical contact just made the feelings intensify?

"For now," Manialua said, "probably not much. Nikiani, did you tell the others about this last night?"

"I told them about the darkness," Nikiani replied, "which was all we knew about it at the time. I think we're going to have to call an emergency meeting about it. If they know, we might be able to start working out a plan. And we need to talk to the Elementals. I don't care how distracted they are right now; they need to know, and anyhow we can't do much without their help."

"I'll get in contact with Kaiko tomorrow," Nico said. "She's usually willing to talk to me. I don't think we ought to do anything this evening. It won't help much to have a couple hours extra, and we all need to rest. There's no need to burden the islands with worries about Harimako until morning."

He rose fluidly and bowed to us. "Thank you for the food and the hospitality," he said. Then he turned and left.

I stared after him for a moment, wondering if his ability was the reason he was so different from other kids. After all, it couldn't have been easy for him to pick up on childish behavior if he couldn't socialize normally without seeing people's whole lives inside his head. He'd said that Kaiko was usually willing to talk to him; I wondered if she was where he'd learned his social habits.

"Nico's right," said Vrenchard finally. "We need to eat, and we need to rest. Tomorrow's another day; we can worry about it then."

I looked down at my plate unenthusiastically. It wasn't that Nikiani's cooking was bad - really, she was a great cook - but finding out what we were facing had destroyed my appetite.

Weren't these islands supposed to be peaceful?

Chapter Eight: The Island Way

We stood shivering at the top of Ea'uaki Pua'e, which stood fourteen thousand feet above sea level as the tallest mountain in Fankaloa. Even though I'd worn my sneakers, a long-sleeved blue jacket Manialua had lent me, and my only pair of long pants, I was still cold - it couldn't have been more than three degrees Celsius up here. A thin and rather pitiful-looking layer of dry snow dusted the ground. I wished that we were back on the outrigger canoe we'd paddled over here. It was tiring work and my back would be sore the next day, but at least it was warm down there.

Ahead of us, at what Manialua said was the exact highest point of the islands, stood Maunei's *nama'ea*. It looked a lot different than Kaiko's. For one, it was a different color: pale gray instead of blue. Instead of pillars and a statue, it had a small plinth, with eight stairs leading up to an empty, flat area at the top.

"There's a small dip in the top," Nikiani told Reubyn and me, the only two who didn't know. She still spoke Fankaloa, just as she had the entire hike to the top. With Niki, learning a language was sink-or-swim. Even though it seemed to work well, it was a little overwhelming. "It changes the wind around it. I guess the people who built it thought it was appropriate, Maunei being the embodiment of air and all."

"Couldn't he have chosen a warmer place to embody it?" I muttered, and then grimaced as I realized that was rude.

None of the others seemed to mind, though. Actually, they laughed. "It's the highest point,"Aiene explained. "That's the idea, because symbolically this is the closest link to pure air on the islands. All the *nama'ea* are positioned as closely as possible to the element their spirit embodies. That's why Kaiko's is on that cliff by the water, Maunei's is up here, Pegu's is by the crater on Kalinuea, and Iemalu's is in a cave on Amikea. It's cold up here, but it's pure air."

Manialua nodded and moved towards the *nama'ea*. "Come on," she said. "We need to talk to him."

She led the way up the stairs, calm and comfortable as could be. I followed behind her with Reubyn and a little more trepidation. Water rescues I could manage, and long-distance chases and fights with criminals, but nothing at the Academy had been geared towards dealing with the supernatural.

Even though we weren't much higher than we☐d been before, it was even windier up on top of the plinth. I shivered and wrapped my arms around myself, wishing I had warmer clothes. Aiene looked at me sympathetically.

"All right," Manialua said. Her voice was much quieter now; I could barely hear it over the wind. "Everyone, sit down. We need to call Maunei."

We sat down in a circle around the dip in the *nama'ea.* "Should we hold hands or something?" asked Reubyn.

"No," said Nikiani. She giggled. "And I'm not sure we ought to, even just for fun. Maunei likes a good joke, but I'd hate to offend him."

So no hand holding, I thought, and couldn't stop the thought *too bad* from crossing my mind. Aiene was sitting next to me.

Manialua told us to be quiet. "Nikiani's better at getting in touch with the Elementals than the rest of us; it's an aliakeanu thing. Hopefully he'll talk if she initiates contact."

"I hope he will," Nikiani said. "He's got a better chance of telling the others than we do."

She closed her eyes and grew still. The rest of us quieted down.

After several long moments, something started materializing in the dip in the center of our circle. My eyes widened.

The shimmering form slowly resolved itself into the figure of a boy in his late teens with long blonde hair, which looked funny against his dark islander skin. As the form grew more defined, I made out his clothes: a sleeveless yellow vest, reaching down almost to his knees, a loose green wraparound shirt, belted at the waist, and loose, sky-blue gathered trousers. He was barefoot.

The wind increased as soon as his feet were corporeal enough to actually touch the ground. I shivered violently as the chill cut through my jacket, and Aiene reached over and put an arm over my shoulder. It helped, since I went hot all over as soon as he touched me.

When he fully materialized, the boy looked around at us. One half of his mouth pulled up in a crooked grin. His voice was half-human, half wind as he said in Fankaloa, "Well, this has to be the worst séance I've ever seen. What happened to hand-holding?"

"I told you," I said, and we all laughed.

Nikiani had opened her eyes, and she told Maunei - still in the language of the islands - "It's good to see you. By the way, we've got a couple of new arrivals." She nodded at Reubyn and me.

"Ai'e," Maunei said, the Fankaloa term equivalent with oh, looking over at us. Then he flicked his hair and said, "Hi."

"Um, hi," I replied. Reubyn greeted him, too. Maunei crooked his grin up another notch, and then looked around again.

"I assume you contacted me for a reason?" he asked. "Unless you just wanted the pleasure of my presence."

I disguised a snort of laughter as a cough and pretended no one looked at me.

"It was for a reason," Nikiani said, drawing everyone's attention to her. "We've got news."

Maunei didn't ask any questions. He sat down where he was and fixed Nikiani with a suddenly serious gaze. "I'm listening."

"Harimako's coming back."

Even the wind went still. Maunei's face wiped dangerously blank.

"What?"

Nikiani proceeded to explain about the darkness she and the others had felt rising, about the *lao kama*, and my visions. When she finished, Maunei's face was still blank, like he was taking it all in. But I could see his fists clenched on top of his knees, and the wind had picked up and whipped around us so fast I feared it might rip someone's jacket off.

"He can't be back," he said. His voice was

low and tight. "He was bound at the end of the last battle. What went wrong?"

I didn't like his tone. It sounded like he was accusing Nikiani of messing up. Before I could stop myself, I spoke: "Well, it's been millennia. Maybe he gathered enough power to break the bond. It's not like the *aliakeanu* skimped on power and let him loose!"

Maunei's eyes flashed. The wind gusted so hard that I felt myself rock backwards towards the edge of the plinth. "Who asked you, *pikali?*" he asked. "You have no right to mouth off at me as though you were my equal!"

My nostrils flared. *Arrogant racist Elemental bastard.*

"I have every right -" I started, scowling, but I couldn't finish, because something clamped my jaw shut. The wind died back down to normal very suddenly.

"Stop it, you two," said Nikiani. She had stood up, and I realized then that she had cast the spell that had shut me up. Her arms were crossed, but she didn't seem angry, just pleading. "We can't afford any arguments right now. There's no way we'll even be able to think about stopping Harimako if all we do is antagonize each other." She looked from me to Maunei. "Please don't argue. It's nobody's fault, and he wasn't suggesting that anyway, Lillia. We're all at a loss about this."

Crap. I couldn't argue with Nikiani when she went all logical; the fact that she looked decidedly young and pleading and lost didn't help, either. Since her spell still had my jaw locked, I just nodded, looking down.

The pressure on my jaw vanished. I opened my mouth and worked it around a few times just because I could. Maunei was looking away, his arms folded.

Finally, mostly to break the silence, I said, "I'm sorry. I didn't mean to snap. It just sounded like you were accusing them, and I'm sure they did nothing wrong. I swear I'm not usually that mean."

From what I could see of Maunei's face, it looked like he'd smiled slightly. "I'm not so sure about that," he said. Then he turned, and I could see that he was grinning. "You're a pain, *pikali*, but I think I like you."

I couldn't help a small smile. "Truce?" I extended my hand.

He regarded my hand for a moment, and then nodded. "Truce." We shook on it.

Reubyn leaned over when I sat back down. "It's good to see that you're making friends with the locals."

"Shut up," I replied, my face going red. Aiene smiled, shaking his head, but didn☐t say anything. We turned our attention back to the conversation.

"- going to need your help," Manialua said. "I know it's been a while, but if we want any chance of saving these islands, everyone's going to have to fight their hardest. We're going to have to work together."

"What about the others?" Maunei asked. "Are they being alerted?"

Nikiani nodded. "Nico - the *pikali* boy with the *kemaua* eyes - he's talking to Kaiko, and Dad's on Amikea trying to get in touch with Iemalu. Mom talked to Pegu yesterday, but that was before we knew the darkness was Harimako and she couldn't get clear contact anyhow."

"I think it was a busy day for him yesterday," Maunei replied. "The eruption was starting to get out of control. It took most of his focus."

I looked at him askance. Aiene took the words out of my mouth: "How? He's Pegu, for the islands' sakes! He is the eruption, I thought."

Maunei sighed. "It's still a force of nature," he said. "Unless we drop our human forms, it's difficult to be in complete community with our element. Pegu's strong, but the eruptions are starting to come under the control of something else." His face darkened. "I suppose now we know what. I'll talk to him."

His form started to shimmer. "Thank you for telling me," he said, looking around at us one last time. "I'll be around. We need to prepare. We've got a lot to do."

Nikiani gave him a respectful half-bow. "We'll look for you."

What remained of Maunei's shape blew away on the breeze.

Manialua rose. "Come on, everyone," she said. "We need to get back."

Later that afternoon, after finishing patrol and my report, I found myself sitting cross-legged on a paddleboard in the channel between Uo'a and Amikea. I needed to clear my head a little.

Carefully, so I wouldn't tip the board over, I lay back, letting the paddle rest across my stomach and putting my hands behind my head.

It was peaceful out there. All I heard were the waves and my own breath.

I still didn't feel right.

Sighing, I looked up at the clouds. It wasn't like I hadn't expected some sort of adventure. I was a Peacekeeper; adventure was pretty much the job description. It was why I'd joined in the first place. But now that it had actually happened, it seemed too much too fast. All control had slipped from my hands, and now something else was running the show.

And then I couldn't contain myself anymore. I needed to do something.

I rose, almost overturning the board, and started paddling at a furious pace. I didn't pay much attention to the direction. I didn't pay much attention to anything. I just went.

I pushed myself harder, paddling faster and more strongly. Soon I cut across the waves, staring ahead and letting the sea breeze blow my eyes dry from the tears that had suddenly appeared. I focused everything I had on the exercise, trying not to think.

When I grew too tired to keep going, I stopped and looked up at the sky.

"Why me?" I whispered. "Why us? There's got to be someone better qualified out there. None of us know what to do. Even with the Elementals and the *aliakeanu* and these powers, how are we supposed to stop Harimako?"

I searched the sky like I might see the answer in the clouds, but I saw nothing there.

Of course not. I never did.

I sighed and slowly turned the board around.

Then I nearly panicked. In my attempt to let out my feelings, I'd forgotten to pay attention to where I was going. It looked like I was out in the middle of the ocean.

I squashed the panic before I completely flipped out, though, and scanned the horizon around me. Finally, I made out several low bumps a long way in front of me. I hadn't realized I'd paddled so far.

I let myself sigh one more time, and then began to paddle towards land. My attempt to clear my head hadn't worked very well, or at least not for long. I was still as befuddled as I had been earlier.

It took me several long moments to realize that there was someone paddling towards me. As the figure grew larger, I realized it was Aiene. I decided to meet him halfway.

"I thought I'd find you out here," he said when he was close enough. "You okay?"

It didn't even occur to me to lie. "Not really." I shoved my glasses up my nose - they tended to slide down, especially when my skin was slick from sunblock - and looked down at the water. I'd never seen it as clear as the sea around the islands.

"You're worried too, huh?" Aiene asked.

I looked up to see his features drawn in compassion. Some of his hair fell into his eyes, but he didn't make any effort to move it away. Despite my concerns, a little bit of warmth bloomed in my stomach. "I'd have to be stupid not to be."

Half of Aiene's mouth pulled up in a wry grin. "That's true," he said. He looked up at the sky. "I keep wondering why Ae Came'a gave us this to deal with. I know he's supposed to give us the strength to get through, but it's tough to keep in mind when everything seems to be hurrying towards hell and Harimako."

I let out a slight snort. "That a common saying here?"

"Yes, actually," Aiene said, his wry expression returning as he looked at me. *"Aua ue Harimako* - that's the original Fankaloa. The expression's been around since the first battle." He sighed. "See, there's that *lao* thing again - I wouldn't have known that otherwise. It feels like I've always known it, but I've never read it anywhere. I never learned about it." He ran a hand through his hair.

"Freaky, isn't it," I said. Aiene was looking out over the ocean, his face in profile to me. I'd thought I was mostly over my crush, but when he looked so serious and faraway I found it unnecessarily difficult not to drool.

This was stupid. We had a ton of crap to deal with - a crush should vanish under those circumstances. Unfortunately, the laws of hormones didn't cooperate very well with rationale.

I scrambled to compose myself as Aiene looked back at me. "What do you think of all this?" he asked.

"Honestly?" came my rhetorical response. "I think it's insane. I mean, look at this place."

I gestured around like I could put all of Fankaloa into that one sweeping movement. "It's so beautiful. And peaceful. It seems like the very last place anything strange could happen. And yet here we are, a couple of *lao*, on paddleboards belonging to the family of a witch, having a conversation about an ancient evil force rising up again. Actually, I take that back," I said, running a hand through my hair. "*Insane* doesn't even begin to cover it." I sighed and looked down at my board. "I half wish I'd never left Plancint."

"You don't mean that," Aiene said. His tone made me look up. It didn't sound like a statement, the way I would have expected. He sounded worried. And he looked it, too.

I let out a breath that sounded like it could have been a laugh. "Not really. I mean, anything's better than living where I did in Plancint. Much longer there and I probably would have ended up in somebody's gang, no matter how much I tried to hold out. You can't reach adulthood in Hartell without taking sides somewhere along the way. Besides, I'm a fighter. I would have joined a lot earlier if I hadn't had Peacekeeping to hold on to."

"Why'd your parents move there, if that's what happens?"

I looked at Aiene in surprise. I'd have thought it was pretty self-explanatory.

"It was cheap housing," I replied. "Neither Mom nor Dad makes a lot of money. We barely had enough to get by. If we'd lived anywhere better, it wouldn't have mattered whether or not I'd joined a gang, because I would have starved before then. As it was we went hungry a lot."

Aiene looked at me for a long moment, expression unreadable. Just to break the silence, I asked, "Um, should we be getting back?"

"Oh," Aiene said, looking back towards Uo'a. "Yeah, probably. I'm actually out here on a mini mission to fetch you."

"Did Vrenchard assign you?" I asked, smiling. When he nodded, I said, "We'd better get back, then. I'm sure he'll be expecting a full report."

"Shorthand and all?" Aiene asked.

I laughed. "Yes," I said, "just to torture you. Race me back?"

Aiene grinned. "Eat my wake."

He took off paddling. I laughed as I hurried after him, trying to see through the salty spray his paddle sent my way.

The whole way back to Manialua's and Vrenchard's, I didn't once worry about what was coming.

When we finally reached the house, both of us were in immensely better moods. Aiene strode in ahead of me after we put our boards away, declaring, "Mission complete!"

I laughed as I pushed through the swinging bamboo curtain behind him. "Manialua, did you know he was such a doofus when you took him on? Because if you did, I think I'm going to have to question your judgment."

Then both of us stopped in our tracks, realizing that there were several more people in the room than usual. Maunei sat at the table with Reubyn, Nikiani, Vrenchard, and Manialua, looking so casual about sitting in a living room that it kind of weirded me out.

There were three other people around the table as well. The most noticeable was a burly man with blonde-tipped, fiery red spiky hair and brown eyes who for some reason had a spear leaned up against the table beside him. The second was a young woman - maybe eighteen years old - with violet eyes and wavy black hair that showed up blue wherever the light reflected off it. The last was a motherly-looking woman with green eyes and a short brown bob and bangs. I recognized them instinctively. The man was Pegu, the Spirit of Fire; the black-haired woman was Kaiko; and the motherly one was Iemalu, the Spirit of Earth.

I flushed. Reubyn, Manialua, and Vrenchard hid smiles. Nikiani had no such reservations. She grinned broadly.

"Hi, guys," she said. "Come here - we need some positive attitude." She patted the empty cushion to her left. Aiene gestured for me to go ahead and take it. He joined us at the table a moment later, after retrieving yet another cushion from a cabinet on our side of the kitchen counter. *How many cushions do the Alindeses own?*

"Um," I said. "So, what's going on?"

Nikiani took control of the conversation. "We were making sure that everyone had all the details of what's going on," she said. "And discussing what we could do about it."

Kaiko nodded. She moved more fluidly than I would ever have thought possible. "Nico told me about it earlier, but I decided to check in with everyone," she said. Like Maunei, her voice was a blend between human and elemental. It reminded me of rain, rivers, and the ocean all at once. "And it turned out that the others decided to do the same, so we began planning. It's nice to meet you, Lillia." At the last sentence, she bowed her head in greeting. I did the same and responded, "You too."

"Have you worked anything out?" Aiene asked.

Pegu shook his head. The way the light caught his hair made it seem to flicker. "These things aren't easy to sort out. There's a lot to deal with."

"We did settle on a couple things, though," Nico said. "You three are going to have to learn how to fight the island way."

I raised my eyebrows, because there was really no other way to react to that. "Is that a different way from how the rest of the world fights?"

Nico almost gave me a look from across the table. "Yes. Harimako's true realm isn't this one; it's the spirit world. And if we're going to fight him, we're going to have to go there to meet him. We're going to have to be in our spirits."

Reubyn, Aiene, and I looked around at each other, and then at the others. "'Spirits'?" asked Reubyn. "As in out of our bodies?"

Nikiani nodded like it was the most natural thing in the world. "Yep," she said. "And spirit weapons, too. It's going to be tough for you three, even you, Aiene. None of you were born here, and you haven't been here for ages like Dad."

"Nineteen years is not ages," Vrenchard said. "Niki, let someone else tell them. Your explanations are impossible to follow."

Nikiani conceded, folding her arms, as Iemalu took up the explanation in a warm, earthy voice. "I'm sure you've already had it explained to you that Fankaloa is much closer to the spirit world than any other part of the physical world. Because of that, not only is it easier for the four of us -" she indicated the other Elementals - "to exist physically in this world, it's also easier for people here to manifest spiritually."

"Out of their bodies," I said, echoing what Reubyn had asked earlier.

Iemalu nodded. "The idea bothers you, doesn't it?"

"A little bit," Aiene said.

"It's nothing difficult," Kaiko said. "I've seen people do it hundreds of times. That was how the first battle against Harimako was fought. It's impossible to travel to the spirit world in a body that belongs to this one."

"And the spirit weapons?" I asked.

Pegu nodded. "Same principle," he said.

There was a silence while the three of us new to this digested the information. I thought about the vision I'd had at dinner the night before. We'd been dressed oddly and carrying weapons. I supposed that made sense now.

I decided I'd absorbed enough to get by for the moment, and asked, "So when do we start?"

"No time like the present," Maunei said.

We followed Pegu's lead in rising. "Kaiko," he said, looking at the black-haired spirit, "I want you training Reubyn. Maunei, you take Aiene, and Iemalu, make sure Vrenchard gets the dust off his skills. I'll take you, Lillia."

Maunei laughed. "Good luck, *pikali*," he said, shooting me his crooked grin. "I'll see you in the spirit world."

That didn't seem encouraging. I struggled to keep my nervousness off my face, but judging by Maunei's continued amusement, I didn't succeed. He laughed again. "Relax a little," he told me. "You'll be fine. And he probably won't kill you too thoroughly."

As he turned to Aiene, sobering rapidly, I hoped he was joking. But the way Maunei acted, I had a feeling that you could never really tell.

I looked up at Pegu. "So what do we do?"

Clearly, my worry still showed on my face, because Pegu's hard features softened. He laid a hand on my shoulder reassuringly, but I noticed that he didn't try to say anything to repudiate what Maunei had said. All he said was, "This."

With his other hand, the one that wasn't on my shoulder, he reached in front of him and pressed his palm into the air. The other Elementals did the same. Kaiko faced me, so I could see that the palm of her hand had gone flat, like she had pressed it against glass. My eyes widened.

Then the air around Pegu's hand started to shimmer and change color. It expanded into something that looked like a portal from a science fiction novel.

"Come on," Pegu said, and he gave me a soft shove in the direction of the portal. I swallowed and, after a moment's hesitation, stepped through.

For a brief second my vision went black, and then the world returned. I stood in a simple room with bamboo walls and woven mat floors - simple, but easily twice the square footage of the Alindes' house. I saw no windows or light bulbs. The light in the room seemed to emanate from everywhere and nowhere all at once.

Then another source of light entered from

behind me, one that seemed like fire instead of sunshine. I turned around to see that Pegu had joined me in the room. But he was different. This was his spirit form.

He still looked like the Pegu who had been in the house, but like he had somehow been crossed with a bonfire or a stream of lava. Warm light flickered in his skin, pulsing in time with what I could only imagine was his heartbeat. His dark eyes smoldered in a way that had nothing to do with romance novels and everything to do with coals and hardening lava on the hillside. But the thing I could most easily identify was his hair. It had turned one hundred percent into spiked-up flames.

"Um," I said, "what is this place?" It was the most coherent thing I could think up in the face of the fiery being in front of me.

"This is a training room," Pegu said in Fankaloa. "It's a middle space between the spirit and physical worlds." His voice had had a hint of flame in it when we'd been in the physical world, but here it sounded like a crackling bonfire.

Then, without any warning at all, he raised his spear and butted me in the chest with the end of the shaft.

The air vanished from my lungs. A strange feeling came over me, like I was stretching like a rubber band from front to back. For a moment, my vision seemed to double up and I saw Pegu stepping out of the way, but overlaid on that was a transparent image of the back of my head almost blocking my view.

Then the rubber band snapped, the overlay image vanished, and I tumbled forwards. "Ungh!"

I rose, hoping I hadn't hurt myself. I stopped in shock as I looked back towards where I had been standing.

I was still standing there.

Well, I supposed that if I could see myself from here, I couldn't call the thing I saw me; it was my body, or at least a perfect replica of it, standing in the exact same position I felt myself in. I took a step towards it, and it took a step the same direction. I raised a hand to adjust my glasses, wondering if I was seeing right, and realized some sort of thin filament connected my right hand to my body's. When I looked, I found four more: one on my left hand, one on each of my feet, and one on my head. Somehow, they made me feel better about whatever had happened. I was connected to my body; that must have meant I was alive. This was freaky, but whatever Pegu had done to get me into my spirit hadn't killed me too thoroughly.

My relief lasted until Pegu stuck his spear

underneath the threads and jerked it upwards. I was yanked off my feet, and so was my body. I heard an ominous snap about a millisecond before I hit the mats.

I scrambled up as quickly as I could to see that my body didn't copy the motion. It lay sprawled on the floor, still as the dead. I looked down at my hands, where I still saw the threads, but they felt slack and when I yanked a hand back, trying to get my body to respond, I found that they'd snapped in the middle.

"Dammit, Pegu!" I snapped, whirling on him. "Those things were keeping me alive! You - you just freaking killed me!"

Pegu seemed completely unfazed, which didn't help me fight back the rush of heat that had begun to spill through my veins. I clenched my jaw to try to brace against it.

"Not technically," Pegu said - still in Fankaloa, I noticed, and scowled deeper. "The strings are still attached to your spirit and body, even though they're broken. You have twenty-four hours before they erode. At that point, you won't be able to return to your body, and yes, you'll be dead. For now your body is just *naekua.*"

I frowned. *"Naekua?"*

"Comatose."

I looked at my body, then back at the Elemental. "Comatose."

He nodded.

"Just comatose," I said in Fankaloa. I figured speaking a different language would help keep my mind focused on something other than my rising temper. "Oh, that makes me feel better! How do I get back into my body so it isn't comatose and I don't die in twenty-four hours?"

I had hoped to get a reaction out of him, something that would break his calm and give me some small amount of vindictive pleasure, but Pegu didn't comply. In spite of the fire visibly burning through him, he looked quite calm. I clenched my fists and tried to ignore my sudden and powerful desire to lunge at him and rip his head from his shoulders.

"There's only one way for you to return to your body," he said, "and that is to materialize your spirit weapon and find your true form."

I bit down on my tongue, trying to control my anger. I couldn't let it win me over. Somehow, trying to kill an Elemental did not seem like the wisest idea I'd ever had.

"And how do I do that?" I asked, struggling keep my voice calm and polite.

Pegu raised his spear and pointed it at my

heart. And what he said made even my hot, angry blood (could I have blood if I was a spirit?) go cold.

"You must fight me, Lillia Anied. And if you can't materialize your spirit weapon in the next twenty-four hours, you will die."

I stared at Pegu, mouth slightly open, as I tried to process what he had just said. Stuck in my head was that word *fight*.

But I couldn't fight. I couldn't. Ever since we'd gotten to the islands, I'd felt my fighting side and instincts getting closer to the surface. If I tried to fight, they might take control.

A part of me, the part I identified with my instincts, went tense with anticipation. The part of me where I could keep rational control balked. My instinctive side was much larger than the rest of me had anticipated.

"Well?" asked Pegu. "Fight me!"

Yeah, sure. I would get on that just as soon as I could move and form coherent thoughts again.

Then Pegu lunged at me. The movement startled me, and for a moment I lost the slight control I had over my instincts. I dodged, then whirled to face him, settling down into a half-crouch that left me poised to strike as soon as I wanted. My eyes darted from place to place, seeking the best spot to attack in order to gain the upper hand. My blood beat to the pace of a sudden energy that hummed hot and bright through my entire body. A fierce smile lit up my face, and I sprang at Pegu, arms extended so that my nails could rip -

No!

The small part of my mind that was still rational lashed out suddenly, and I faltered mid-spring. Pegu batted me aside with the shaft of his spear, and I hit the ground.

My heart beat in my ears as I struggled to keep my instincts contained. Now that they had had a chance to flow free, I found I couldn't shove them aside so easily. I gritted my teeth and stood. I wouldn't be ruled by my instincts. I had to use my head.

Pegu stabbed for me again. I dodged more clumsily this time, but I managed to do it, stay in control, and have enough presence of mind left over to try to meet him halfway through his follow-up motion with a quick left hook.

Only it didn't quite work out that way. I did dodge, and I punched, but Pegu caught my fist in his hand and jammed the butt of his spear into my gut. I collapsed backwards, gasping, and another blow from the spear sent me sprawling on the ground. He pinned me down, the spear pressing into my sternem. I was breathing hard, or would have been if the spear hadn't been pushing down on my lungs.

"Stop fighting," he said.

I looked up at him, managing to find room for

surprise. "But you said -"

"You're fighting yourself," Pegu said. "Stop. A warrior whose main battle is within is worse than useless in a fight - she's a liability." He put more of his weight onto the spear, and what little air remained in my lungs huffed out. "You have to trust your instincts, not fear them. You have the instincts of a killer? A hunger for battle, a thirst for blood? The will, even the desire to crush and mangle, to rip and tear and shred? Good! Use it!"

I couldn't breathe. I stared up at Pegu, feeling his words pound their way into my head, where they pulsed to the beat of my rush of energy. But I couldn't - *couldn't* - let myself give in.

"You're trying to fight with reason," Pegu said. "That's not enough. How can you fight with only one foot to stand on?"

My vision began to swirl black. I felt the two tides fighting for control of the current in my head. As the blackness encompassed the last of what I could see outside, my sight turned inwards and I saw them.

Red and white crashed together against the black - blood and water, war and peace, bloodlust and the urge to protect.

Instincts. Fight. Reason...

The tides swirled around each other, mixing

together but never fading into one another. The white stayed white, and the red stayed red.

Reason. Hunger. Kill...

Something seemed strange about the tides. I spent far too long trying to figure out why: they weren't fighting each other like I'd first thought. They moved together, supporting one another. They were opposites, but they coexisted.

Kill. Shred. Can't give in...

"You dumbass," said a voice that made my eyes go wide with recognition. "Come on, think. You're a fighter. You said it yourself earlier. Why can't you just accept it?"

A teenage girl approached me from across the tides. I recognized her, but she looked as different from the girl I knew as Pegu's spirit form had from the Pegu I'd met at the house. The girl wore an asymmetrical white shirt, jagged at the edges like it had been ripped in half just above her waist. Where it dipped down on the right side, I saw the top part of some kind of too-short cuirass made of black iron. A long piece of red fabric was knotted at her left hip, making an almost ankle-length skirt with a slit all the way up to the knot. She was barefoot. A katana hilt poked over each of her shoulders - one of white metal wrapped with black, the other of black metal wrapped with white. The straps connecting their sheaths - again, one black and one white - met in the middle at a yin-yang symbol. She wore square, black-framed glasses in front of brown eyes, and kept her blonde-streaked auburn hair braided away from her face. She didn't flicker with light like Pegu did, but I sensed a hot energy burning beneath her skin nevertheless. It felt intensely familiar.

My spirit self reached the edge of the tides and stood there, arms folded.

"Listen, genius," she - I - said. I recognized the tone. It was the one I used with myself when I felt like I was being an idiot. And what did you know - she/I spoke Fankaloa, too. *Great.* "So you've got instincts. They're nothing to be scared of if you work with them. Are you scared of being a blonde? Naturally, at least," she/I said, looking wryly at the dye job. "They're part of you right down into your genes. You just have to deal."

At my look of doubt, her/my expression softened. "You're not going to believe me, are you," she/I said. "Fine. I guess I'll have to do this the Pegu way."

She/I settled back into a fighting stance, drawing the katanas. "Come on," she/I said. "Fight me. And don't hold back!"

I bit my lip. The tides of red and white still swirled around us/me, lighting the blackness. If she/

I let the instincts in, and she/I wasn't a crazy killing machine, then they couldn't be too dangerous. But I'd spent my whole life trying to resist the influence of my instincts. There had to be a reason I felt like I needed to.

She/I gave me a look over the top of her/my glasses. "What's the matter?" she/I asked. "Not scared, are you?" She/I grinned, and I remembered Reubyn saying those same words on our first day at the Academy, down by the lake.

"Of course not," I replied, almost grinning.

"Then let's go," she/I said. "There's not much time left in our twenty-four hours."

That made absolutely no sense, until I realized that I could have been standing among the tides with words floating through my head for any amount of time at all. Time in this place seemed subjective. I shoved down a flutter of panic and dropped back into my own fighting stance.

She/I sprang. Even as I dodged, I registered the smooth grace of her/my movements. She/I seemed completely in control.

I spun around to counter but found that she/I was waiting with a roundhouse kick at my chest. I grunted and stumbled back.

She/I was fierce, I had to admit. I could see in her/my eyes that whatever strange, ferocious joy I'd found in the brief moments my control had slipped wasn't just a one-time thing. She/I felt it every second of our fight.

I didn't know how much time passed while we/I fought. It could have been five minutes; it could have been a full day. But finally, the force of my instincts grew too strong, and they broke through.

The instant they did, energy surged through me, rushing fierce heat through my veins. My senses seemed to heighten, colors and sounds and sensations going impossibly vibrant. I could see the dark inner world around me, but I could also see the training room and Pegu kneeling above me, watching me with concern in his burning-coal eyes, spear laid aside.

I jabbed my knee into her/my gut and, now that I could see, also into Pegu's. The inner world faded; I had just enough time to see her/my expression of approval before it disappeared. I felt the approval, too, like it came from me...which I supposed it did.

I sprang up from where I lay on the floor and reached to my shoulders with both hands. The katanas were there. *Yin-Yang. That's their name.*

I had found my spirit form.

"Do you still want to fight?" I said. My voice

carried more than I was used to.

I could feel the currents of energy inside me, the red and the white, swirling together. I had never expected this. Sure, I could kill with it, that would have been easy, but millions of other possibilities lay within my grasp. My heart hammered with fierce happiness like nothing I'd ever imagined.

Pegu rose to his feet, wincing slightly but otherwise not showing any effects from my bony knee having been rammed into his gut. He grinned.

"Let's see what you've got!" he cried, raising his spear.

I grinned and drew my blades with the same quick motion she/I had before. This time, uninhibited by fear, I struck first, slicing my swords around from the right. Pegu blocked them with the shaft of his spear and stabbed at me. I knocked his weapon away with one of my swords.

How was I ever afraid of this?

It felt as natural as breathing. I had two swords in my hand, two currents in my blood, but they worked as one, opposite but together - left and right, blood and water, war and harmony, like the yin-yang symbol that bound the straps together.

I knew what Pegu would do an instant before he did it. I didn't know if it was *emakalao* or my heightened senses or maybe a combination of the two, but it lent my attacks a sense of ease that amazed me. My body thrummed with energy. I could have fought forever.

"Ahem," came a voice, making us stop way too soon. We looked over to see Maunei, leaf-bladed sword in hand, standing in the room in front of another portal. Everything loose on him, from his hair to his trousers, blew in a breeze I couldn't feel. "If you two are ready to take a break, we're planning a *peguiki.*" He shot me a crooked grin. "See, *pikali*, I told you he wouldn't kill you too thoroughly. The form suits you."

"Thanks," I replied, sheathing my katanas. "I was afraid for a little while there he'd killed me completely. I got no warning before he snapped those strings. Scared the hell out of me!"

Pegu laughed. The fight seemed to have put him in as good a mood as it had me. "She found her way. That bony little knee of hers made itself quite a niche in my stomach."

I grinned. "So what's a *peguiki?*" I asked.

"A fire gathering," Pegu said. "Right through, Maunei?"

Maunei nodded. "The others are already there. They've been waiting."

He stepped through.

I followed Pegu through the portal and came

out in the dark. Well, it was almost the dark. We were in a forest someplace - maybe Kamo Nakae, maybe somewhere else - but ahead I saw a clearing with a fire and people. Maunei pushed through first, announcing that he'd brought us.

Pegu and I joined everyone in the clearing.

"Finally," Manialua said. Her shoulder-length dark hair was pulled back into a knot at the back of her head. She was draped in some kind of loose, gold-and-black martial arts robe, like a wise sensei from stories, and I saw white wraps around her hands, especially her knuckles. "You'd been gone so long we started to worry that you hadn't managed to materialize your spirit form." She was speaking Fankaloa, too. It looked like I would be using that all night.

"Well, it took a while, but I did," I said.

Pegu snorted but didn't say anything else.

"You look...very Lillia," came Reubyn's voice. I had to look to find her. She leaned up against a tree at the very edge of the firelight, hands clasped in front of her. Her hair was loose underneath a thin, silvery headband, and fell around her face. She had on a knee-length lilac dress, belted at the waist and with long, loose sleeves. I could see the edges of a shield poking out from behind her. There was something about the way she looked, whether it was the firelight or her delicate features or something else entirely, that reminded me of an elfin princess from fantasy novels - soft, graceful, gentle, but intensely powerful beneath it all. "The swords just figure, don't they?"

"What's that supposed to mean?" I asked.

Reubyn laughed, and it made me feel better. She hadn't laughed much since we'd reached the islands. "Just...the way you act, something about you, makes me think of swords. Though I didn't expect two."

"Uh-huh," I said doubtfully. "And what about you is supposed to make us think shield?"

As soon as the words were out of my mouth, I realized just how stupid that question was. I knew Reubyn; we'd roomed together for a year, and she was my best friend. Of course I knew why she would materialize a shield. I'd known it since the mock-up.

She knew when I figured out the answer, and stuck her tongue out. I rolled my eyes. "Come in to the fire, freak," I said. "Do we have any marshmallows?"

"Shoot," Aiene said. "I knew I forgot something."

I joined the others around the fire, taking the free stump next to Aiene, who had on blue and black and a quiver full of arrows. I was aware of him watching me as I sat down, and I looked at him, feeling myself go warm. "What?"

"Nothing," Aiene said. Did I imagine it, or did his skin go a shade darker? "Just...you do look very Lillia."

Somehow, the words had a completely different effect coming from him than they did from Reubyn. I felt myself flush, and the two of us exchanged smiles.

Nikiani beamed. She was dressed pretty normally, for her, though instead of a shirt and long skirt she had on a long silver dress patterned with dark blue stars. I could see the edges of her anklets poking out from underneath her skirt, and she had on matching leafy bracelets. Instead of the usual hibiscus behind her ear, she had a wreath of them around her head. "Now that we're all here, let's have some fun!" she said, grabbing the dark wood staff, topped with a silver stone, that lay on the ground next to her.

"Uh-oh," Nico said. "I think I'll sit out whatever you have in mind, Niki. I'm scared of what you find fun."

I almost laughed at Nico's spirit form, because it looked so exactly the same as his physical one. He even had the fishing pole, although the string had vanished and it looked more like a stave.

Nikiani stuck her tongue out at him. "I was thinking," she said, "that we could have a tournament fight! Since we've all got weapons and stuff."

"I'm not sure that's such a good idea, Niki," Vrenchard said. He had a hammer, which he had tucked into the obi sash that tied the waist of what looked like an ancient Japanese hakama (I had gotten bored in history class during the Old Continents unit and started surfing the Interweb - that was the only reason I knew what a hakama was). He had his suddenly long ginger hair tied back in a thick ponytail. "We've got work to do, and whaling away at each other with spirit weapons isn't high on the list of priorities."

An image flashed through my head of a big group of people standing by a cliff, and my stomach flopped. "We're going to be talking in front of a lot of people, aren't we?" I asked. I hated speaking in front of groups. I could do it, but I hated it.

Vrenchard nodded. "We need to call a *peguiki,*" he said, rising. "It's time the islanders know what's coming. Where should we call it?"

"The area by my *nama'ea* should be large enough," Kaiko said. In her spirit form, I could see where the sculptors had gotten the inspiration for the water beneath her waist on the statue. That was exactly what she looked like now. "Aiene, get up; we need something long-distance to get the message out."

Aiene did as Kaiko said, drawing an arrow from his quiver. "Which way should I aim?"

"Straight up," Pegu said.

Aiene nocked the arrow and aimed up. I couldn't help staring. He narrowed his eyes, taking aim. Then Nikiani raised her staff, and a burst of silvery light leapt from the stone at the top to Aiene's arrow as he let it fly.

"Ooh, ahh," I muttered, grinning, as the arrow-flare exploded a couple hundred yards above the forest. "I didn't know we'd have a fireworks show."

"To the *nama'ea*, then?" asked Manialua, rising. "The people who live in Laneke'a will probably get there soon."

Kaiko raised a hand and made another portal. We stepped through into what looked like another training room. Eleven bodies lay on the floor: mine and everyone else's.

"Let's get back in," Iemalu said, heading straight for her body. She had a more solid, more steady look to her in her spirit form, though I didn't quite know how. She stepped carefully onto her body's feet and seemed to melt into it. Then her body moved, pushing itself up off the floor and brushing off the front of her dress. "Come on, don't leave me alone here."

We all moved over to our bodies. I looked around at the others, who were already going back, before I copied their movements and placed my spirit feet in my physical ones. For a second, all I felt was a weird stretching sensation, like I was being taffy-pulled again. Then I blinked and realized I was lying on the ground, and got up. Sure enough, I was back in my body. I hadn't changed since paddleboarding, so I still had on just my swimsuit and the old T-shirt/cover-up.

It seemed odd seeing everyone back in their physical bodies, after seeing their spirit forms. It felt like we'd all removed a step from who we really were.

"I'll let us out," Maunei said, opening up another portal. "We'll be right by Kaiko's place. With any luck, we'll be there before the islanders."

We were. When we stepped through, the *nama'ea* was completely deserted. It was also dark.

I volunteered to gather kindling when Vrenchard suggested it, and Aiene went with me. We were silent for a little while as we searched around using a small, bobbing light Nikiani had set us.

After I'd gathered a few sticks, I glanced over at Aiene. "So I've been wondering," I said. "You've lived here for what, a year and a half?"

"Yeah," Aiene said. "Why?"

"How did you not know about any of this stuff?" I asked. "The magic, witches, stuff like that. As close as you all live, it seems like you'd have to know."

He shrugged. "I just assumed they held strongly to their mythology," he said. "There are lots of places that do. And Niki does so much between her schooling and her social life that I never noticed that she was out at the full moon, because she was out half the other nights as well. It was stupid, but I mean, what else would I have thought? You don't read Old Continent mythology and assume Zeus and Hera still live on top of a mountain in what used to be Greece."

"That's true," I admitted. "I guess I'll let you off the hook."

He chuckled. "Oh, thank goodness," he said. "I was so worried."

I smiled. "Well, next time, pay more attention."

"You got it. Next time I accidentally end up somewhere where myths and legends and magic are real, I will definitely notice. But what are the odds of that?"

"I dunno." I leaned down and grabbed a stick that I could break up into lots of little kindling pieces. "After this place, I don't think I can rule anything out."

"That's true."

We fell back into silence, but only for a moment. Then Aiene said, "You seem different."

I looked up. "How do you mean?"

He shrugged. "I don't know. It's been all of ten minutes since you came back from training with Pegu, but you're...more relaxed? Like you'd been worried about something, and now you're not."

I couldn't help it. I laughed.

"What?"

I shook my head. "You're a lot more perceptive than I thought."

"Hindsight is twenty-twenty. Especially for me," he added, grinning. "So what is it?"

I stooped to gather a couple more sticks. "I had to work through some stuff in there, that's all. It's bothered me for a while, and I'm glad I finally resolved it."

"Mm."

"What's that supposed to mean?" I asked.

He shrugged again. I rolled my eyes and kept

working.

"What did you work through?"

I grimaced. "It's kind of personal."

In the dim light, I saw his cheeks darken. "Sorry."

We collected in silence again. Then I said, "Sort of...anger issues, I guess."

Aiene looked up. "Really? I wouldn't have guessed that. You seem pretty calm to me."

I snorted. "Are you kidding? This morning I snapped at an Elemental."

"Aside from that."

"I also yelled at Pegu in the training room."

"And you're still alive?"

I chuckled. "Only just. But yeah, I've had trouble with it for a long while, and to be honest, it kind of scared me. Now it turns out I don't need to worry about it, so I'm relieved."

I saw him smile. "I'm glad."

"Hellooo!" Nikiani called. Aiene and I both jumped and turned towards the sound of her voice. She waved at us through the trees. "Does it take that long to get kindling?" she asked when she got closer. "People are showing up, but we haven't got anything to set fire to. Not even Pegu can get a fire going without something to burn!"

"We've got some," I said. "See?" I held out

my handfuls of twigs.

"Okay," Nikiani said. "Come on; we need to get the fire started so we can actually have a *peguiki* like the *uiniko* - that flare message we sent up - said."

She turned away, and after Aiene and I glanced at each other, we followed her back to the *nama'ea*.

Someone had already cleared an area of grass in preparation for the fire, so Aiene and I just had to pile up the sticks and let Pegu take charge. He touched the kindling and it burst into flame.

Aiene and I stood back and watched the flames lick up the twigs. Well, Aiene watched it. I watched Aiene. The firelight flickered across his face and danced in his eyes, and something about the way it made his features seem to move kept me entranced.

Then he looked at me, and both of us flushed a little as our eyes met. I looked away quickly, smiling for some reason I couldn't identify.

It took a surprisingly short time for the small crowd by the *nama'ea* to multiply. I pulled my mind away from Aiene long enough to try to call back what I'd learned about Fankaloa in school - both the Academy and the one in Plancint. About fifteen thousand people lived on the islands. Clearly, not all of them were there - there were maybe a hundred people around the *nama'ea*.

"Think they can all hear what's going on?" I asked. Maybe the crowd didn't make up even a tenth of the full population, but there still seemed like a few too many people for them all to be to hear well.

Reubyn nodded. "Nikiani cast a spell while you and Aiene were gone," she said. "It'll let everyone here hear what we're saying, and those who didn't come will know what's going on, too. Nikiani said it was kind of like a radio - the *aliakeanu* who came will hear what's happening, and through them the people at home will hear it, too."

"You're interested in this stuff, aren't you?" I asked.

She shrugged, but I could see in her face that I was right. "I don't know that I have the ability," she said. "But yeah, I'm interested in it. I'm thinking about asking Nikiani if she'd help me try my hand at a couple simple spells, just to see if I have the skill for it."

"I think you'd be good at it," I told her. "With any luck, you'll have time to learn before...well."

"Yeah." Reubyn looked at the fire. "But I think we'll have time. We're not ready to fight yet."

Then Nikiani stepped up behind the fire. "Hi, everyone," she said in Fankaloa. Her voice carried, but I noticed a distinct lack of her usual cheer. I couldn't blame her.

"I know you're all curious about why we called a *peguiki*, when there hasn't been one in so long. Well, I'm sorry to say this, but it's bad news." She looked back, tiny features pleading, at her parents. Vrenchard took pity on her and stepped up to the plate. Nikiani retreated to her mother. Nico moved over to touch her shoulder sympathetically.

Most of the time, despite her energy and her tiny frame, I had a hard time remembering that Nikiani was only twelve; all her joking aside, she was more mature than a lot of people eight or ten years her senior. But there in the low, flickering light, with her mother's arms wrapped around her and the top of her bushy hair hardly reaching Manialua's shoulders, she looked extremely young. Seeing her like that felt like someone had thrown a bucket of ice water over my head.

Vrenchard looked around at the crowd of waiting islanders. It seemed to take him a few moments to be able to speak. When he did, he only said four words. "Harimako is rising again."

I could practically feel the shock rippling through the crowd. It got noisy very quickly -

everyone started shouting out questions at the same time. It took Pegu yelling for silence to get them to calm down enough for Vrenchard to continue.

He explained about the vision I'd had, though thankfully he didn't mention me by name. Then he continued, talking about the growing darkness that the *aliakeanu* and everyone else with any kind of present-sense had felt. I could see understanding bloom onto the faces of a couple people who were closer.

"I guess forms of *emelao* are pretty common," I murmured.

"Mm-hm," said Aiene, nodding. "*Lao* powers aren't as uncommon as Niki made them out to be. Almost everybody has a little bit of them inside - they manifest as déjà vu, intuition, stuff like that. And of course, since people here have such a close connection to the earth, the powers can sometimes manifest a little more clearly. But they're only considered *lao* if all three abilities show up at once and they're all prominent, like ours."

Vrenchard finished speaking, and the babble broke out again. I only caught a couple questions out of the bunch - mostly variations of "What are we going to do?" Vrenchard put a hand in the air and waited for them to quiet down before he continued.

"I know this is shocking - beyond shocking.

But we can't let ourselves get panicked; we have to keep our heads and prepare. No matter how young, how old, how fit or otherwise, we all have to be ready when the time comes." He looked back at Pegu, who nodded and stepped up, and the last murmurs in the crowd died away. Every face turned forward.

"Not all of us are going to fight," he said, "I know this. You have families and other responsibilities in this world to attend to. But we need people to go with us to face Harimako's army. We need warriors; we need *aliakeanu*; we need Fankaloa. The soul of these islands must go with us to fight, because without it, we'll never be able to defeat the darkness that threatens us. With it, we can do anything."

I smiled. "If he had been a human," I said, "he'd probably be the leader of some country."

"If he had been a human," Aiene said, "he wouldn't be here to lead now." He looked at me wryly. "But I understand what you mean. He knows how to bring the fight back into a group."

"If you choose to fight with us, shoot off an *uiniko*," Kaiko said. "Or find someone who can set it off for you. But we need to know soon; there's no way for us to be exactly sure when the battle will start, and we need to have as much time as possible to train." She closed her eyes and looked down. "And pray for us, please. Whether you fight with us or not, we need all the help we can get."

That seemed to be the end of it. The islanders started leaving. Some walked off, heading back to paddleboards or canoes or their homes around Uo'a; others met up with an *aliakeanu* or two and jetted off.

Iemalu smothered the flames with several fistfuls of dirt, then brushed her hands off on her dress and said, "You all ought to get some rest. I'll return to my place; you know how to get in touch with me if you need anything."

The other Elementals left, too, leaving the rest of us standing in the dark by the *nama'ea.*

"You know," I said after a long moment, "I'm suddenly very, very hungry."

Dinner was a hurried affair, and none of us stayed up for very long afterwards. We retreated to bed in silence. I curled up on my futon, pulled my blanket over me, closed my eyes, and sighed.

I was bone-tired. I hadn't slept in over twenty-four hours, and I felt every second of it. But I couldn't get my mind to settle down enough to let me fall asleep.

I had had songs stuck in my head every day

since the second grade, but never until now had I had a conversation stuck there. But every word that Aiene and I - okay, mostly Aiene - had said in the woods was playing through my head like someone had caught it on tape. *I'm glad.* He said he was glad. What did that mean?

God. What was wrong with me?

I rolled onto my back, slapping my hands over my face. *I need to sleep,* I moaned to myself. *This is ridiculous. He's just a boy! There are more important things to think about.*

Not that those more important things would help me get to sleep any better.

I looked up through the skylight so I could see the stars. There was supposed to be someone up there to help when the going got tough. Where the hell was he now? Hiding behind a spangled curtain? Some god he was.

I sighed again and closed my eyes. That wouldn't help.

As I finally began to drift off, a tired, half-muddled thought made its way across my mind.

Please be out there, God. Because if you're not, I don't know what we're going to do...

Chapter Ten: Ridiculously Tired

"Form up!"

I stopped doing jumping jacks and scrambled into formation with the other seventeen islanders in the room. We ranged in age from seventeen to fifty-three, and looked like the cast members of eighteen wildly different films. I'd never seen such a bizarre group in my life.

An aliakeanu named Eaumu was in charge of today's training. He patrolled around our six-by-three person block, one hand on the faintly glowing dagger he had slung around his hips, and when he was satisfied with our arrangement he walked back around to the front of the room.

"All right," he said in Fankaloa - the go-to language for island matters. If things continued at this pace, I'd be fluent by the end of the week. "We've got lots to do, and no guarantee of how long we'll have to do them, so we have to work quickly. Today we're going to be training for the battle. Harimako's army isn't made up of people like you or me, or even things that take the form of people. It's an army of strange creatures, and so strange creatures are what we need to learn to fight."

He drew his dagger and closed his eyes, lips moving. The dagger flashed so bright that for an instant I had to close my eyes, and when I reopened them, something stood next to Eaumu that looked like the snaky cousin of a Komodo dragon. It hissed, revealing a mouthful of sharp fangs. Either those were poisonous, I thought, *or else that whole mouth is a breeding ground for quick-acting bacteria.*

Within about a second, I noted its potential weapons (the fangs, its claws, the tail that looked like a heavy whip), its areas of weakness (its eyes, the gap between the scales on its neck), and ranked it on some internal potential danger scale I didn't even know I had. It was a mid-level threat: strong and probably quick, but not likely to be very smart.

Well. I stopped. *That's different.* I hadn't even had to think about it.

Eaumu had started talking again. "This is one of the main beasts in Harimako's army," he said. "Its main weapon is its size and strength; *rinko* aren't known for being very smart. Now, does anyone want to try to fight it?"

My hand shot into the air the second he finished talking.

None of the others seemed eager to fight the *rinko*, so Eaumu nodded for me to come up. I left Yin-Yang in their sheaths.

Eaumu stepped back when I reached him. Out of the corner of my eye, I saw that the others did, too. But most of my attention was focused on the *rinko*. It seemed to be sizing me up. Its tongue flicked out like it thought I was its next meal.

Then it lunged, and I realized my initial assessment had been right - it was fast. I barely avoided having my hand bitten off. I drew Yin-Yang as I dodged to the side. Then I lunged back, blocking the tail with one sword and stabbing at that gap in its scales with the other.

I missed by about a centimeter, but I'd clearly hit a sensitive spot. It hissed and glared at me with its flat orange eyes. I could see the dent in its throat scales where the sword point had landed.

The *rinko* snapped at my midsection. I leapt backwards and swung the swords out towards its rapidly moving neck. A heavy jolt ran up my arms as the blades sliced through and clashed together in the center. The *rinko*'s body stayed standing for a second, and then toppled in what was very nearly slow-motion - either that or my senses had sped up. It was hard to tell.

As soon as the *rinko* collapsed, it vanished. "A little lacking in finesse," came Eaumu's voice from behind me, "but effective. Aiming for the neck first was good."

I turned to see the *aliakeanu* smiling in approval. "And for a first-time fight, of course, it was excellent. You have good reflexes."

"Um, thanks," I said. Eaumu dipped his head and waved me back to my place in the block, and then continued our lesson.

We all reached the house at about the same time that afternoon. All the others looked as exhausted as I felt, and Reubyn seemed depressed on top of it all.

"It's nothing," she said when I asked her about it. "Trying to be an aliakeanu is just harder than I thought it would be."

"Are you having any luck?" I asked.

She shrugged, wrinkling her nose. I knew that expression.

"Not really," she said. "I'm hoping it's just that I've never tried before. It's kind of tough, you know? It takes a lot of concentration. I'm not used to using the parts of my brain that magic takes." She paused, then laughed tiredly. "No, wait. That makes me sound stupid."

"Yeah, well, the truth has to slip out occasionally," I said, grinning. "Don't feel bad. I think we've all been worked about to our limits today."

I ran a hand through my hair, and then heard a buzzing sound from upstairs. "Oh, no," I said. "I must've missed a call. I'll be down in a sec."

Reubyn made some kind of noise of assent as I hurried up the stairs. The library was a mess, as usual, so it took me a while to find the Vcomm. I finally found it tucked up behind the futons and bamboo screens in the corner, but by that point, it stopped buzzing. I sighed and switched it on, sitting down.

"Crap," I muttered. An icon flashed between *Missed Call* and *Mom and Dad.* I selected it and the icon vanished, replaced with the call details. They'd called only a couple minutes before I got back. I glanced at their names on the Contacts list. They weren't online anymore, but I hit the icon anyway. I at least needed to leave them a message.

The Vcomm kept ringing until I got to vid mail. "Hey, guys," I said, "sorry I missed you. We were out. I'll keep this with me, so if you call back I might pick up." I laughed, but even to me it sounded a little forced. "Love you guys. 'Bye."

I hit End Call and set the Vcomm down, sighing. We'd been playing phone tag for a while now, and even when we did happen to hit each other I felt like I was holding a lot back. It felt wrong. I'd never felt the need to tell them everything that happened in my life, but I'd never turned into the secretive teenager either, and I hated not being able to talk to them about something so big.

At least I'd been able to talk to Dad alone a little bit. My dark dreams had come to visit almost every night since we'd found out about Harimako, and I needed to talk to him about them. When they'd bothered me in Plancint, he'd told me that he had the same dreams sometimes. He would always let me crawl into bed with him and Mom if I'd had a particularly frightening one.

"Hey," came a voice. I twisted around, already knowing who I would see.

"Hi, Aiene."

"Something wrong?" he asked, taking a seat next to me.

It was a long moment before I said anything. Even then I didn't answer the question directly. "Have you ever talked to your parents about all the spiritual stuff that goes on here?"

Aiene blinked. "Yeah," he said. "I mean, not about it being real, but I talk about it. You're having issues talking to your mom and dad, huh?"

I nodded. "I feel awful about it," I said. "I mean, I know they'd think I've been out in the sun too long, but...it doesn't feel right, you know?"

"I guess not," Aiene said. "I've gotten kind of used to it. It's still no good, but what else can you do? Plus, if my parents knew what was going on, all they'd do is worry about me, and I don't want that."

"Yeah," I said. Then the Vcomm started ringing, cutting off anything else I might have said. It was Mom and Dad.

"Hi," I said as their faced filled the screen. "I'm sorry I missed you earlier."

"So are we," Mom said. "I must have just turned it off when you called. But it vibrates when you miss a call, so once we figured out what the noise was -"

"We decided to call back and bother you for a bit," Dad said. He looked towards Aiene. "Is this the mystery boy you keep mentioning?"

I flushed. "Um, yeah," I said. "Mom, Dad, this is Aiene. Aiene, these are my parents, Unrich and Hattis Anied."

Aiene smiled. "Nice to meet you, Mr. and Mrs. Anied," he said. "Lillia was just talking about you."

"It's nice to meet you, too, Aiene," said Mom. She smiled.

Dad, on the other hand, looked serious. To break the tension in my mind (and to forestall any embarrassing questions), I asked, "So Dad - Mom told me the company put you in charge of one of the work teams. How's the project going?"

That was exactly the right thing to say. Dad launched into a discussion of the project, as I knew he would, Mom rolled her eyes good-naturedly, and I smiled.

"So how's it going on your end of things?" asked Mom loudly, cutting in on a description of the difficulties Dad's build team had encountered trying to lay the foundation. "Oh, let it go, Unrich, she's hardly told us anything."

I wrinkled my nose. "Sorry," I said. "We've been kind of busy the past little while."

Dad raised his eyebrows. "Though Fankon was peaceful."

"With an emphasis on the *was* right now," I said. "There's a little bit of trouble, nothing to be worried about. Reubyn and I are learning plenty about the islands' history and legends. And we're learning the language, too."

"Really?" asked Mom. "Could you speak some?"

"Sure," I said. "Um..." Naturally, my mind went blank.

"'Ua iniki ku?" said Aiene. Are you warm?

I looked at him and smiled, giving the Fankaloa equivalent of "yeah": a short nod and a half-grunt from the airway behind my nose. *"Ainame."*

Mom and Dad waited. Mom raised her eyebrows. "And what did that mean?"

"I asked if she was warm," Aiene said, "and she said yeah, thanks."

Dad gave an *okay* look. "Sounded good to me."

I laughed. "Geez, I didn't even need to make an effort," I said. "Everyone here speaks it; I'd almost forgotten you guys didn't! I could have just made a string of random noises."

Mom laughed. "That's what it sounded like," she told me. "Vowel-heavy random noises."

"You should try some of the other words," I said. "Like this island's name - it's all vowels. It's a little crazy, but really fun to say once you've figured out how to pronounce the vowel combinations without going tongue-tied."

"Have they let you speak anything else?" Dad asked.

I laughed. "If it were up to Nikiani, we wouldn't," I said. "Vrenchard's and Manialua's daughter - she's the one who's been teaching us. She's a very enthusiastic teacher."

"Which is the understatement of the century," Aiene said. "She taught me when I got here a year and a half ago, so I know firsthand. She's good at it, but it's a real headache."

As she laughed, Mom looked away. She shut up quickly.

"Shoot," she said, "I'm going to be late for my shift. Love you, Lil, love you, Unrich. Good meeting you, Aiene." She gave Dad a kiss and blew me one, then hurried away.

"I probably have to leave soon, too," Dad said. "Listen, Lillia..." He hesitated, glancing towards where Mom had disappeared, and then looked at me. "I know something's going on there. Don't argue," he said, seeing me open my mouth. "I can tell. Your mother hasn't seen it, but I know. And I don't want to know what it is. Just...be on your guard. And watch out for each other." He looked at both of us when he said that, and I felt my cheeks start to burn.

"We will, Mr. Anied," Aiene said. Somehow, the don't-worry-sir-I'll-get-her-home-safe voice didn't make it worse. He sounded one hundred percent sincere.

Dad looked at us for a long moment. Finally, he said, "Good. I love you, Lillia."

"Love you too, Dad."

He hung up before I could get to the button.

I sat silent for a long moment, at which point my stomach decided to let loose with a monster growl. Aiene laughed and touched my arm as he got up. "What do you say we raid the pantry?" he asked. "There's plenty in there."

"Sounds like a plan," I replied. I turned off the Vcomm and put it back where I'd found it, and then joined Aiene as he headed downstairs. We passed Reubyn about halfway down.

"Hey," I said. "Where're you going?"

"To take a nap," Reubyn replied. "I'm ridiculously tired."

"Okay," I said. "Don't let the bedbugs bite, I guess."

Reubyn laughed, and I worried about how it sounded. I couldn't tell if it was exhaustion or worry or what, but it didn't sound like her. She smiled slightly and continued up.

I looked at Aiene, feeling my brows knot up. He shook his head slightly, shrugging and looking just as worried as me. "I don't know," he said quietly. "But there's nothing we can do now. We might as well let her sleep."

I bit my lip. "I just wish I could help her," I said. "It's awful, seeing her like this and not being able to do anything about it. I mean, if we can beat Harimako, then things ought to get calmer, but until then everything's going to get worse. Reubyn's tough and she's got a good shield - no pun intended," I said, recalling her spirit weapon. "But I don't know that she can keep up with all this if it gets any worse."

Aiene shook his head. "I don't know," he said, "I really don't know. The only thing I can say is imagine how much worse it would be for a regular *lao*. They'd have to deal with all our times at once."

"Ugh," I said.

The others were spread out around the ground floor. Manialua was in the kitchen, fixing some kind of fruit smoothie; Vrenchard was sitting at the table, looking at his omnipad like he was trying to think of something to do; Nikiani was staring out the back window. I grabbed a granola bar out of the pantry, and then joined her.

"Hey, Nikiani," I said.

She jumped a little and turned. "Oh," she said. "Hi, Lil. What's up?"

I shrugged, leaning up against the wall. "Dunno. How did Reubyn do today?"

Nikiani wrinkled her nose. "Not very well," she said. "It's kind of weird - she can sense the world around her all right, better than me even, and she can feel the energy inside herself no problem - but she can't get to it. I don't understand it. It's there and she knows it's there, but she's kind of blocked off from using it." She shrugged. "I'm not really sure how to explain the energy thing. It's something you can either sense and use or you can't - or at least, that's what I thought. It's weird."

"I'll have to take your word for it," I said, "because I'm pretty sure I fall into the second category."

Nikiani gave a snort that passed for a laugh. "How are you doing with all this?" she asked.

I shrugged. "Not bad. Not good, obviously, but I could be worse. I'm just a little weirded out by it all. You know, spirits and legends and weird little witch girls."

"Don't even go there. I'll turn you into a frog or something." She grinned wickedly.

There was no safe response to that, so I decided not to say anything. We stood there in silence for a long moment. I ate my granola bar.

"It's clouding over," I said as I swallowed the last bite, a little surprised. It rained a lot here, but the rain came almost exclusively at night. I'd never seen the sky with so much cloud, not here.

"Mm-hm," Nikiani said. "It has to rain sometimes, you know. Even in paradise."

About that time, the first drop fell.

Something in that drop made it all become too much. I shoved myself away from the wall. "I'm going for a walk," I said, and strode out of the house. The others stared at me as I left, but I ignored them. I wasn't in the mood.

For a few moments, I strode blindly across the

already-dripping landscape as the rain continued to come down. It took all of thirty seconds to soak me to the skin. When the deluge eased, I slowed and looked around. I had wandered into Kamo Nakae. The trees didn't stop the rain entirely - when I looked up, I still managed to get several drops on my face - but the branches thinned the fall.

I sighed and leaned up against one of the trees. What was the matter with me?

Hormones, came my first disgruntled thought. *Hormones and stress.* It would just figure that they'd start kicking in at a time like this, when I most needed to keep my head clear. They couldn't have gotten out some other time, could they?

I closed my eyes and leaned my head back. It was peaceful out here, at least. The little rain that made its way through the canopy splashed onto my face and onto the ground around me. I concentrated on the noise and the feeling, ignoring my thoughts. I had to focus myself for a few minutes, but soon they melted away. The rain pattered down on me and around me. The tree branches blew in the breeze. A stream ran somewhere behind me. Waves crashed on the beach.

I relaxed against the tree and let myself drift away.

It could have been five minutes, five hours, or five equally rainy days before conscious thought returned and I opened my eyes. The forest seemed different, somehow, more alive. For all I knew, it was just that I could finally see again. But somehow, it didn't seem that way. The world just seemed a little more real.

I pushed off the tree and looked around. I'd wandered far enough into Kamo Nakae that I couldn't see the end of the trees, but I could tell about where I was. The waves crashed to my right, so I faced south. For a moment, I considered going back to the house, but I decided to finish my walk first. Even in the rain, the island was beautiful. So I set out, walking south.

It took me about an hour to get back to the house, by which point I was too wet to even think about staying in the same clothes. I toweled off, changed into dry civvies, and headed back downstairs to join the others.

I found Aiene at the table, playing a game of chess with Vrenchard. I sat down next to Aiene to watch.

He glanced up. "Hey," he said. "Good walk?"

"Yeah." I glanced down at the board. "I'll play winner."

"All right," he said. "Sounds like a plan."

So we sat and played and talked, and all the while the rain came down around us.

Chapter Eleven: Courage or Idiocy?

"Anyone ready?"

I could hear the nervousness in my voice. And by the lack of response, I guessed that the answer to my question was *no*.

Nikiani looked around at us. "Come on, guys!" she said. "I told you, it's fun. Would I suggest it if I thought anyone was going to get hurt?"

"Then why aren't you jumping?" asked Reubyn. "If it's so great, you can go first." She crossed her arms and stepped away from the cliff edge. "Go ahead, have your fun."

"Fine," Nikiani said. She stepped to the very edge of the cliff, so close that her toes hung out over the drop. She shot the three of us a mocking look, then turned around and jumped.

I had to admit, it did kind of look like fun. Our particular part of the cliff sat about twenty meters above the ocean. Nikiani backflipped twice within the first three - "Show-off," muttered Aiene - and then righted herself to go feet-first into the water, a neat, simple pencil jump. When her head popped back up above the surface, she looked up, and I would have sworn I saw stuck her tongue out at us.

"Well, meh to you, too," I said.

Aiene laughed. "You both realize you've just been shown up for courage by a twelve-year-old girl, right?"

"Courage or idiocy?" I asked. "That's the distinction, and there's a pretty fine line."

Reubyn snorted. "Well, I'm going," she said. "That felt awesome, and I wasn't even the one jumping." She grinned. "See you at the bottom if you work up the nerve!"

With that, she backed up a couple paces more, and then sprinted for the edge. She flung herself into the air, and as she started to fall, she screamed, "Wahoooooooo!"

"A twelve-year-old and a nervous emelao," I sighed. "Okay, now I'm embarrassed."

I considered following her down, but the thought alone made my heart jump into my throat and my stomach drop out. It wasn't that I was afraid of heights; as a matter of fact, I loved them. I'd never seen anything that equaled the view from up high. I was, however, terrified of jumping from them. I had no idea why, but whenever I tried to jump from anything higher than about a meter - unless I'd jumped from it once or twice before - I froze up. It took me forever to get up the nerve to make the leap.

"So who's going first?" Aiene asked.

I looked down at the water, where Nikiani and Reubyn waited away from the landing zone. "Dunno." I swallowed and looked up. "What do you think?"

"I think this is crazy," Aiene said, and laughed once. "But it's also a lot of fun, so you ought to at least try."

"Yeah," I agreed. "Just give me about twenty minutes to convince myself I'm not gonna die."

Aiene laughed. "Coward."

"When I jump off cliffs, yes."

My heart jolted as Aiene grabbed my hand and pulled me to the edge. "We'll go together," he said.

He didn't give me time to object. As the last syllable left his mouth, he jumped, and I had no choice but to follow.

We raced towards the ocean, wind whipping past at speeds that would have ripped my glasses off if I hadn't left them on top of the cliff with my satchel. It felt like I'd left my stomach up there, too. But it wasn't terrifying - it never was, once I passed my initial fear at the top. It was exhilarating.

I screamed, and the wind tore it away as it tried vainly to push Aiene and me back to the cliff edge. I wouldn't have imagined that the wind could get so strong, but later on I decided it was probably the effect of the speed. Aiene and I hurtled towards terminal velocity.

Then, in a wet, slightly painful, and impossibly quick moment, we hit the waves. Water rushed up my nose as the two of us sank down toward the bottom.

My feet hit sand. I pushed off, and a moment later my head broke the surface. I wiped my eyes and looked around.

"See, that wasn't so hard!" said Nikiani, swimming over to us. "It was fun, wasn't it?"

"Shut up," I said. "Do you always need to be right?"

"I always am," Nikiani replied. "There's a difference between needing to be and just being." She flashed me a grin and back-flipped away.

"Show-off," I said, echoing Aiene. He smiled. "Told you."

"You're just as annoying as she is, you know that?"

Reubyn rolled her eyes. "Stop flirting, you two," she said. My cheeks went furiously red. Still, it was nice to have her teasing me again. She hadn't done it since we'd arrived.

Then she turned towards Nikiani, who had surfaced about ten feet away. "How do we get back up to the top?"

"Magic," Nikiani replied, flicking her hair out of her face. "And a little muscle. See that path up there?"

It wasn't a path so much as a particularly rough part of the cliff that was a little less vertical than the rest. "We have to climb?"

Rock climbing scared me even more than jumping off cliffs.

"Yeah," Nikiani said. "Don't worry, it's not as hard as it looks. Plus if you fall, you'll have a nice water landing."

"Unless you crack your head open against the cliff side," I muttered, but I decided not to argue too much. The only other way up was to swim halfway around the island to the nearest beach.

Nikiani led the way up the cliff, and I headed up the rear. Once I finally reached horizontal ground, I stood and hoped I wasn't shaking as much as I felt like I was.

"Who wants to go again?" asked Reubyn. Her eyes were bright.

I had to laugh. "You're crazy," I said. "Twenty vertical meters down and back up again, and you're going to voluntarily put yourself through it a second time?"

"It's fun," Reubyn replied. "Not my fault you're a fraidy-cat."

"Just for that, I'll push you over the edge," I said, laughing.

"You'll have to catch me before I jump." She flashed a grin and ran for the edge again. Several seconds later, a loud splash cut off her screen. I glanced out over the edge to watch her pop back up and grin tauntingly.

Except she didn't.

Well, she came back up, but by the time she did, she was much further out than any of us had gotten after our jumps. Even from twenty meters up, I could see the panic on her face as the current swept her away from the cliff edge.

"Riptide!" I said. I panicked for a second, and then grabbed my satchel.

"What are you doing?" asked Aiene as I yanked it open and tore through the contents.

"Getting these," I said, pulling out my goggles and my Aquabreath. I put the goggles on as I said, "Somebody get me Reubyn's Aquabreath, quick. I don't know if she'll need it or not."

Nikiani didn't bother with the manual search. She cried, *"Hani ae Aquabreath!"* and Reubyn's Aquabreath zoomed out of the bag and into her hand. She gave it to me as I put my own into my mouth.

"Be careful," Aiene said. I couldn't talk

through the Aquabreath, so I just gave him a thumbs-up. Then I leapt off the edge and into the current.

Damn, this thing was strong. I knew from experience how well Reubyn swam, but even so, I saw her struggling as she tried to cut across the current. I'd read somewhere that riptides were narrow, and since Reubyn's progress could be measured in inches per minute, I really hoped that was true. I didn't want to think about what it might mean if it wasn't.

Then I heard a voice: "Hey!"

I slowed and glanced around. I didn't know that voice.

When I looked forward again, I realized that someone else had caught up to her - the person who had yelled, without a doubt. All I could see from my angle was wet black hair and fair skin.

Whoever it was, they were a strong swimmer than Reubyn. The two of them made it out of the current in less than a minute. I struggled my way out, too, and found the edge a lot closer than I'd expected.

The guy - I realized now that it was a guy - who had saved Reubyn swam my direction, back towards the cliff. I met them halfway.

"Thank you," I said, taking out my

Aquabreath. "I was afraid I wouldn't reach her in time. Reubyn, you okay?"

"On top of the world," she replied weakly, rolling her eyes. "Ugh, I'm tired."

"We'll get you back to shore," the boy said.

I gave Reubyn her Aquabreath, which was soaking wet but still perfectly useable, and the boy and I swam back towards the cliff.

Nikiani waited up at the top. "Wait down there just a second," she called. A moment later, I felt myself being pulled out of the water. When the three of us reached the top, my legs almost collapsed beneath me before I got control.

"Are you okay?" asked Aiene, hurrying towards us. Nikiani followed, slower and out of breath.

"I think so," I said, "but Reubyn's pretty tired."

Reubyn made a face and took out her Aquabreath. "Can you blame me?" she asked. Then she looked up at the boy who, I realized now that we were standing next to each other, was even taller than me and Aiene. "Thank you so much. I was getting exhausted trying to swim. I'm Reubyn." She didn't put a hand out to shake - I guess she figured it was a little late for that, since the boy had an arm wrapped around her in support.

"Mukon," the boy replied.

Nikiani and Aiene introduced themselves, and then it was my turn. "Lillia," I said, extending my hand. When Mukon took it, I went cold all over.

For a split second, my vision went black, and something icy and ancient and hateful bore down on me. I heard someone crying.

My vision cleared quickly enough that no one else noticed anything. I hid the horror I knew wanted to take over my face and shook Mukon's hand. "It's nice to meet you." Which was a flat-out lie, but what was I supposed to say? *Aaugh, it's Harimako!*?

As soon as that thought crossed my mind, I went cold again, but it wasn't a vision. It was just horror.

Because that was who Reubyn's handsome rescuer was.

If anything was worse than meeting Harimako, it was having no one else seem to realize it. At first, I thought they were all just hiding what they'd realized, like me; between all our various powers, I didn't think there was any way they couldn't have noticed who he was. But Reubyn kept clinging to him like he was the only thing keeping her on her feet, and the glances she threw up at him when he wasn't looking didn't look remotely like horror.

I thought once or twice that maybe I'd just imagined it, but halfway to the house, I accidentally brushed against his arm. My vision didn't black out this time, but I saw enough in the brief flash to know that I hadn't been mistaken. The only question was how the others hadn't seen it.

Harimako went with us all the way back to the house, and if I needed any more proof that none of the others knew who he was, I got it when Nikiani invited him in.

As we headed in, I braced myself and touched Harimako on the arm. He looked at me. "Mm?"

"I'll take Reubyn upstairs," I said. "You've got to be tired after helping her all this way. Enjoy your hero's welcome." Despite the warmth I tried to put in my voice, I felt myself staring ice daggers at him.

He looked back at me for a moment. "Thank you," he said, transferring Reubyn's arm from his shoulder to mine.

"Anything to help," I replied. "Come on, Reubyn. Let's get you to bed."

"I can get up the stairs on my own, Lillia," Reubyn said, "come on."

I didn't say anything, just let go of her and stepped back. She almost fell over on her first step, and I caught and steadied her.

"Point taken," she said. "Upstairs it is, then."

Manialua and Vrenchard came inside just as Reubyn and I started up the stairs. Nikiani got their attention and started telling the story.

"Sit down," I said when we reached the top. "I'll get the bed together."

I turned away and headed for the futons, finally letting my emotions show up on my face. *What the hell?*

"Reubyn," I asked, trying to be conversational about it. "Did you feel anything...weird about Mukon?"

"Um..." Reubyn said. "No. Lillia, are you okay? You seem pretty... I don't know. What's the matter?"

I forced a laugh. "Really," I said. "You just got caught in a rip current and almost dragged out to sea, and you're worried about me?"

I couldn't lie to Reubyn. Not only was she my best friend, but she was an *emelao*. She'd know if I didn't tell the truth.

"I don't know. But when I shook his hand, I got something really bad."

"I didn't sense anything," Reubyn said. "Don't worry, Lillia. You were probably just imagining things. If there were anything bad about him, Nikiani or I would have sensed it."

"Mm." I laid a sheet out on the futon. "You're probably right."

Reubyn laughed a little, and I felt her hand touch my shoulder. I straightened up and turned around. "What?"

"I know you don't believe me," she said. She smiled. "Just trust me. Mukon helped too, remember? He's not a bad guy."

The hell he's not.

"Trust me!" Reubyn said. She all but fell onto the futon. "If I'm not awake in an hour, wake me up, would you?"

"No," I said. "I'm going to let you sleep all day if that's what you need. You didn't swallow any water, right?"

"Of course not," Reubyn replied, pulling her sheet up over her. "I was at the Academy lessons, too. Don't worry, Lillia - about me or Mukon. Go downstairs. Do you think you get extra points for jumping into a rip current to help someone?"

I laughed. "I'll ask Vrenchard," I told her. "Go to sleep, okay?"

"Mm." She closed her eyes and rolled onto her side. Within seconds, her breathing slowed to an even rhythm. She was asleep.

"'Night, Reubyn," I murmured. "Sleep tight."

I looked down at her for a few seconds

longer. Asleep, she looked peaceful, more like she had before Harimako had started stirring up trouble. My jaw tightened. I didn't know why Harimako had come, or why he had decided to try and make us trust him, but he'd be sorry if he tried to pull anything. If he did, I would kill him - with my bare hands, if I couldn't get into my spirit fast enough.

"See you when you wake, Reubyn."

Downstairs, everyone was partway through their lunch, except Nikiani, whose food had already mysteriously disappeared.

"Did I miss the story?" I asked, sitting down on the empty cushion next to Vrenchard.

"Yep," Nikiani said. "But not the food. I restrained myself long enough to save you some." She pushed a plate my direction. I pulled it the rest of the way, examining the contents - chicken sandwich and some of Manialua's homemade applesauce.

"Thanks," I said. "I know it must have been hard."

"It was," Nikiani said. She grinned. "So eat up, or I'll eat it for you."

I immediately started in on my sandwich. "By the way," I said between bites," I don't think I thanked you properly for saving my friend." I looked at Harimako. For the islands' sakes, I felt forebodings about him from the opposite side of the table. How could none of the others sense who he was?

He dipped his head and smiled. "What else could I do?" he asked. "You tried to do the same thing. Or at least I assumed you were trying to save her, and not swimming through the rip current for fun."

I noticed that his sandwich was untouched. Everyone else had eaten at least a couple bites.

"Still, thanks. You ought to eat some of that; Manialua's a great cook. You'll enjoy it."

Harimako's gaze lingered on me a second or so longer than it really needed to. Somewhere in the depths of his blue eyes, I saw a flash of something like a crystal of ice.

"Actually," he said, sounding embarrassed and glancing up the table at Manialua, "I'm vegan. I'm sorry, I should have told you; you were just so polite about offering it, I felt embarrassed to refuse."

"That's all right," Manialua said.

I bit back a smile. Trusting my instincts seemed to work.

Manialua offered to get Harimako something non-meat to eat, but he shook his head. "No, I really should be going," he said. "My grandparents will be wondering where I've gotten to."

Nice cover. "I'll walk you out."

Harimako was rather pleased with himself. Several millennia of careful thought and theorizing had paid off: his hypothesis was correct.

From the moment he realized the binding was beginning to weaken, he had known he would one day be able to reemerge, and it was his determination that he should return to his rightful place as ruler over the islands. To that end, he had set about analyzing the two main causes of his defeat.

The first was that he had underestimated the strength and will of the islanders, which would not happen again.

The second was that the damned *lao* had seen through his disguise. It should have been impossible, and so Harimako had devoted much of his time to figuring out why.

He had determined that she could not have sensed him through *emelao*. His spell had been far too complete for any to penetrate through normal means; even an *aliakeanu* of the most sensitive abilities would have been unable to sense him. He had hidden his true self completely, and since he knew the value of the past in creating a being's present, he had hidden that, as well. So it could not have been her *ealao* ability. However, he could not hide himself from senses in the future, for he would not remain in disguise forever; and so the *lao* Simai had been able to sense him. And since the binding had grown weak enough for him to finally break it, he had decided to do so in order to test his hypothesis.

And the events of the morning had proved him correct. The *emelao,* the girl Reubyn, had been unable to see through his spell despite the strength of her power and the close quarters in which they had been. The *ealao* Aiene and the strangely powerful young *aliakeanu* had been similarly blind. But the red-haired *emakalao*, the angry girl Lillia, had recognized him the instant their hands touched. He had sensed her fear and anger all the way back to the *aliakeanu's* house and even when she had gone upstairs to help the emelao to bed.

Lillia watched him out of the corner of her eye as she walked him out of the house. As they stepped outside, she pulled him out of view of the people still inside and fixed him with a fierce glare.

"I don't know what you think you're doing here," she hissed, "but don't think I don't know who you are."

Harimako kept his expression neutral. "There is no need for such hostility. I came here to observe, and I have seen all I need." He spoke in Fankaloa, forcing the girl to switch languages. She scowled and obliged.

"Good. Leave."

"You're an angry being, girl," Harimako said, smiling coolly. "What is it about me that so offends you?"

Lillia glared at him, and though Harimako did not show it, the ferocity of the fire in her eyes surprised him "What is your problem?" she asked. "You're causing enough trouble here already without even being present. Get out."

"What if I choose not to leave?" Harimako asked coldly. "Fool. You might have some small power, but I have lived thousands of your lifetimes. And none of your friends can see the truth about me. What can one puny seventeen-year-old *emakalao* hope to do against me?" As he spoke, he allowed his assumed form to waver for a brief second, revealing his true shape. To Lillia's credit, she scarcely flinched, and the anger in her eyes only grew stronger.

"I don't know," Lillia replied. "But I do know this: hurt any of these people - spill a drop of Fankaloa blood - so much as break one hair on somebody's head - and I will destroy you, no matter how long you may have lived or how strong you are.

That's a promise." She jerked her chin up so she could look him directly in the eye. Harimako's human shape was taller than Lillia, but the power of the anger flowing through her filled her out until she seemed twice his size. "And stay away from my friends."

Harimako scarcely admitted it even to himself, but the girl's angry resolve shook him. He had not seen anything like her in millennia. He had wiped out all of her kind with his own hand. The fact that one had appeared again, and so firmly set against him, caused him to worry.

"I make no promises," Harimako said, keeping his face clear. He had had no intention to remain in the islands once he had finished his observations, but to say as much to Lillia would be akin to giving in to the force of her anger.

With his final words, he turned on his heel and walked away from the house, leaving the oblivious family and the fuming girl behind him.

An idea began to take shape in the depths of his mind.

As Harimako disappeared into the trees, I leaned up against the house and ran my hand through my hair. I let out the shiver that had been trying to fight its way up my spine ever since Harimako had flashed his true form.

It had been gratifying to see how rattled Harimako seemed by my anger. I would have expected, him being ancient and evil, that he'd have seen a lot of anger more frightening than that of a lanky and overemotional teenage girl. The fact that I'd unnerved him made me smile in a way that had less in common with happiness and more with a wolf catching the scent of prey.

Then I sighed. Much as I hated to admit it, Harimako had been right: none of the others could tell who he was. And though I knew they trusted me, I doubted they would believe me if I told them that Reubyn's handsome, kind, mysterious rescuer was Harimako, the worst threat the islands would ever face. I was on my own.

I took another second to compose myself, and then headed back inside. I couldn't do anything at that exact instant. Besides, I was hungry. I wanted lunch.

And then, I decided, it would be time to do some research. I needed to know as much as I could about Harimako. And what better place to start than at home?

"Hey," Aiene said when I sat back down at the table. "Something wrong, Lillia?"

I wrinkled my nose. I didn't want to lie, but

who was going to believe me? "Something seemed...off about Mukon," I half-lied. "Did any of you notice it?"

"He refused Manialua's chicken," offered Vrenchard. "Even a staunch vegan shouldn't be able to resist something like that."

I smiled as I bit into my sandwich. "That's true," I said as soon as I swallowed. "But I meant something different. I got a flash of something bad when we shook hands."

Nikiani stayed quiet for a second, thinking. Then she shook her head. "I didn't sense anything," she said. "Did you ask Reubyn?"

"Yeah," I replied. "She didn't sense anything, either. Aiene, you get anything weird?"

He shook his head. "Not a thing."

I sighed. "Yeah, I didn't think so." I wondered if that had anything to do with the observations Harimako had talked about. Last time, Simai had been able to tell that Harimako wasn't who he seemed to be. It made sense, then, that all three of us with *lao* powers should be able to tell, but for some reason that wasn't happening. I took a half-hearted bite out of my sandwich and then set it down, feeling a little drained.

"Are you feeling okay?" Aiene asked.

"Dunno," I replied. "I think I'm gonna go

upstairs for a little while. Sorry to waste your chicken, Manialua. You want it, Niki?"

"Not if you're sick," Nikiani said, then reached out and snagged my plate. "Don't worry, I won't let it go to waste."

"You're a little pig," Vrenchard said as I headed upstairs. I smiled a little.

Now, where's that book?

I scanned the loft, looking for the most likely place. Reubyn, Aiene, and I hadn't seen it when we'd looked for books after my first vision, so it couldn't have been anywhere obvious. After a moment, I decided to look on Manialua's work table. The thing was in dire need of organizing; there could have been three books of that thickness buried in all the papers and no one would ever know.

But I only found papers, unrelated books, and an inch-long dead cockroach that almost made me scream. I managed to get my head just in time, though, so I just flailed angrily and jumped back. Then, making a face, I scooped it up on a piece of paper and flung it out the open window. *Yuck.*

Sighing, I turned to face the room. *Use your brain, idiot,* I thought. Manialua had said that it was one of the oldest books written on Fankaloa lore, so it would need special care. I stuck my hands in my pockets and leaned up against the wall. So if I wanted to take special care of a book, where would I put it?

Not on that desk, that's for sure.

I surveyed the room. If neither Aiene nor Nikiani had known about it, it must have been pretty thoroughly hidden away.

An irregularity on the wall opposite caught my eye. I headed over, stepping carefully around Reubyn, and examined it closer. One thirty-by-thirty centimeter section pushed out from the rest of the wall by about half a centimeter. When I felt around it, I discovered a little depression in the side. I pressed it. There was a tiny click, and the panel opened.

Geez. Who would have thought there would be a secret panel in this simple little house?

My shadow fell on whatever sat inside, but I could tell that something was in there. When I reached in to get it, my hand felt about five degrees cooler, and the humidity vanished. Yes, this would be the perfect place to keep an old book.

I pulled it out, closed the panel, and climbed carefully out the window and onto the roof so I could read in private.

This is the book, all right, I thought. I opened it, praying I wouldn't break it by accident, and started scanning the pages.

As I read, I realized that Manialua must have paraphrased what she'd told us about Harimako's reign. The book devoted nearly two hundred pages to it. I checked, and when I realized how much I had to read - and in Fankaloa, no less - I moaned and let my head fall against the book.

"What's wrong?"

I lifted my head from the pages to see Aiene's head sticking out the window. "Oh," I said. "Hey. I'm just trying to do some research."

"Pretty heavy reading," Aiene said, climbing onto the roof to join me. "This might be a stupid question, but why now?"

I bit my lip and glanced down at the yellowed pages. "It's Mukon," I admitted. "I know none of you sensed anything, but when we shook hands, I got more than just a flash of something bad. It was... God, it even sounds stupid in my head." I took a deep breath. "It was Harimako."

Aiene's expression slowly morphed into an interesting combination of shock, disbelief, and worry.

"But..." he said. "I don't...no." He shook his head. "Lillia, I trust you a lot, but there's no way. Besides, none of us sensed anything."

"That's not the point," I said. "Maybe he cast

a spell or something. But I talked to him - well, confronted him really - when I walked him out. Believe me, it's him. I saw how he really looks." I hid the shiver that went through me when I thought of those horrible red-and-black eyes. "It was like the description in here, only about a thousand times worse."

Aiene's face contracted in worry, but when he spoke, my heart fell. "Lillia, are you sure you didn't hit your head or something when you jumped? Maybe you ought to go to sleep, too."

For once, I didn't appreciate the concern. "I'm not imagining things," I snapped.

"I didn't say you were," replied Aiene.

"What, then?" I asked, sitting up and glaring at him. "That I'm just making this up? I wouldn't say something like this unless I was absolutely sure!" He'd thought I didn't have anger issues? Well, he'd change his mind after this, that was for damn sure.

"You know what, this wasn't helping anyway," I said, and slammed the book shut. Aiene winced, but I didn't care. I shoved the book at him and slid down off the roof.

"Lillia," Aiene yelled, but I strode away from the house, in the direction of Makanea Pua'e. "Lillia!"

But he didn't come after me.

I didn't notice tears building up until they slipped onto my cheeks and started to bunch up in my throat. I kept walking, wishing I could punch a wall, wishing I could run to someone and throw my arms around them and have them tell me everything would be okay. I couldn't do either, and knowing that made a sob rip itself up out of my chest.

I reached a small grove and sank against a tree to cry. My shoulders heaved, and the tears left salty tracks when they dripped off my chin and the end of my nose.

"I was just trying to help," I whispered into my knees. "I was just trying to help!"

I kept on sobbing. And no one came out after me.

Chapter Twelve: I Call Steerer

Things didn't get any better.

Aiene relayed what I'd said about "Mukon" back to the others, so worried glances followed me from the second I got back to the house. When Reubyn woke up, they told her. She didn't take it any better than Aiene. Actually, she took it worse. The two of us didn't speak much over the next week or so.

And, just to top it all off, Harimako stuck around. The day after he'd first shown up, he came to the house, and Reubyn lit up like a firefly. I tried to stop her when he asked her to go swimming with him, but the instant she realized what I wanted to say, she snatched her hand away.

"What's your problem?" she snapped. "Why can't you just let me enjoy myself? I really like this guy, Lillia, okay, and I don't see why you're trying to screw this up. It's not my fault your temporary insanity scared off whatever ghost of a chance you had with Aiene. This is my life, my business, and my relationship. You think you need to protect me or something, but I have news for you. I'm tougher than the poor, weak little ditz you have me staked out as. And if you don't like it, well, fuck you!"

I stood there, shell-shocked, as she stormed

down the stairs to where everyone stood staring. "I'm sorry, Mukon," she murmured. "Let's go."

They left, but not before Harimako had a chance to glance in my direction. I saw the laughter in his eyes, and my face hardened. Then I turned on my heel and stormed up the stairs.

I'd spent the week and a half since becoming more and more isolated from the others. I didn't even join them for dinner most nights. I woke up and went to bed early, and spent most of the day avoiding anyone who I'd told about Harimako. I had plenty of time to patrol and to train, but I would have traded that in an instant for someone who would believe me. And Reubyn had been right: my attempts to tell everyone who Mukon really was had destroyed whatever had tried to start between Aiene and me.

Mom and Dad had called a couple of times, and Valie called once, but talking to them didn't help much. I couldn't really explain what was going on to any of them except for Dad, who by some miracle hadn't freaked out when I told him the truth about everything, and even when we had time to talk alone, I had a hard time opening up. Besides, even though I loved Dad, it wasn't him that I really wanted to talk to. I wanted to talk to someone who was physically with me, someone who could hug me when he told me it would be okay. I wanted to talk to Aiene.

And I'd never had so many nightmares in my life. I felt tired from the moment I woke up until my head hit the pillow and I found myself back in the otherworld.

It sucked.

"I just don't understand," I said. I sat alone at the foot of a tree, a few meters back from the waves on the west side of the island. My Vcomm sat balanced on my knee. Dad's face filled the screen.

"Well," Dad said, "didn't you say that Harimako can cast spells?"

I blinked. "Yeah, I did, didn't I? God, I'm an idiot - I never thought of that." It explained a lot. However in love Reubyn was with "Mukon," she wasn't stupid, and we'd been friends for long enough that she trusted me. And none of the others had reason to insist that there was absolutely no chance of "Mukon" being Harimako. "You're pretty good with this stuff, considering you just found out about it all last week."

Dad half-smiled. "No need to sound so surprised," he said. "Just be careful, Lil. If Harimako did cast a spell, it was probably for a reason, and if I had to guess I'd say that reason would be to alienate you from the others.

Remember what I told you?"

"'Don't let yourself be absorbed by anger." Yeah, I know. You say it every day."

"There's a reason for that," Dad said. "Anger's a natural thing, but you can't let it take you over, especially now that you're letting yourself use those instincts. If you did, you wouldn't be any better than Harimako."

I smiled grimly. "I know. Geez, Dad, you should have been a psychologist or something."

Dad chuckled. "No, I shouldn't have. In this job I can yell at people if they do something stupid. I don't think psychologists are allowed to do that."

"Probably not," I replied.

We were both silent for a minute. Then Dad said, "I'm sorry I can't be more help, Lil."

"You are helping."

He looked at me sympathetically. "I know I'm no replacement for having someone there with you, but I'll be here if you need me, and I'll keep the Vcomm on. And in the meantime...just know I'm proud of you. You're strong. I couldn't imagine tackling something this big on my own. Keep your hopes up. Maybe a solution will reveal itself."

I smiled, blinking back the tears that had been just below the surface ever since I'd finished crying over Aiene. "Thanks, Dad. I'll keep my eyes open." I glanced down at the clock icon. "I'd better start patrol. Give Mom a kiss from me."

He smiled. "You got it. Chin up, little warrior. I love you."

"Love you too, Dad. "Bye."

We hung up. I sat there for a minute, looking out over the ocean. Then I smiled and got up to head out on patrol.

After patrol, I found myself wandering again. I'd gotten into that habit recently, especially when I had nothing to do. Dad's words ran through my head. *Just try to make things better. Chin up, little warrior. Maybe a solution will reveal itself.*

I stooped and grabbed a couple long sticks off the ground. They weighed maybe a quarter as much as Yin-Yang, but I couldn't train with my swords outside of spirit form, and I hadn't yet mastered the effort it took to change forms on my own. I settled back into a fighting stance and started to move through a couple basic forms. Moving helped my brain settle down.

Halfway through the second form, I stopped dead. *Of course! How did I not think of that before?*

I dropped the sticks and headed southeast, towards the sound of running water. I needed to talk to a certain someone with a fishing pole.

I had a much more difficult time finding Nico than I'd expected. My original plan had been to look by the water in hope of finding him fishing, but even though I could see all the way both up and downstream and I had a clear view of several other streams and a stretch of beach further south, I saw no sign of him.

I tried Kaiko's *nama'ea*, but the only signs of life there were a couple of seagulls. I paused by the edge of the blue stone and sighed. What had made me think the homeless boy would be easy to find, anyway? He could be anywhere on Uo'a - maybe anywhere on the islands. However well-known Nico was - and however well *pikali* like us stood out against the dark-haired and -skinned islanders - finding him wouldn't necessarily be easy.

And naturally, at that exact moment, his voice piped up from behind me. "Searching for something?"

I spun around on a sudden rush of energy, and very nearly punched him by accident. I stopped myself at the last instant. "Nico! You scared the hell out of me."

"I'm sorry," said Nico, approaching the *nama'ea* to stand beside me. He seemed completely unperturbed by the fact that my fist had almost buried itself in his nose. "Were you? Searching for something, that is."

"Yeah," I said, "you. There's something I need to talk to you about. Have you heard about what happened last week when Nikiani took us cliff diving?"

"In bits and pieces. I haven't been over at the house to discuss the full details with any of you yet. Why?"

I started on the story, trying and failing to quash a sense of hopelessness. No one else had believed me. Who was to say Harimako hadn't magicked everyone on the islands?

Nico looked a little doubtful, but I'd learned what concern for my sanity looked like, and Nico's expression wasn't it. "Are you sure?" he asked when I finished talking.

"One hundred percent," I said. "Do you think you can help me out? Because so far, only you and Dad out of the people I've told about this have even thought about believing me, and I've got to do something. I don't know what Harimako thinks he's doing here, but I have to stop him before someone gets hurt." *Especially Reubyn.*

Nico hesitated. Then he said, "Show me."

I blinked. "Huh?"

"Show me how certain you are," he said. "I need to be absolutely positive myself before I can even think about doing something."

"Oh," I said. Bracing myself - though I didn't know what for - I shifted my gaze slightly to the side, so that Nico and I made eye contact. I'd never realized how vivid his eyes were. It felt like someone had aimed a couple of green lasers into mine.

I shivered.

It started dimly, a sense of something dark and warm and enveloping. Then something jolted, and I felt myself moving.

It sped up. I emerged into light, felt someone hold me, saw blurry images and heard half-formed noises. The sensations sped by faster and faster as the island disappeared. My first year passed in thirty seconds, my second and third in twenty apiece. A line of white fire flashed across my arm as I broke it jumping off a swing at the age of five. I got in my first fight and won in the time it would have taken me to blink if I could have. First crush at seven. Hungry in second grade, when Dad lost his job. Everything impossibly fast and impossibly clear. I'd forgotten so much of it. Every writing assignment, every friend, every cut and bruise and fight and dingy street and hungry night and gunshot and gang fight and meal and drink and nightmare and battle with my instincts - the trip to the Academy, my fights with Reubyn, lessons and mock-ups and thin ice and homework and silly jokes and graduation - balmy days and a stormy night, the islands, Aiene, Reubyn, my vision, the *aliakeanu*, *lao*, Harimako, Maunei and training and my mental otherworld with the tides, training and soreness and worries and chess and rain and cliffs and riptides -

The stream of memory almost broke when Harimako and I shook hands and Nico recoiled from the rush of ice and blackness. A few seconds later, the stream jerked back into real time.

Nico ripped his gaze away, running a hand through his messy hair. He closed his eyes and shook his head like a dog ridding itself of flies. "Wow," he said. His mouth worked for a minute like he wanted to speak, but couldn't quite do it. Finally, he managed, "And you're...you're sure no one's believed you?"

"Positive," I replied, surprised. "Why?"

He half-laughed. "You don't know how strongly your emotions communicate," he told me. "I can't believe they didn't break through the spell." He blew out a sigh. Then he looked back towards me. "I'll see what I can do to help. We need to go to the house. Nikiani will listen to me, spell or no spell."

I nodded and checked my watch. "Fourteen

hours fifty-five," I said. "Somebody ought to be there, at least. Come on."

I wanted to run, but Nico seemed comfortable at a quick stride. I didn't push the pace - so far he was the only person in the islands who believed me, I wasn't going to do anything that might piss him off - but it took every ounce of self-control I had. It seemed to take an eternity to reach the house, and every step of the way, I felt my stomach knot itself tighter and tighter.

It was Reubyn. Something was going to happen.

I led the way in, making the bamboo curtain wave around wildly. Nico followed, pausing to lean the fishing pole up against the doorway.

"Lillia," Aiene said. He'd stood up from the cushion the second I'd entered. "What's up?"

"Where's Reubyn?" I wanted to talk to Aiene, but there wasn't time. Reubyn wasn't there, and that frightened me.

"She and Mukon went on a walk about a half-hour ago," Nikiani answered. "He wanted to show her a good view of the islands. I think they might have paddleboarded over to Eilani."

"Oh, no," I whispered. "Come on, we have to find them." I made for the front door.

"Lillia, what's going on?" asked Aiene,

grabbing my wrist as I passed him. He spun me around to face him, and I chose to ignore the fact that my heart chose that moment to do wind sprints. "This isn't more of your Mukon-is-Harimako bull, is it?" He looked worried, and more than a little annoyed.

I pretended that the sudden wetness in my eyes was just because Aiene's grip was tight. "It's not bull," I snapped, yanking my hand away. "Just trust me for five seconds, would you?"

That stunned him enough to keep him from saying anything else. "If you don't believe what I tried to tell you about Ha - about Mukon," I corrected myself, "then at least listen to this. I've got a really bad feeling about whatever's going to happen on Eilani. Forget the question of my sanity for a second. I just want to make sure she's...that they're okay." I met Aiene's eyes. "Please."

He hesitated, biting his lip. Then he said, "Okay. The canoe's down at the docks in Laneke'a. We'll go over and check on them." He glanced at Nikiani and Nico. "Are you two coming?"

Nico nodded.

Nikiani shrugged. "Well, somebody has to keep things sane," she said. "I call steerer."

"You can have it," I muttered. "Come on. Let's hurry."

We scrawled a quick note to Manialua and Vrenchard *(Gone to check up on Mukon and Reubyn - be back soon)* and left. It took us about forty-five minutes to paddle to Eilani. There, we left the canoe on the sand and followed Nikiani to the place she said Harimako had taken Reubyn.

When we finally reached the cliff, I decided that Nikiani had been right: the view was gorgeous. But it gave me a funny feeling. Something seemed familiar about it.

As I stood there, something stirred at the edge of my sight. I turned to look, expecting to see a bird fluttering out of the bushes. But there was nothing there. And we were the only people here. Reubyn and Harimako - if they'd ever been here at all - were gone.

Disturbed, I looked back down at the islands.

That was when I realized why this seemed so familiar: it had been the scene of my first vision.

"Oh, my god," I whispered.

"What is it?" asked Aiene, looking at me.

"My dream," I said. "The one I told you about in the library."

Nico's eyes went wide, and his head snapped around so he could scan the view. "That's it," he said.

My stomach seemed to have vanished. "They're gone," I whispered. "Harimako and Reubyn."

And that was when the ripples started, far out to sea.

"No!" I exclaimed. The four of us on top of the cliff exchanged frantic looks.

"Those ripples," Nikiani said. "Do you think we could use them to get to Harimako's realm?"

They seemed to believe me now.

"It's worth a shot," said Aiene, squaring his shoulders. "Come on."

We hurried back the way we had come, towards the ripples. They were getting closer. I couldn't hear screams like I had in my dream, not aloud; but somewhere inside of me I felt something every time the ripples hit. And it was getting cold.

When the first of the ripples hit land, the ground shook a little. We grabbed onto each other so nobody would fall, and when we'd righted ourselves Aiene didn't let go of my hand.

As we reached the area where we'd had to climb, the earth shook again. The ripples were close enough now that if we jumped from the cliff, we'd probably land in the next one.

"Aelikio!" Nikiani cried. A bright light flashed around us, and then it cleared to reveal our bodies

lying collapsed at our feet. I couldn't feel the warmth of the day anymore, just the spiritual cold that came with the ripples. And now, I realized, I could hear the screams.

I shivered.

"Come on," I said. Another ripple yawned toward us. "One - two - three - go!"

We grabbed hands and leapt for the blackness beneath us. It felt physical, thick and cold and gelatinous, and it dragged us down like quicksand. We hit something hard and let go of each other. I ducked my head and rolled to absorb the impact, then stood and looked around.

My eyes went wide in horrified recognition. We still stood on Eilani, but it had changed. All round us, the plants had shriveled and browned and the rich earth had gone dry and crumbly. The ocean in the distance ran thick and dark, like blood, the same color as the tired sun in the black sky above us.

I knew this place.

It was the dark otherworld of my nightmares.

"Ugh," Nikiani said. She shivered in her thin silver dress. "This place is awful."

"Yeah," Aiene agreed. He looked at me with half a wry smile on his face. "Anytime you want to say 'I told you so,' I will be ready to hear it."

I smiled grimly, suppressing a shudder. "I told you so."

"Thanks."

"You got it."

Nico looked up the cliff behind us, and his usually serious features darkened further. "There it is," he said. "Harimako's palace."

It looked exactly like it had in my vision and my dreams, right down to the monster guards on patrol outside. I scanned the walls, trying to find the place we'd entered in my vision. Everything here felt too familiar. "I think I know which way to go. Come on."

I led the way up the mountain towards the palace, keeping my eyes half on the guards, half on the place I remembered the entrance being. Nobody questioned how I knew what to do. Nikiani murmured a quick spell to keep us hidden from the guards.

We were about twenty meters from the walls when I hissed, "This way. There's got to be a way in."

We moved around the palace, Nikiani's spell keeping the monster guards from noticing us. Then I heard her voice. "Lillia," she said quietly, "what if we don't find her?"

I straightened my shoulders. "We will," I said.

"I don't need a vision to tell me that. Come on," I said then. "Follow me."

I led us across the darkly familiar landscape to the palace. When we reached the wall underneath a carving, I ran my hand along the stone, searching. Then my fingers caught on a round bump, and I grinned. "Excellent," I said. "Got it."

I pushed on the bump. It yielded, sinking into the face of the rock. Lines spiderwebbed outwards until they reached the edge of a rectangle. The cracked rock flashed white, then vanished, revealing a passageway even blacker than the rock.

"Nice!" said Aiene quietly.

Nikiani murmured a word in Fankaloa, lighting the stone set into her staff. We stepped through the doorway, into the palace.

At that moment, Nikiani's staff went out. She inhaled in a sharp, angry hiss. Again, she said the word to light her staff, but nothing happened. She tried a third time. Still nothing.

"Shoot!" she hissed. "Something's blocking my magic." She muttered another spell - *"Ua'aki pegu apea iki,"* light a fire before us - but it didn't work any better. There wasn't so much as a spark. She said something in Fankaloa that I recognized as "Dammit."

"It looks like we'll have to do this the manual

way," Nico said. I heard him fumbling around, and then he said, "Got something. No one would happen to have the means of lighting a torch on them, would they?"

"Sure, just let me grab my tinderbox out of my pocket," said Aiene sarcastically. The silence that followed led me to imagine Nico staring daggers at Aiene.

"Thank you," Nico said. "But I don't think this is quite the time."

"Sorry," muttered Aiene.

"Let me try something," I said. "Um, how to do this...well, guys, move away from my voice. This could get ugly if someone gets in the way."

I heard three sets of feet retreat.

I drew Yin-Yang and felt better with their weight in my hands. "Okay," I muttered. I held one of my swords out in front of me, and then raked the edges against each other like a flint and steel. Sparks bounced off the blades.

"Good thinking," said Nico's voice. "Don"t do anything just yet. Talk so I can figure out where you are."

"Um, okay," I said. "Uh, hydrogen. Helium. Lithium. Beryllium..."

I couldn't hear his footsteps, but I knew it when he tapped the base of the torch against my leg.

"Grip it," he said. "You're going to have to do this on your own, because I like having my head attached to my shoulders."

"Got it," I replied. I adjusted the torch so that the end to light would be beneath where the blades would meet, and I moved them apart while Nico retreated again. "Haah!" I yelled, for no apparent reason, and struck.

It took three tries, but eventually the sparks fell onto the kindling at the top of the torch and caught. I grinned and sheathed Yin-Yang, grabbing the torch. "Shall we?"

We looked both ways down the corridor. One way ended abruptly - the entrance had closed behind us when we stepped in. The other way stretched out beyond the reach of the firelight. "Nikiani, you sense anything?"

She shook her head. "I don't think it's just my magic that's being restrained in here," she said. "I can hardly sense you guys, and we're right up next to each other. We're going in blind, I think." The flickering light from the torch seemed to highlight the motion of her throat when she swallowed. "It feels really weird. I don't know how it's being blocked. I've heard of blocking magic, but not to this degree. And I've never heard of any spell blocking off an *aliakeanu's* senses."

That wasn't good. I closed my eyes and tried to cast my power out ahead of us.

"Um, Lillia -" Aiene said, but I held up my free hand to cut him off. He didn't say anything else.

I fumbled around, trying to see ahead. There was a clash of weapons and scales and skin; something black flashed by me and impaled itself into something that rushed towards me. Things flickered in torchlight, and then the light went out. I saw white skin striped with black, and heard a cold voice speaking in Fankaloa, and felt a tight feeling around my throat.

When the images and feelings faded, I opened my eyes. The others looked at me oddly.

"What was that?" Aiene asked.

I blushed a little. "Something I was working on while I was on my own," I said. "Sort of projecting my powers, trying to see at will. I thought it might come in handy."

"That's pretty cool!" said Nikiani. "Did you see anything?"

"Not much," I admitted. "I'm not very good at it yet. Most of what I got was flashes. But I think we're going to end up in a fight at some point."

"Why am I not surprised," Nico muttered, rolling his eyes. "Well, if it's going to happen we might as well meet it head-on. Let's go."

I hefted the torch higher as we headed down the corridor. Our feet padded against the stone, but to me it sounded like they slapped it with every step. My breath echoed in my ears like the droning of a nervous vacuum. I could see every mortar line and carving in the stones. Energy thrummed through me.

We would rescue Reubyn. I'd hack Harimako into pieces if that was what it took.

I might do it anyway.

Soon we reached a choice: the corridor broke off to the right, leading up a spiral staircase, while in front of us it ended in a doorway covered by a black curtain.

"Up," I said without pausing.

Aiene raised an eyebrow. "Was that in your vision?"

I shook my head. "I know this place. This is where we need to go." I gestured towards the stairs.

"Wha... Never mind. Up'll do." Nikiani sighed. "You'll have to go first, Lillia."

I led the way up the staircase.

And up, and up, and up and up and up until I was thoroughly dizzy and my thighs started to ache. "Doesn't it ever end?" complained Nikiani from behind.

"Logically, yes. In practice, maybe not." I almost grinned, and I glanced around to see her sticking her tongue out at me. "Nikiani, you have the soul of a five-year-old."

"Yeah, because you're so much better."

I shook my head but didn't reply. As I continued up and around, I spotted a landing materializing at the edge of the torchlight. "We're almost at the end," I said.

"Thank god," Aiene said. "I feel sick."

We made it to the top, only to discover a black door blocking our path. Nico tried the knob.

"Locked."

Nikiani muttered a quick spell, but nothing happened. She made a face. "I hate this."

"Let me try," I said. "Can someone hold this for me?"

Aiene took the torch. I touched the knob and heard a quiet click. I opened the door.

"How'd you do that?" asked Nikiani.

I bit my lip, thinking about my dreams. Somehow, this didn't seem like the best time to discuss them. "Just...luck, I guess."

"Maybe," Nico said, but he glanced my direction. My stomach dropped. I'd forgotten that he'd looked me in the eye. He knew about my dreams.

But he didn't say anything.

Aiene passed the torch back to me: "Since

you've had good luck so far." As I continued leading the way through the palace, he took my hand. He didn't say anything, but it made me feel a little better.

Then I froze. I heard the sounds of claws on stone. "Something's coming," I hissed. I glanced around and, spotting a free bracket, set the torch down in it. All four of us prepared to fight.

I recognized the *rinko* when it sprang into the light cast by the torch. An arrow hissed an inch to the right of my cheek, impaling itself directly into the *rinko*'s left eye.

"Nice shot!" I said to Aiene. As the rest of the guards rushed into the torchlight, I drew Yin-Yang, and the four of us rushed into battle.

It was fierce but brief. Within five minutes, all six of the guards that had attacked lay dead in the corridor. I'd killed three - two of them with one strike from Yin-Yang. As my heartbeat slowed back down and my senses returned to normal - or as close to normal as they seemed to get in here - I grabbed the torch out of the bracket. "Come on," I said. "I don't think it's much further."

We went down the corridor. I led us down the second left, up a thankfully short flight of stairs, and to the right when the corridor forked off again. About thirty meters down, it opened up into a big rectangular chamber. Two black stone doors, covered in carvings, were set into the wall opposite. Two monsters stood guard: *hukulili*, skeletal, dragon-like creatures. They growled when they saw us.

I swung the torch forwards, knowing that they wouldn't like it. They had large eyes, adapted for seeing in the dark. A flash of bright torchlight wouldn't feel too good.

Sure enough, they reeled back, shrieking. Nikiani smashed one of their wings. I pitched the torch at the other one and drew Yin-Yang.

To stop *hukulili*, you had to sever their heads, but they were tall enough that that was a problem. I took out a leg and the one hissed at me, but it limped on.

Nico's stave swung up and rammed into one of the *hukulili*'s skulls. I heard a nasty cracking sound, but the head didn't come off. One of Aiene's arrows hit it right in the eye on the same side, causing it to shriek and rear back. It whacked its head on the ceiling and, with a final crack, its skull fell to the floor. A moment later, its body collapsed into a pile of bones.

We finished off the other one, but none of us put away our weapons. Aiene retrieved his arrows and picked up the barely-burning torch. In spite of his best efforts, it went out a moment later. But along the bottom of the double doors, I could see a strip of firelight.

I heard someone crying inside.

The four of us approached the door as quietly as possible. I ran my fingers over the carvings, trying to figure out what they were. Aiene's hand joined mine, but as soon as he touched the stone he sucked in a pained breath and snatched his hand back like it had been burnt.

"I hope you know what to do with that," he said. "I'm definitely not going to be any help."

I looked at him, my fingers still on the door. "That bad?"

"It remembers," he said. "Objects don't usually have memories like that." He shivered. "I can't see through it all to find the code."

I touched his hand gently. Yin-Yang's right blade pressed up against my leg. The feeling of Aiene's hand and the cold weight of the blade made an odd combination, but it wasn't unpleasant.

"This is Harimako's throne room, no doubt about it," I murmured. "You ready?"

"As ready as I can be," he replied. "What about you?"

I hesitated. "I hope so." I swallowed. "I'm scared."

"We all are." Aiene put his hand over top of mine.

The image of Harimako's true form flashed through my mind, and I shivered. Then I took my hand away from the door. "I know how to open it," I said. I looked around at the others. A part of my mind registered that Nikiani and Nico had taken each others' hands, and for a second, a smile almost made it to my lips.

"Are you ready?"

Three heads nodded in agreement.

The movement as familiar as if I'd done it a thousand times, I touched a carving on the left-hand door: a lion with two eagles' heads, beaks open in an angry screech. I pressed down. The carving depressed itself into the door, and I moved on to the next carving in the sequence. There were twenty-four.

When the final carving sank into the stone, the doors began to rumble and tremble. I stepped back, gripping Yin-Yang. "Here we go," I whispered.

The four of us stood together as the doors shook and the rumbling grew louder. Then, with a horrible groaning noise, they sank down into the floor, and I got my first glimpse of Harimako's throne room.

No, not my first glimpse. My dreams had taken me here, too. I knew every detail of this place intimately: the windows set into the black walls, showing different parts of Harimako's realm; the thirteen torches burning on the walls; the dark carpet running the length of the room, embroidered with the same sort of designs that had been on the door, and the black throne opposite us, upon which sat Harimako.

He watched us out of the black-and-red pits of his eyes, which burned with an icy fire from under his blood-matted, shoulder-length black hair. Black stripes like a tiger's crossed his arms and face, which were white as first snowfall. His long white hands and their pointed black nails rested delicately on the armrests of his throne, and leaning against the right arm was a blood-encrusted silver sword. Black lines that looked like what happened when someone cried with eyeliner on ran from his eyes to his jaw. His lips were red as blood. They looked wet.

Reubyn sat at the foot of the throne, arms and legs bound, eyes red and damp like she had been crying. When she saw us, her eyes went wide.

"No -!" she choked out, but at a slight motion of Harimako's pale hand anything else she might have tried to say seemed to literally die in her throat. Reubyn looked at us imploringly and mouthed, *Run! Now, before it's too late!*

"We won't," I said, looking her directly in the eye. I knew it would irk Harimako to be ignored in favor of the girl bound at his feet. "We're not letting this overgrown playground bully mess with us anymore."

"Is that so?" asked Harimako. His voice sent shivers down my spine. It was icy cold and sharp enough to kill. I looked away from Reubyn to meet Harimako's eyes. God, his eyes. They made me want to curl into a ball and cower away.

"Yes," I said, "it is."

Phantoms of dreams overshadowed my view of the room. I saw figures kneeling on the carpet before the throne and screaming islanders writhing under a spell or blades or one of a million other methods of torture that I recognized from seventeen years of nightmares. I'd writhed there more than once. Even more than that, I'd knelt and wielded the blade myself.

I forced the images out of my head and led the way into the throne room, hardly flinching when doors shut behind us with a rumbling groan and a loud thud. Aiene was on my left; Nikiani and Nico were on my right. Their presence buoyed me, and I managed to sweep away the memories of the dreams.

"I confuse you, don't I?" I asked. "You don't understand me. How can anyone be angry instead of terrified - isn't that what you're thinking?" The words seemed to be coming from somewhere deep inside of me. I wasn't sure where, exactly, but I trusted them. I let them ring into the throne room, defying the fear that gripped me when I looked at Harimako.

"This stupid plan you have - it was doomed from the start. You should have realized that the *aliakeanu* would have sensed your presence when you started getting stronger. There was never a chance that you would be able to appear from the darkness and take the islands back. Just give it up."

The words were less an offer to let him lay down arms peacefully than a challenge to face us in battle. Harimako rose smoothly and touched the hilt of his sword.

"Brave words," he said. "But before you speak any more, I would advise you to look and see what's happening in the world outside." He gestured with one tiger-striped arm to the window to my right. I glanced over out of instinct, and my heart dropped into my stomach.

The islanders had massed and followed us into Harimako's realm. Outside, on a plain I identified as part of the twisted version of Haliuku, the oldest of the islands and the most flattened by the elements, the army of spirit warriors had met the much larger force of Harimako's monster army. Dead monsters littered the plain, and for a moment the lack of human bodies made my heart lift. But then I saw one of the islanders killed. The body - the spirit - dissolved into silvery dust and then to nothingness. Half the islanders could be dead and we wouldn't be able to tell from a body count.

"Yes," Harimako said. "It's a valiant effort. But it will be a waste. You have already felt that your magic is useless here, Nikiani. The other *aliakeanu* will realize it soon. And your army of islanders, determined as they are to save their home, is nevertheless far too small. They cannot destroy a force the size of mine.

"And so," he continued, "it is good that the five of you, those with the strongest and most...*unusual* gifts, are here, in no danger of accidentally having your throats ripped out before I could reach you."

He raised a black-nailed hand in our direction, and something invisible but extremely solid hit me in the chest and flung me back against the door. Yin-Yang clattered to the floor. I slid down the wall to join them.

Aiene started towards me, but a sharp gesture from Harimako stopped him in his tracks. Harimako didn't so much as look at him as he crossed the throne room. He paused, looming over me, arms folded. I glared up at him, because I couldn't do anything else. He'd done something to paralyze me.

"A familiar face, perhaps," he mused. "Yes, that could be interesting." His tone made my innards pull a disappearing act. Then he turned, and a spasm of horror ran through me as I realized I wasn't paralyzed. Harimako had my body - my spirit, whatever the hell it was - under his control. Despite my mental shouts at myself to stop, I rose and followed him to one of the other widows, leaving Yin-Yang on the floor behind me.

He forced me to look out.

It was the fight again, only here the window seemed to open right into the middle of it all. I couldn't hear anything, but it didn't take a lot of imagination to think what it must have sounded like. A thousand kinds of weapons clashing on scales and bones, flesh and sinew; claws and teeth and tails ripping through skin and clothes. I could all but hear the screams - human and monster - as the battle raged.

Then I saw something that would have made

me recoil in horror if I'd been able to move. There, in the middle of the battle, fighting back-to-back with several islanders, were Mom and Dad.

Mom's long, dirty blonde hair, shot through with streaks of gray, flew loose around her face as she whaled away at a *rinko* with a heavy oak staff. Her blue-and-gray striped dress spun as she fought. Dad fought next to her in a sleeveless leather jerkin and black pants, slicing at the monsters with two long, cruel, curved blades. My heart thumped erratically as I saw the look in Dad's eyes. It was the instincts. He had them, too.

But instincts or no, they were surrounded by monsters on every side. I couldn't bear to watch - I wanted to look away and cry, or sprint out to help them, or maybe both. But I couldn't move. Harimako had me bound tight.

When a thickset, ogre-like monster brought its club down on Mom's shoulder, I shocked myself and everyone else in the room by screaming "Stop it!" and breaking free of Harimako's control to slug him in the face.

He stumbled back, probably stunned more by the surprise than the force of the blow, and I took advantage of the moment to scramble for Yin-Yang. When he turned to face me, finally showing a little bit of emotion, I was already in fighting stance. He lunged. I spun aside, making it out with just a shallow cut on my upper arm, and raised Yin-Yang to strike back.

I drove him recklessly, momentarily forgetting that I had no armor except a too-short cuirass. I gave myself over to the force of instinct, intent upon stopping Harimako through whatever means necessary. Everything that was happening here - Reubyn's pain, the battle, the fact that Mom and Dad had been dragged into this, *everything* - was his fault. If I could destroy him, it would be over. Everything would be peaceful again. Everything would be right again.

Harimako made a formidable opponent - I would give him that much. When he moved, his feet hardly seemed to touch the ground, and he met my two blades with his one like it was nothing. But where he was glacial, an icy blizzard, I was a tropical hurricane with the full force of its winds. Yin-Yang wove a black-and-white steel tapestry around him, forcing him back towards the wall. Then I twisted his blade with the flat of my left-hand sword, spinning it out of his hand, and pinned him against the wall, one of Yin-Yang's blades on either side of his throat. I gripped the blades, my palms on the dull edge, and forgot to care that the sharp edge pressed somewhat painfully into the pads of my fingers. I had him.

"It's over, Harimako." I saw exactly where I needed to strike to make everything end.

But Harimako didn't look as perturbed as I would have expected. "I understand you better than you would think, *emakalao*," he told me. "Would you like me to tell you something about these instincts that serve you so well?"

I blinked, very nearly relaxing my guard. But Harimako didn't take advantage of it.

"They came from me."

I froze.

"Millennia ago, I chose two dozen of the strongest young islanders and endowed them with the abilities that you now possess. They were raised as warriors to protect my realm - powerful, merciless fighters, hungry for battle. For generations they bred and protected my realm, until I decided it would be prudent to destroy them before they grew consciences. Clearly, however -" he glanced coolly towards the window through which I could still see Mom and Dad fighting - one escaped. His blood and his ability carried down through the generations, to your father and to you. Haven't you wondered why you always dreamt of this place? Why it seemed to draw you in?"

He gazed down at me coldly, but his eyes

glinted with a bright, sadistic pleasure.

"My realm is your home."

"No," I whispered, shaking my head. Then more forcefully: "No! You're lying!"

Harimako smiled coldly, revealing a line of sharp teeth. "Pity," he said. "You seemed like a very sensible girl. It's too bad you don't believe the truth when you hear it."

"Shut up!" I shouted. I felt myself trembling.

No. It was impossible. I'd finally accepted these instincts as something that wasn't evil. They couldn't have come from Harimako. If they did...

That was when Harimako hissed the words of one of his spells and flung me backwards. I landed heavily against the other wall. Yin-Yang fell from my hands and clattered to the floor again.

"Lillia!" shouted Aiene, but as he started towards me, Harimako thrust out a hand and Aiene went flying back, too. I winced as he hit the wall with a very solid thump. Harimako froze Nikiani and Nico in their tracks, and they collapsed to the floor like someone had hit them in the backs of their knees.

I tried to move towards them, but Harimako crossed the room with a few quick strides and grabbed my jaw, forcing me to look at him. He regarded me for several seconds and then forced me to the floor. I grunted as my head whacked against the stone.

"As it should be," he said, looking down at me coldly. "History does indeed repeat itself, Lillia Anied. It will return to the darkest days of my reign and this time, they shall not end. And all will bow to me...starting with you."

Then one pale, long-nailed hand wrapped around my neck and squeezed. My eyes popped wide as I struggled for air.

Harimako dragged me into a sitting position.

"Bow to me, Lillia Anied," he hissed, his terrifying face centimeters from mine.

"Lillia!"

Harimako's expression didn't change, but he let go of my throat. He gestured sharply, and I watched in horror as Aiene's hands scrabbled at his neck, like he was being strangled.

Then he collapsed to the floor, gasping.

"Poor children," Harimako said, and my innards writhed at the icily scathing tone. "Misguided creatures, believing that you could defeat me alone - that this determination to save your poor friend could carry you to victory - when in truth it merely carried you all into the palm of my hand."

A hissed spell picked me up and dragged me

to the middle of the throne room, squishing me against Aiene, who was squished against Nico, who was squished against Nikiani. We were held together as Harimako crossed to Reubyn, bound and spell-gagged by the foot of the black throne. Her head was bowed in something that looked very much like shame. *What? I don't understand...*

Harimako traced a finger along Reubyn's jaw and lifted her chin ever so gently. "Little sparrow," he whispered mockingly. "Little sparrow Reubyn, tell me about your friends."

Tears streaked down her cheeks. She looked at us pleadingly. *I'm sorry, she mouthed. I am so, so sorry...*

"'Lillia's such an idiot,'" Harimako said, mocking Reubyn's nasal tones. "'Just because she can fight, she thinks she needs to protect me... I swear she's jealous of you, Mukon. Just because someone else cares about me... I can't believe her. It's ridiculous.'"

My throat went tight, and despite myself I felt my eyes sting with tears.

She shuddered as Harimako stroked her hair. "Yes," he said quietly. "Our little sparrow was quite the font of information about you all. How ironic, that such a powerful *emelao* should be fooled by such a simple piece of magic...simple, and yet far beyond the reach of even my spells... Love...

"'Nikiani's just unbelievable,'" he said then, returning to his imitation of Reubyn. "'She's so little, but everyone says she's the most powerful *aliakeanu* in the islands. And I've felt it, too. You have no idea!'"

Reubyn's shoulders shook. I swallowed hard. Harimako's silencing spell didn't stop the broken sounds of Reubyn's sobs.

"'You think about past-sense and it doesn't sound all that awesome, but it's pretty neat. Aiene knows practically everything there is to know about history - more than Manialua, even. And I'd never tell Lillia, of course, but he worries about her all the time, now that she's gotten so weird.'"

Aiene blushed furiously. But Harimako didn't stop.

"'Nico - don't get me started! I've never seen him use his ability, but Niki's told me all about it. The poor guy, though... *Emelao*'s bad enough. I can't imagine never being able to look anyone in the eye.'"

Nico looked away bitterly.

"'And Lillia...'"

I looked up.

"'It's really annoying sometimes, but the way she is... You know you'll always be protected. She'll do just about anything to keep her friends safe.'"

"Yes," Harimako said, returning to his usual tone. "Quite the font of information." He smiled coldly and stroked Reubyn's neck. "A sparrow - a songbird."

I saw Reubyn's mouth move.

"What is it, sparrow?" He touched her throat.

Apparently, that ended the silencing spell, because Reubyn burst out, "Don't touch me!"

Harimako gazed at her coldly and said, "Very well."

Reubyn looked up at the rest of us, trapped together by Harimako's spell. "I'm sorry... Niki, Aiene, Nico... Lillia... I'm so, so, so sorry..." Her face crumpled with sobs.

"Reubyn," I whispered.

"Now," Harimako said, gesturing. Reubyn was jerked to her feet and pulled along next to him. "The most powerful, the most unusual abilities...are here."

He smiled coldly and touched Nikiani's face. She strained to back away, but she couldn't move any more than the rest of us.

"It doesn't matter what happens to us," she told him. "They won't stop fighting just because of five kids."

"I am afraid I must argue that point, young

aliakeanu," Harimako said, exposing his sharp teeth. "Think you, Nikiani, that the islanders will fight when such a powerful *aliakeanu* as yourself serves me? That the *aliakeanu* will not quail when faced with attacking me, with you by my side?

"Nico - think you that your precious Elementals will not pause when they know that I will not hesitate to destroy friend or foe, innocent or evil, in order to further my cause?" Harimako didn't touch Nico - probably a smart move, since Nico looked like he'd probably bite if Harimako got too close.

He moved on to Aiene. "Think you, Aiene, that your teacher and her Peacekeeping husband will not stop fighting when they realize their daughter, their apprentice, their fellows and their ward are in my grasp?"

I glared at him as he stepped towards me and felt a fierce pleasure at seeing that he stayed a safe distance away. "Will not your father be horrified when he knows the origin of your powers, Lillia? Will not your mother be revolted?"

"You leave my parents out of this," I snarled.

Harimako laughed, a cold, icy sound that grated on my eardrums. "None will fight," he said. "Not when I have the power of the past - the present - the future - the strongest human mage - the most potent of knowledge - in my control! □" As he named off powers, each of us received a corresponding blow across the face.

I struggled against the spell holding me trapped. "We'd never serve you, Harimako," I growled. "Never -"

Then I was pulled forwards, away from the others.

"You will be the first to serve me," Harimako corrected. "You will bow to me - you will swear your loyalty - and then you will watch as, one by one, your friends do the same. And then I will watch as you go out on my orders and fight for me, destroying the precious army you trained so hard with. Bow to me, Lillia Anied!" he cried then. "Bow to me and acknowledge me as your master, as did your ancestors!"

I spat in his face.

He glared at me icily. "You - will - bow -" he hissed, and something began pushing down on my back. I strained every muscle I had trying to struggle against the force. *No. Never.*

The pressure on my back grew stronger and stronger, until I was sure my spine would shatter if I kept trying to resist.

"No!"

Suddenly I broke free of the pressure,

shoving myself fully upright and then beyond as the resistance vanished. I fell backwards and hit the ground hard.

Harimako strode over to me and grabbed my hair, pulling my head up to face him. "I will break you," he hissed. "Willpower is useless - it will only extend your pain. If necessary I will subject you to so much that you are left as nothing but a husk, an empty shell with a few useful features. But I do not wish to do that." He pulled my head closer to his. I fought back the tears that sprang into my eyes as I felt chunks start to pull out of my scalp. "I want to see the pain in your eyes when you must carry out an order. I want to see how much it hurts when you do my bidding - when you kill for me, when you capture and torture and maim for me. I want you broken, not destroyed. And when you are broken, your friends will know they have no hope." Then he picked me up my hair - I gasped - and flung me against the wall with no more effort than I would have used to throw a rag doll. I hit hard and slid down into a heap on the floor.

He gestured, and pressure appeared around my throat like someone was choking me. I spluttered, hands scrabbling at my neck like I could somehow tear off Harimako's magic. Then I was picked up and bashed against the floor, the wall, the throne. When the pressure vanished, I collapsed to the ground. My head spun. I felt sick.

And then a burning sensation hit me all over, and I screamed. Every part of me felt like fire - my bones burning logs, my skin scraps of paper in a raging bonfire, the blood in my veins lava. I would have happily leapt into the crater on Kalinuea to cool myself down. I writhed, screaming, like that would somehow help put out the flames. It didn't.

When it stopped, it was sudden. I lay there on the freezing stones, gasping for breath. My whole body trembled. I'd never hurt like this in my life. I had blood in my mouth, dripping down my face, running from sword wounds and the four small marks on each of my palms where my nails had dug in while I burned. Tears ran out onto the floor, and I bit back sobs. I hurt enough that the pain in my lip seemed like nothing.

"Oh, God, help her," I heard Nikiani whisper shakily. And then Harimako: *"God?"*

I forced my eyelids up so I could see the scene in front of me. Harimako advanced on the others, still bound together by his spell.

"Tell me, Nikiani, what does your God know of this world?" Harimako asked. "Your God of mercy, of light, of compassion, of love - what does He know of the power I wield? The power of darkness?"

"'The light shines forth in the darkness, and the darkness has not understood it...'"

I didn't realize until Harimako turned to me that I'd actually said the words aloud. He crossed to me in three strides and stood there, looming over me. I cowered, and then felt sick with myself.

"Who are you," he said quietly, "to speak of light? You, who have had darkness in your veins from the moment you were conceived - you can know nothing but the power of the dark!"

And then he stomped on my leg so hard that I heard a loud crack.

A half-second later, I registered the pain, and my throat almost tore from my scream.

Another spell flung me at the wall, and even though I didn't hit my leg, I jolted it, and the pain throbbed. When I hit the floor, I curled everything but the broken leg into a ball and lay there, sobbing, praying that it would end.

"You see now how this will end," Harimako said. "Perhaps you are strong, perhaps you can bear this, but you cannot bear everything. Bow to me now, and it will be over. Your pain will be gone."

There were no words for how much I hurt - no words for how desperately I wanted it over. But I couldn't. I couldn't. *Help me,* I prayed wildly. *If you're there, God, please, please - help me!*

"Bow!"

Slowly, I raised my head from my fetal curl. My voice shook and cracked and burbled with blood, but it was audible enough. "There is nothing...nothing you could do to me, Harimako...that would ever make me bow...to you..."

Harimako's pale nostrils flared. "Is that so?" he asked. My stomach dropped at the cruelty in his tone. "Then perhaps I ought to do nothing to you."

He gestured and pulled Aiene forward. One pale hand grabbed his hair, pulling his head back and exposing his neck. Another gesture brought his sword back to his hand, and, ever so gently, he set the blade across Aiene's throat.

My eyes were wide. "No," I whispered.

A glitter of pleasure lit Harimako's dark eyes. "As it would be futile," he said, "I will do nothing more to you. But you know, I have little need for a historian in my court. Perhaps it would be simpler if I simply took care of him now." He pressed the blade into Aiene's neck, and I watched in horror as a few drops of blood appeared.

"Stop it!"

"Lillia, shut up!" Aiene gasped. "Don't - you can't let him win!"

Harimako yanked on his hair, and Aiene groaned. "I win either way," Harimako hissed. "Either your death breaks her, or you live and she becomes mine."

I stared at Aiene in horror. I couldn't - I *couldn't* let him die. I would have rather died myself than let that happen.

The blade pressed deeper into Aiene's flesh. "I can't," I whispered. "Stop it. Stop!" I tried to pull myself forwards, but the pain in my leg surged and I cried out.

Aiene's neck was bleeding hard now. A few more seconds - just a little bit deeper - and he'd be injured beyond repair. He'd stopped struggling. He knew as well as me that if he moved, he was dead.

"I give up."

The words passed my lips and dropped into the suddenly silent room. Aiene, Nico, Nikiani, and Reubyn stared at me in horror. My head dropped. I let my face rest against the cold floor for a moment. It felt good against the swelling I knew had appeared, and I longed to never get up again.

But I couldn't stay down. This was the only way.

I lifted my head to look Harimako in the eye. "I'll do whatever you want." My gaze shifted to Aiene, and although the tears in my eyes made it blurry and hard to tell, I thought he was crying. "Just□don't hurt him."

"Lillia..." Aiene's voice was quiet. "No..."

Harimako removed the sword from Aiene's neck and dragged me closer with a spell. I whimpered as my broken leg dragged on the floor.

"Kneel before me," he commanded.

Between the pain and my pride, it took every iota of willpower I possessed for me to force myself to do it.

"And now repeat what I tell you..."

The words he spoke were dark and twisted, but I recognized them. This was the language of Harimako's realm - a twisted version of Fankaloa. I could feel them settling in around me as I repeated the oath, line by line, binding myself to Harimako's will.

"Until death shall loose my bonds," he said coldly, the final words of the oath.

I took a deep breath. I'd spoken too much already to escape.

"Until death shall loose my..."

I broke off, looking up, as the short hairs on the back of my neck rose. My eyes went wide. I knew this feeling: it was *aliakeanu* magic!

But it wasn't coming from outside, or from Nikiani - she was looking around for the source.

After a moment, I realized. It was coming from Reubyn.

She looked as surprised as the rest of us, but she seemed to be going with it. At a whispered word, the ropes around her wrists and ankles slid off. She slipped the shield off her back.

"Reubyn!" Aiene exclaimed.

Reubyn closed her eyes. I felt the magic in the air increasing, coalescing, gathering itself into a deadly point around a focus.

Reubyn's.

She stood perfectly still, but her hair and skirt wreathed around her like she was standing in the wind.

Harimako looked like he stood in the wind, too. He looked down at himself and then at Reubyn with a combination of shock and horror on his face.

"Nikiani," I gasped. "Help her -" And then I doubled over, screaming, as I felt why Harimako had made me swear in his language. Every wound I'd ever felt in my life, every headache, every broken nose, every sunburn, every aching stomach, every cramp, every bruise - if they'd all risen up and throbbed together, they'd have been maybe a thousandth of this. There was no way I could go on defying him. There was no way I could do anything.

But it was too late: Nikiani had heard me. The room started humming with the energy she and Reubyn fed into the spell. It kept increasing until I realized that even Nikiani couldn't be the source of so much energy - there were more *aliakeanu* helping, too.

"Damn you, girl," Harimako hissed. "I shall teach you to obey me -" He kicked my broken thigh. I screamed and fell onto my side, where I lay moaning softly.

"You leave her alone!" yelled Reubyn. The energy focusing in the room sharpened, refining its aim.

Harimako looked at me then, and the look of sudden inspiration in his eyes made my stomach drop out. He said the words to one of his spells - I couldn't hear it over the humming suffusing the throne room - and disappeared. As soon as he did, my vision blurred and doubled. I went cold, and then shuddered as I recognized the presence that had leapt into my mind.

Harimako.

The phantom sensation of the cold blade lingered against Aiene's throat as he watched Lillia give herself up to Harimako. As she struggled to kneel and began repeating the phrases of twisted Fankaloa, he wished he could trade her surrender for the blade back again. She couldn't have suffered everything Harimako had done to her and then have given in so easily for his sake!

But there she knelt, giving her oath. Aiene shuddered at the words. He knew a promise in that language couldn't be broken.

He had been as surprised as the others when Reubyn had suddenly developed magic - and when Harimako disappeared from the throne room. At that moment, Lillia's head went back and her eyes went wide. But when she opened her mouth to speak, it wasn't her voice that came out.

My mouth was moving. My mouth was moving and it wasn't because of me. Harimako's voice passed my lips, and there was nothing I could do to stop it. "Very well, then. Cast your spell, if you wish. Destroy me. But think about the spirit in which I reside!"

Reubyn had stopped, eyes wide. "No," she whispered. "Lillia...!"

Harimako's presence in my mind made it hard to think. He bore down on me, pushing me from my ability to talk. I struggled against the force, but it was almost impossible. Finally I managed a word.

"Reu...byn..."

A snarl from Harimako, a sharp throb of pain. An involuntary moan escaped my lips. And then a sudden forceful scream: "Don't stop!"

Then I recoiled as Harimako bore down more heavily on me. Fragments of memories, snatches of dark thoughts, powerful, icy hatred and strength: thousands of years of evil bore down on my mind and soul, crushing me.

"I can't!" Reubyn said. Her voice broke. "Lillia!"

Nico struggled fruitlessly against the bonds of Harimako's spell. Hearing his words out of Lillia's mouth sent shivers down his spine. Reubyn seemed to fracture faced with the decision of destroying Harimako now, with his spirit inside of Lillia's.

He knew more intimately than he would have liked just how terrible that would be for her. He hated how much he knew about Lillia's pain - how exactly he knew what being in service to Harimako did to her.

Oh, it had been brave, and crying out for Reubyn to cast the spell was too, and he knew she thought it would be worth it, but he still thought it was stupid.

She couldn't be thinking of sacrificing

herself!

Beside him, Nikiani watched like her eyes were glued to the scene. She shook her head. "It's the only way," she whispered. It sounded like she was choking back tears.

"It can't be!" snapped Aiene. There was a tear track down one of his cheeks, and his eyes glimmered wetly. He was as stuck as Nico or Nikiani, but he kept struggling. "Reubyn!" he shouted. "Don't do it!"

Reubyn still stared at Lillia. She had her mouth covered with both hands, and Nico could see the tears in her eyes.

Then Lillia managed to speak out again. "Reubyn, cast the spell!"

Reubyn shuddered at the mass of emotions swirling around her. Anger, fear, desperation, anguish - they threatened to overwhelm her. And then Harimako - she could sense him, too, not strongly but enough. *How is Lillia standing this?*

She knew the only way to end Lillia's pain - and her oaths - was to destroy Harimako. But how could she destroy him when she knew the spell would probably kill her best friend, too?

"Quickly!" Lillia screamed. "In a few minutes, your magic will -"

And then her eyes snapped wide and she let out a long, low, broken moan.

She shivered.

What was she going to do?

I couldn't hear. I couldn't see. I could hardly breathe, and even though I wanted to scream, I couldn't manage anything more than a weak moan. Harimako was crushing me. I couldn't sense anything but him - him and the pain. They were everywhere, pushing down on me with an unbearable weight. All I had left for myself were emotions, and they left me as desperate prayers that earned Harimako's disdain and more pain: *please, please, stop him, help her, let it end, O God, let it end!*

I knew I was moving. *I* was moving, not Harimako. My leg screamed in protest, but I couldn't fight it. Not anymore. The torture I could have stood, maybe Harimako's presence in my mind, maybe even the pain of breaking the oaths; but all of them, together, and the threat of more - it was too much. I had no chance of beating him anymore. So I walked and I raised Yin-Yang and I screamed inside and struggled - not to fight, not to defy the orders to move forward and stop Reubyn's spell by any means necessary up to and including killing her, but just to survive, to keep myself in some semblance of a whole beneath the hatred and the pain and the horrible energy that still flowed through me even though I could hardly move. It was all too much. It might kill me. I'd have been happy if it did.

And then a bold of destructive energy pierced me through the heart.

I gasped and fell as my pain and Harimako's rushed together into something thousands - millions! - of times worse than anything from before. It was a physical impossibility - fire burning at ice, not melting it, but cracking it and breaking it and burning it into nothingness. I could feel Harimako's pain - his terror - as Reubyn's spell sought his spirit and burned it away.

It burned me, too. I was caught between burning ice and burning fire as they warred deep within my spirit, in Harimako and also in me.

I gasped for air and the screaming started, Harimako's voice combining with mine in an agonized harmony. The pressure of his mind lifted, burning away, but he was still inside me, and because he burned I burned too.

The pain grew; it became impossible to bear; but it didn't diminish or stop. It kept growing, burning through my blood and my bones, destroying and cleansing. Our combined screams reached a crescendo, and I couldn't breathe. Everything was red and black. My fingers and toes, my skin and everything on my outside froze, and on the inside I burned alive. I didn't know if the others were there; I didn't know where I was. I didn't even know whether I was alive or dead.

I felt a final scream from Harimako, a sound of pure anguish, and then nothing but a strange sense of freedom. I fell into an extinguishing blackness.

There were voices above my head. I didn't know who they belonged to, or what they were saying. But they seemed concerned.

After a time, I could make out different voices. There were eight of them. Two belonged to grown women. Two to grown men. One was a teenage boy. One was a teenage girl. Two more were younger, maybe twelve or thirteen. One was a boy and one was a girl. I still didn't know what they were saying.

The first time I understood words, they came from the teenage boy, who hadn't spoken as much when the other voices were around. But when it had just been his voice, he had spoken to me in tender, quiet tones.

"Nikiani," his voice said, "she's been out for almost a week. What...what if..." He didn't seem able to finish the sentence.

The young girl spoke next. "She's going to be okay," she said. "Can't you feel her heartbeat? It's been getting stronger all week." But there was doubt in her tone.

The voices were quiet for a moment. I strained my memory, trying to remember who they were. I knew them. I knew all the voices. I just couldn't remember how.

"Go get some lunch," said the boy's voice finally. "I'll stay here and watch her."

"You need to eat too, Aiene," said the girl. "I don't think you've had more than a couple bites all week."

Aiene. *Aiene.* I knew that name. I strained my memory further. There was something there, just out of reach. All I had were flashes. Dark eyes. A wonderful laugh. A sense of long-reaching protection.

Nikiani. A never-ending appetite. A confident, mischievous smile. Immense power juxtaposed with a tiny, cheerful shape.

I grabbed at the threads of memory, trying to catch them and resolve them into some sensible order.

Fear. Annoyance. Love. Excitement. Warmth. Pain. Anger. Embarrassment. Friendship. Wonder.

They didn't make any sense. I could only see flashes. Getting annoyed, I made another snatch.

Disdainful blue eyes. A redheaded girl in a mirror. Blonde hair with streaks of gray. Piercing green eyes staring into my soul. White skin with black stripes.

When I finally managed to grab onto one of the threads of memory, it all came crashing down. I was Lillia Anied. I was a Peacekeeper, an *emakalao*, a warrior. I remembered who the voices belonged to. I knew Aiene and Nikiani; I knew the owners of the traits I'd seen. I remembered the emotions and the situations that had brought them on. I remembered everything.

With the memories came fear. Had Reubyn's spell destroyed Harimako like it was supposed to? If it hadn't, why were the others with me? If it had, how was I not dead?

I tried to move, but even though my neurons were firing at top speed, my body felt like lead. I couldn't even twitch a finger.

"I don't want to leave her until she wakes up," Aiene said. My heart swelled.

Nikiani sighed. "Fine," she said. "I'll bring

you up a plate. And then I'm not going to leave you alone until you eat it!"

She sounded like Manialua. I smiled inwardly as her footsteps receded.

A gentle hand touched my cheek and brushed a lock of hair off my face. "Wake up, Lillia," Aiene murmured. "I'm waiting."

I was awake, I wanted to tell him, but I was too tired. As Aiene's hand stroked my cheek, I fell back into the comforting darkness of sleep.

When I woke up next time, I felt much better. The backs of my eyelids were dark orange, so I decided that it was daytime. I heard several people beside me eating and talking quietly.

"I don't know," Manialua said. "Nikiani says that she'll be all right, but I'm not so sure. The only problem is that I don't know enough about magic to be able to tell."

They were silent for a moment. I heard the sound of a fork against a plate, but it sounded halfhearted. Then I heard Mom's voice: "But she can't be all that bad, I think. Her leg's healed, her heartbeat's strong, and her color's gone back to normal. She looks a thousand times better than when we first got here."

"But she hasn't woken up," said Dad.

There was someone eating closer to me - all but sitting on the bed, I thought - who wasn't saying anything. It was Aiene, I was sure. I didn't know whether he'd even left since the last time I'd woken up, whenever that was. Judging by what Nikiani had said to him, my bet would have been no.

I wasn't tired anymore, but I ached and getting my eyes open was a struggle. I supposed it was because they'd been closed for so long. How many things *didn't* you have trouble with when you didn't use them for a week?

My fingers twitched in annoyance, and there was a gasp from beside the bed. I had been right: it was Aiene.

"Lillia!" he exclaimed.

I struggled all the harder against my lids. Finally, slowly, they fluttered open. Aiene was leaning over me, concern and relief prominent on his face. I lay in the loft of Manialua's and Vrenchard's house. Sunlight streamed in through the windows and skylight.

Aiene's face broke into a smile, all the concern draining away. "Thank god," he said. "You're awake!"

I wasn't sure if my eyes would open again if I closed them, so I didn't blink. "Yeah," I said. My mouth was dry. "I...what, what happened?"

"A lot," said Aiene. "Dammit, Lillia, I...I thought you weren't going to wake up!"

"Well, I did." Slowly, I sat up. Geez, everyone was in here.

And they all rushed me at once. Within a second, I found myself enveloped in a massive group hug. Voices muffled by arms and shoulders floated to my ears:

"We were so worried about you."

"Thank goodness you're all right!"

"You were asleep for so long, I thought..."

"Oh, sweetie..."

"Lillia."

The hug broke off eventually, and I found myself facing Reubyn. She had a horribly guilty look on her face, and her eyes were red. "I'm so sorry," she said. "I...I didn't know he was Harimako. I betrayed everyone... I almost killed..."

"Reubyn..." I said.

She wiped her eyes with her arm.

I couldn't think of anything to say. So I stood - very shakily - and hugged her.

"It's okay," I whispered as her shoulders shook. "You didn't know. And it all worked out, remember? We destroyed him. *You* destroyed him." I pulled back, my arms on her shoulders. "Okay? It wasn't your fault."

"That's what they keep telling me," Reubyn replied, smiling slightly. "It doesn't matter. I still feel guilty."

"You're an idiot," I told her. Then I hugged her again. "But you're my best friend, so I'll forgive you this once."

"You'll forgive me every time," Reubyn mumbled into my shoulder. "Because you think I'm just that amazing."

I laughed. "Glad you're back, Reu."

We broke apart, smiling. Then Reubyn started. "Food!" she exclaimed. "You've got to be hungry. I'll grab a plate."

She hurried off down the stairs.

"I'll go, too," said Manialua. She squeezed me in a hug. "I'm glad you're okay, Lillia."

One by one, the others left, each of them giving me a hug on their way. Finally it was just Aiene and me. We stood there awkwardly. I shifted from one foot to the other.

Finally, I said, "Thank you."

"For what?" Aiene asked. His brows pulled together.

"For staying with me," I said. "I heard you and Nikiani talking one time."

His skin darkened. "Oh," he said. "Yeah. I...it was nothing. I just didn't want you to wake up alone."

I smiled. "Thank you."

Aiene smiled, too. "You're welcome."

We stood there for another moment. I twisted my hands behind my back. Somehow, after everything that had happened, I felt no less awkward than ever.

"Maybe you should sit down," Aiene said after a moment of the silence. "You can't be recovered yet."

I shrugged. "I feel okay," I said, but sat down on the futon anyway. Aiene sat next to me.

We sat silently for a minute, leaning up against each other. The conspicuous lack of anyone coming up with food made me think that they were deliberately giving us time alone.

"I really am glad you're okay," Aiene said suddenly. I looked up at him. He blushed. "I mean...I don't know what I'd do if you weren't."

I went warm. "Thank you," I said again. He smiled. I leaned up against him, nestling my head on his shoulder. Something about the warm comfort of it made my thoughts start to settle down into a recognizable order.

"Are you gonna be okay?" murmured Aiene.

I hesitated. "I think so. There's some stuff I need to work through. But for now...I think I'm all right."

"Good," Aiene said. When I turned my head to look up at him, he was close. Gently, he touched my cheek, just like he had before.

And he kissed me.

Epilogue: An Entirely New Shorthand

"C'mere, you," I muttered, grasping the tree branch with my legs as I reached up towards Ika Ame'ei's cat. This was the third time since we'd gotten here that the crazy old tabby had gone up a tree, and he wasn't any happier about coming down this time than he had been any of the others.

He hissed and swatted my hand, claws outstretched. I yelped as his claws dug into my hand and snatched it back, glaring.

Ika Ame'ei watched nervously from the ground. I wasn't sure if she was concerned for me or her furry lunatic.

I climbed a branch higher, still holding the cat in my glare. Maybe it was just my imagination, but he seemed to glare back.

I got my balance, and then lunged after him. "Gotcha!" I yelled, yanking him in. Then I missed my landing and fell out of the tree. The cat and I both yowled as we fell, and I grunted when I hit the ground. The cat shook off my arms, righted himself, and stalked off, throwing me a disdainful look that I probably earned from having landed on my back instead of my feet.

"Thank you!" Ika Ame'ei said, scooping her lunatic up in her arms. "I'm so sorry, *'ema*. Are you all right?"

"Fine," I said, pushing myself up. "Just watch him, would you? This is the third time in the past month and a half." Not to mention that I would soon have a big mottled bruise up my back to match the yellowing collection all over the rest of my body.

"I know," she replied, looking down at the cat in concern. "He just loves to wander around on his own - I hate to take that right away from him."

Well, I couldn't argue with such a sweet old lady about the state of her cat's sanity. I just nodded. She thanked me again, and I left.

I checked my watch as I headed back towards the house. Eleven hours forty-three - lunchtime. Patrols were usually short, and this was no different.

Everything had been peaceful since Reubyn's spell had destroyed Harimako - twelve days, though I'd only been conscious for six. Ika Ame'ei's cat was the most dangerous thing we'd had to deal with that whole time.

Aiene had told me about what had happened while I'd been out. Vrenchard had ended up taking over most of the patrol duties, since Reubyn had been prone to crying randomly and without warning. Not that I could blame her. If I thought I might have killed my best friend, I'd be teary, too.

They had been around the islands checking for damage or injuries, but fortunately, no one who had stayed in the physical world had been hurt. Apparently, though, physical bodies reflected wounds they got in spirit form, because everyone who had come back from the fight had at least three injuries. The *aliakeanu* had several under intensive care. Nikiani had been running all over, trying to take care of everyone at once - including me, which apparently had involved her and Reubyn working for almost five straight hours to heal the myriad fractures in my femur and the lacerations to the surrounding muscles, plus the time it had taken to heal the shoulder that had popped out of joint one of the times I hit stone and the concussion I'd gotten against the arm of Harimako's throne. None of my other injuries had been serious enough to need more than a little peroxide, a few bandages, and some ice.

This time, none of the *aliakeanu* had burned out their powers on the spell, which left me very impressed with the amount of finesse Reubyn could apply to spells. She wasn't as strong as some, but her senses were even better than Nikiani's thanks to her being an *emelao*.

Then there was the situation between Aiene and me.

I supposed the technical term for what was going on between us was dating. We didn't go out to restaurants or to see films, but we spent a lot of time together and once we'd had a not-so-romantic attempt at a picnic on the roof. We were still finding bits of chicken in the grass in front of the house.

But I was happy, and I could tell Aiene was, too. That was all that mattered.

When I got back to the house, everyone was home. I joined Reubyn and Vrenchard at the table to start writing my report. As I pulled up the screen, my eyes flickered down to the date-and-time bar on the bottom.

"Crap," I said. "It's October tenth."

Reubyn and Vrenchard both stopped dead in the middle of typing. "Oh, no," Reubyn said.

"October...oh," Nikiani said. She grinned wickedly. "I'll clear out before you start. Dad makes enough profanity on his own dealing with that."

"I do not," said Vrenchard, shooting her a

look over the top of his glasses. "I'll thank you to not spread rumors."

Nikiani adopted a fake chastened expression. "But I love you, Daddy."

We all laughed. Nikiani slid off the counter and left, calling, "Nico and I'll be looking in on some of the injured people."

"You could look in on your own family first," muttered Manialua good-naturedly. She and Vrenchard had both been injured in the battle, though not badly compared to some of the others. All Vrenchard's bandages were gone; Manialua just had one, on her left calf. Mom and Dad had left the day before, both with thankfully minor injuries.

I tapped the icon with the formatting for the monthly report as Aiene sat down next to me. "Have you got anything in that shorthand for "Harimako?'" he asked. "Or 'magic,' or 'dark cold spirit world?'"

We all laughed. I took Aiene's hand.

"'*Ema*, for this we're going to have to invent an entirely new shorthand."

Kiliopi

End

Acknowledgements and About the Author
Sara Dotson

I was born in Chesapeake, Virginia, and spent
several years in Hawaii and Germany as a military
child. I'm now back in Chesapeake and using my
writing to help me survive the last few years of high
school. I'd like to thank my parents, Greg and Amy
Dotson, for supporting me in everything that I am
and do; all the friends who have read my work and
given me the pep talks I need to keep going; the
dozens of authors whose books inspired me to write
my own, among them J.K. Rowling, Stephen King,
and C.S. Lewis; and the almighty search engine
Google, through which I have somehow always
found what I needed to know.

I'm an indie author, so I couldn't have done this
without your support, my dear reader. Thank you
for having the courage and curiosity to pick up a
book from someone you've never heard of and
letting it become a part of your life. I believe that a
story is the most powerful way to connect hearts and
minds, and I'm more happy than I can express that
you chose this one. May these characters live in
your imagination forever, just as they will in mine.

CPSIA information can be obtained at www.ICGtesting.com
Printed in the USA
BVOW03s1222260715

410116BV00001B/3/P